The Grace Mysteries

ASSASSIN and BETRAYAL

The Grace Mysteries

ASSASSIN

BETRAYAL

Patricia Finney is writing as Grace Cavendish

DELACORTE PRESS

Assassin and *Betrayal* text copyright © 2004 by Working Partners Ltd.
Cover art copyright © 2010 by Aleta Rafton

All rights reserved. Published in the United States by Delacorte Press, an imprint of Random House Children's Books, a division of Random House, Inc., New York. This omnibus edition comprises The Lady Grace Mysteries: *Assassin* and The Lady Grace Mysteries: *Betrayal,* each originally published in hardcover in the United States by Delacorte Press in 2004.

Delacorte Press is a registered trademark and the colophon is a trademark of Random House, Inc.

www.randomhouse.com/kids

Educators and librarians, for a variety of teaching tools, visit us at
www.randomhouse.com/teachers

Library of Congress Cataloging-in-Publication Data for the hardcover editions of *Assassin* and *Betrayal* is available upon request.

ISBN 978-0-385-74005-0 (tr. pbk.)
ISBN 978-0-385-90821-4 (lib. bdg.)
ISBN 978-0-375-89879-2 (ebook)

Printed in the United States of America

10 9 8 7 6 5 4 3 2 1

First Omnibus Edition

Random House Children's Books supports the First Amendment
and celebrates the right to read.

Assassin

To Meg, with many thanks

I am supposed to use this book to write all my prayers and meditations in. That's what Mrs. Champernowne said when she gave it to me for my New Year's Gift—and that I could make one of my beautiful embroideries for its cover, which I shall do, because I like making pictures with stitches. But why should I drone on like Lady Hoby about Improving Passages and Sorrowful Meditations on my sins? How boring!

Anyway, I don't commit any very terrible sins, apart from once ruining my gown when I jumped off a log. And losing things. That's why I haven't written anything in this before—I lost it under my bed for a while. But now I've found it I'm going to write everything in it. It can be a book about me, Lady Grace Cavendish, Maid of Honour. And all my favourite things. Why not?

My favourite person (apart from my mother, who is dead, God rest her soul) is Her Majesty the Queen. She's a bit old, which you're never supposed to say or she might throw a shoe at you. She is thirty-six! Even for a great lady, that is almost too old to get married and have children—as Mrs. Champernowne complains when she thinks nobody is listening. I think Mrs. Champernowne's pate is addled: why would a queen want to marry and gain a king she'd have to obey? In fact, why would anyone want to get married if they didn't have to?

Unfortunately, I have to. The Queen says so.

The most exciting day of my life is probably tomorrow. The Queen's Majesty has arranged a St. Valentine's Ball and I must choose one of the three suitors the Queen has selected for me, to be my wedded husband. We'll be handfasted once the lawyers have finished the contracts, and then I shall marry whoever it is properly when I'm sixteen. All three suitors are now at Court, ready for tomorrow.

I wish I didn't have to marry. I feel far too young to do so but, being an heiress, I must—though if I were a commoner I could wait until I was as old as five and twenty!

Mary Shelton just came in and made moan to me

about Lady Sarah not wanting to walk the dogs—
even though it is her turn. I see an opportunity. I
must run!

Later this Day

I am writing this in bed because Lady Sarah and
Mary Shelton aren't here yet and I cannot sleep.

My favourite place in all of Whitehall Palace is
behind the compost heaps at the end of the
Orchard. I must have a care when I go there
because if the other Maids of Honour or Ladies-in-
Waiting knew about it, they'd tell the Mistress of
the Maids, Mrs. Champernowne. And then she
would tell the Queen, and Her Majesty would have
to know about it officially, instead of just unofficially
as she does now.

So when I want to go there, I generally volunteer
to take the Queen's little dogs for a walk. Everyone
knows I'm the only one of the Queen's
Gentlewomen who actually likes them. They're
small and hairy and smelly and quite fierce and a bit
snappy if they don't know you—but I never have any
trouble with them. They like me.

That was why I had to stop writing earlier: I had

to run downstairs and find (my very pretty Lady and doesn't she know it?) Sarah Bartelmy. She was standing by the door to the Privy Garden with her face as sour as week-old milk, because *she* had been told to walk the dogs.

"What is wrong?" I asked, though I knew because Mary Shelton had told me.

Lady Sarah tossed her shiny copper hair and sighed. "The Queen bade me walk her dogs."

"Oh, what fun!" I declared, knowing she wouldn't agree. We play this charade with great regularity.

"But the wind is raw and there's a frost upon it," she complained. "And my mother sent me rose-water and almond oil to see if that will help my spot, and now I'll not have time to try it!"

Lady Sarah does have a spot on her nose, but it's not that big. She makes such a fuss about spots.

"Please don't trouble yourself. I will take the dogs out for you," I said kindly. "You must look your best for the ball."

For a moment Lady Sarah smiled at me quite pleasantly. Only for a moment, though. "I suppose you like galloping around with the horrible smelly little creatures," she observed.

"Yes, I do," I agreed. "Wait here, I'll get changed."

I ran up to our bedchamber—I share it with Lady Sarah and Mary Shelton—to change into my old green woollen hunting kirtle that's a bit short for me now. I couldn't walk the dogs in my white damask bodice and kirtle with the false front embroidered with roses. It was embroidered by my dear mother and is precious.

I didn't bother the tiring woman to help me—I can do it myself since I have all my bodices lacing up the front. I left my damask on the bed because I was in a desperate hurry to get out in the Orchard before it started getting dark. I pulled my boots on, grabbed my cloak, then rushed back downstairs again.

This time Mrs. Champernowne caught me on the back stairs. I think she lies in wait for me. "Lady Grace!" she shouted. "Lady Grace! Stop at once and wait!"

She's Welsh, you know, and very strict. But I have to be respectful to her, because she's served the Queen longer than anyone else—since Her Majesty was just Princess Elizabeth and everyone thought she'd be executed. So I stopped and curtsied. I knew exactly what she was going to say. And she did.

"Lady Grace! When will you live up to the pretty name your poor mama gave you? How many times do I have to tell you not to clatter down the stairs like a herd of cattle?"

Silly old moo, as if cows could run downstairs.

"Sorry, Mrs. Champernowne," I said meekly, though I wasn't sorry because I *don't* clatter. I was going as quietly as I could and it's not my fault my outdoor boots have hobnails in them.

"Now walk, child, look dignified. What would the Queen say if she saw you like this? Why cannot you be more like Lady Sarah?"

Oh yes, be like Lady Sarah Copper-locks Bartelmy and squeal every time I see a spider and have nothing in my head except how white my skin is and how shiny my hair is and whether some idiotic young gentleman is writing stupid sonnets to my chest. Hah!

I didn't say that, though it was a struggle. I said, "Yes, Mistress Champernowne." And curtsied again and walked as gracefully as I could with my knees bent, so she wouldn't spot just how too short my old kirtle is and make me go and change again. Then once I was round the corner I ran even faster to make up for lost time.

I came puffing out into the Queen's Privy Garden, which is all formal and deadly dull. Lady Sarah was standing under a tree, her face covered with a scarf to protect her complexion, scowling at Henri, who was lifting his leg against one of the roots.

"What took you so long?" she sniffed.

"Mrs. Champernowne caught me running and told me to be graceful like you." I said this with a straight face so she couldn't be sure whether I was being sarcastic or not. Though I'm not sure Lady Sarah Bartelmy actually knows what sarcasm is.

She sniffed again, gave me the leash, and hurried off back to the palace before the cold air could damage her white skin any more.

I kept the dogs on the leash in the Privy Garden so that they couldn't go digging up hedges from the maze as they did last time. They were so happy to see me; they were barking and bouncing round me and bringing me interesting sticks. I walked as sedately as I could down the path, past the big fountain that was still frozen, and on to the gate into the Orchard.

One of the Queen's Guard was there, guarding the gate from ferocious apples probably. He was looking miserable, his nose bright red and dripping from a cold. It was his own fault: he was too vain to put on his cloak and hide his wonderful crimson doublet and puffed velvet hose, and his white stocking hose on his handsome legs and his smart, polished high boots. I expect he was hoping Lady Sarah would walk past him, or maybe that the Queen would come by and admire how handsome he is—all the gentlemen hope for that.

"Will you open for me, sir?" I asked with a curtsy.

He sighed, turned the key, and opened the gate. He didn't even bow! He would have for Lady Sarah, I believe, if only to get in a stare at her dugs. Not for me, though. My body hasn't started to develop in that way yet. So I curtsied to him anyway, because the more you curtsy to people, the more they'll do for you, so it's worth the wear on your knees.

"Will you be riding with Sir Charles later today, my lady?" he asked me.

I'd completely forgotten about it. Hell's teeth! (It's a good thing Mrs. Champernowne can't see how much swearing I do in my head.) I don't really like horses much, but Sir Charles is one of my suitors and he's quite fun, even though he is old and plump and puffs a bit. Really he is happiest when he is at home on his country estates. He never feels very comfortable at Court, but he has been staying here to teach me to ride better—the Queen doesn't want me falling off again the next time we go hunting. And he's a good teacher. He never shouts and he explains things as often as I need, and the horses really like him. But as a husband—Lord preserve me! (That's not swearing, I checked.)

"Later," I said, and swept past with the dogs towing me excitedly.

The Orchard isn't nearly as tidy and formal as the Privy Garden. There are apple and pear and cherry trees—some of them quite climbable if I hitch up my kirtle over my belt—and redcurrant bushes and raspberries and brambles and some herbs that escaped from the kitchen gardens. Most of the time you can't be seen from the palace.

Well, the Queen can see from her bedchamber window, if she's standing in the right place. She saw me playing in the Orchard once, sword-fighting with a raspberry cane, which amused her. She has ordered that the gate be kept locked except to me, mainly to keep the older Maids of Honour and their gentlemen out of it—because they are empty-headed nitwits who are liable to ruin their whole lives for a pretty locket and some bad verse. Or that's what the Queen says.

Once I am out of sight, I often go to see a particular cherry tree that reminds me of my mother. In spring it has blossom the exact same colour as a silken gown she wore in summer. My mother died only a year ago, saving the Queen's life, and she wasn't like some of the other girls' mothers—all angry and fierce and strict. She was lovely.

The tree has tiny buds but nothing more yet. I let the dogs off the leash and they went scampering off on their short hairy legs, barking wildly. I knew why, because I could see little drifts of smoke coming from behind the compost heaps right at the end of the Orchard, near the river. The dogs yipped excitedly and disappeared behind the nearest heap. Henri came back out with a bright red shiny juggling ball, glittering with glass chips.

I grinned as I heard Masou's singsong voice saying, "Unclean beast! Get away from those. Come back, spawn of Shaitan!" Masou is my good friend, and the best boy acrobat in the Queen's Court—or so he says.

I took the ball from Henri's dribbling muzzle and went round to the hide I had made with Masou and

Ellie, my other good friend. She is a laundrymaid. We have furnished the hide to look like just another compost heap.

I have to be careful nobody finds out about our friendship or they would get into even worse trouble than me—and probably they would get beaten with birch twigs for not knowing their proper places. I hate it when they have to bow and curtsy to me in public, and call me "my lady" and "mistress." And it's very difficult not to laugh when Masou winks at me. Behind the compost heaps we can be just Ellie and Masou and Grace and nobody has to curtsy or bow to anybody.

(I had decided to write this secret information with Seville orange juice so it could only be read if the page is warmed. But when I visited the kitchen, I found that Cook has already used all the oranges for marmelada. Fie! I shall just have to be careful to keep my daybooke from prying eyes.)

Masou had lit a little fire just outside the hide, which is a dangerous thing to do, except that compost heaps do smoulder sometimes when they get too hot. He was cooking some crayfish out of the river, spitted on twigs, and Ellie was sitting over the fire warming her poor chapped hands. She works in the Whitehall laundry and, as she's an orphan, she sleeps there, too, in one of the storerooms, and she never ever has enough to eat. I feel guilty that she has to work so hard. I wanted her to be my tiring woman to take care of my gowns, but my guardian, Lord Worthy, who is one of the Queen's most trusted Privy Councillors and in charge of looking after my estates, said it was an unnecessary expense. *I* think he just wanted it to be a girl of his own choosing—so I share Fran with the other girls.

Masou was juggling absent-mindedly with his glittering red and yellow balls. When I threw him the third, he just caught it and mixed it in with the others, along with a knife and a cup and a horn spoon. I really like Masou. He's a little shorter than me, though we think he's about the same age. He comes from the south, where they're burned by the sun, and his skin is a lovely colour like a wooden casket. As he's a tumbler for the Queen's Troupe, he wears a brilliantly coloured tunic made of dozens of different brocades and velvets. He has two: a new one for performing and an old one for the rest of the time.

The dogs came scampering up, barking. Ellie scooped up Eric to give him a cuddle and then tried to rub the paw marks off her apron. I felt in the pocket of my petticoat for the couple of manchet rolls and sweetmeats I'd saved for her.

Masou sprinkled pepper on the crayfish and he and Ellie started stripping off all the legs and chewing on the bodies. I don't like crayfish—I've never even tasted them, but the look of all those legs puts me off.

"What will you perform at the St. Valentine's Ball?" I asked Masou.

He winked and made a throat-slitting movement with his finger. "Can't say," he said. "Hanged, drawn, and quartered for telling you."

I know that the Queen has devised a riddle for me to solve at the ball. I have some reputation at Court for fathoming riddles, puzzles, and the like. I am very curious (and not a little nervous!) about this one, so I thought I would see if Masou had heard anything of it—the Queen's Troupe is often privy to the Court gossip, especially if the Queen has planned a special entertainment.

"The Queen said she's got a little riddle for me—do you know what it is?" I ventured.

Masou put his hands on his chest and looked wide-eyed and innocent. "Me? Why would a poor tumbler know?"

"Lord Robert's had a bath specially," said Ellie thoughtfully. "He went down to the stews yesterday to get ready for it."

I laughed at this. Lord Robert Radcliffe of Worcester is another of the three suitors the Queen has chosen for me. He must be anxious to look—and smell—his best.

"His heart burns with passion for the beauteous Lady Grace and so he must quench it!" Masou said dramatically, so I had to kick some earth at him for making fun of me.

"Well, I think it was gentlemanly of him," said Ellie. "Very considerate. He can't afford new clothes at the moment—all the moneylenders are after him. Sir Gerald Worthy's arrived, too, and he's got a new shirt *and* a new velvet suit for the dance."

Sir Gerald Worthy is my Lord Worthy's nephew and my third suitor. I have hardly ever seen him because he has been travelling round Europe. Lord Worthy doesn't have any children and his wife died young. Sir Gerald is his only heir, which is one reason why he would be such a good match for me. I've heard he is quite handsome and that is all. I was just going to ask what else Ellie had heard about him, when I heard someone shouting my name at the Orchard gate.

I jumped up, and the dogs all started barking madly, just like we've taught them. Masou scuffed earth over the fire, Ellie gulped down the last two crayfish legs whole, and the two hid in the little compost-heap house, while I ran up through the trees.

Sure enough, Sir Charles Amesbury was standing there, big round face all red. "Come along, my lady," he said, patting his stomach. "Remember how important it is to ride every day so you become used to it." He smiled fondly. "At least you remembered to wear your riding kirtle, Lady Greensleeves."

Yes, but please, please don't sing it, I thought.

"Alas, my love, you do me wrong," carolled Sir Charles as we went through the Privy Garden and down the passageways leading to the Tilting Yard. *"To cast me off discourteously, When I have loved you so long . . ."*

In fact Sir Charles has a very nice deep voice—very tuneful. He often sings for the Queen with other Court gentlemen. It's just embarrassing being sung at by a man who's old enough to be your father but wants to marry you—especially when it's such an old-fashioned song. Doesn't he know any Italian madrigals?

Two horses were saddled and waiting in the yard. I

took the dogs on their leash over to the groom. Henri started growling and snapping at Doucette's hooves, which just shows you how stupid lapdogs can be.

Sir Charles caught the horse's bridle just as she started tossing her head. "Now then," he said. "Now then, Doucette, you could squash that little dog with one foot. He's quite beneath your dignity. Gently now. See, my lady? See? With horses you move slowly and gently and so . . ."

I moved slowly and gently to pat Doucette's neck. Then Sir Charles cupped his hands for me to mount, and I managed to get myself hooked over the side-saddle without going right over the other side and falling flat on my face as I often do.

Once I had my front foot arranged, the other one firmly in the stirrup, and my whip, Sir Charles climbed up, puffing, onto the other horse. Then, suddenly, he was a completely different creature— straight and relaxed and quite at home. I'm sure that's how he looked when the Boy King was alive and Sir Charles was known for his prowess at the Tilt.

"*Greensleeves was all my joy, Greensleeves was my delight, Greensleeves was my heart of gold . . . ,*" he sang as we trotted off, and I tried not to tense up and bounce, but just to rock my bum into the saddle with the horse's movement.

While we trotted the horses to warm them up, Sir Charles talked to me. He does it so I won't think about falling off so much. Today he told me something quite sad: his twin brother died recently fighting the religious wars in France.

"I had the letter last night," he said, looking sombre. "Just the bare news of it. Alas, Hector and I were not good friends when he left and I would it had not been so. In truth, he was always the black sheep of the family—and oftentimes up to no good—but he was my brother still."

"I am sorry. Was he fighting for the Protestants?" I asked gently.

"Ay, against the foul Papist Guises," he replied grimly.

I frowned at the name of Guise. I hate them, too, and I have good reason: my mother died in one of their wicked plots to kill our Protestant Queen and put a Catholic monarch in her place.

Sir Charles distracted me then by telling me the proper way to ask a horse to canter. We practised and then tried it and dear Doucette went from a trot to the slowest canter, which was just like a hobbyhorse and not frightening at all. In fact, it was almost fun to go cantering down one side of the Tilting Yard, round the fence, and then up the other side. It's the first time I've managed a canter without falling off! I was so proud!

Sir Charles laughed at my flushed face. ". . . *And who but my Lady Greensleeves,*" he sang, and gave me a kiss on the forehead as he helped me down. "Well done, that was very good, my lady. We'll have you out-riding the Queen yet."

"Better not let her hear you say that," I told him, and couldn't help smiling as he pretended to be dismayed.

"Oh, you wouldn't tell her, surely?" he said. "Please don't. I beg you. Shall I kneel down and beg you that way?"

I tried not to laugh. "I don't want you to hurt your poor knees," I said.

He looked cunning. "Good thought, my lady, and I must keep my hose decent for tomorrow. Are you looking forward to it?"

"No," I said, because I'm too lazy to tell polite lies. "I am not sure I am ready to choose a husband and married life."

"Small blame to you," Sir Charles sighed. "But not all ladies can be like the Queen, you know. If only you would marry me—darling Grace, Lady Cavendish—I should treat you no differently than I do now, until you were grown to your proper womanhood."

I sighed. I do like Sir Charles, but even though he's one of the three suitors the Queen has chosen for me, I don't want to marry him.

———

I just had to go and get some more ink. When I started I didn't realize how much there is to say about even a dull day.

The next thing that happened as soon as I got back from my riding lesson was a gentleman telling me the Queen was already in her chamber and I was bid attend on her. So I had to run upstairs and change into my damask again and then run to wait on the Queen.

I got there and curtsied. One of the Wardrobe tailors was kneeling in front of the Queen, sweating.

"But wherefore is Lady Grace's kirtle still not finished, Mr. Beasley?" the Queen asked disapprovingly. "Surely this is not your wonted service to me. Why so long a-making? I had desired to see it before she wears it."

"But Your Majesty," the tailor said desperately,

"the beauteous Lady Grace keeps on growing, but the cloth does not!"

I could see the Queen wanted to laugh at that, but she only told him he had her permission to burn ten more wax candles, to save his men's eyes while they sewed another hem tonight, and sent him off.

The Queen is very grand and frightening. She has red hair and snapping dark eyes and a lovely pale complexion, apart from a very few, very tiny small-pox scars, from when she was so sick while I was a little girl. She's about middling size for a woman—though she seems much taller, especially when she is displeased! And she wears the most glorious gowns imaginable, all made for her by the men of the Privy Wardrobe. She's very clever and it pleases her that I am quick enough to learn to read and write and so on. She says that she is bored by girls who can only think of jewellery and clothes. She likes me especially because she's known me all my life and my mother saved her life a year ago.

"What have you been doing to make your cheeks so red, Lady Grace?" the Queen questioned.

"I managed to canter on Doucette, Your Majesty," I told her excitedly. "And I didn't fall off once!"

She clapped her hands. "You must be tired then,"

she said. "You shall have a little light supper and go straight to your bed, for tomorrow will be a long day."

I didn't really want to be alone but there's no point arguing, so I had my light supper of pheasant pasties and salt-fish fritters, with a couple of sausages and manchet bread and some overcooked potherbs, and went to our bedchamber.

And here I am at last, in my shift and three candles lit. I'll just say my prayers and

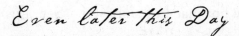

Even later this Day

I had to stop because there was a tap at the door. Ellie and Masou crept in, looking very furtive.

"You shouldn't be here, you'll get in terrible trouble," I told them.

"Fie!" said Ellie. "Look, mistress, I'm delivering your nice new smock for tomorrow, isn't it lovely?"

"Rude!" said Masou. "It's very rude to say smock. She should say shift. Isn't she rude, my lady?" He was wagging his finger at Ellie.

"Yes, and don't call me 'mistress,' or 'my lady,'" I growled.

Ellie stuck her tongue out.

"All right, let's see it," I said eagerly.

It was a beautiful smock, in fine linen, embroidered with blackwork. I recognized what Mrs. Champernowne and the Queen had been working on all autumn and smiled, feeling quite touched. The Queen was as excited about the St. Valentine's Ball as if I were her own true daughter.

"We just ironed it. Look at all them ruffles—I did 'em myself," said Ellie, who was learning to be a proper laundrywoman. She folded it neatly and put it in my clothes chest.

Masou came over and sat on the bed. He had a little tiny pot made of alabaster. "See, this is kohl," he said, opening it. "If you put a little, just a very little, around your eyes, they will look beautiful and sparkling."

"I don't like wearing face paint," I said, and pushed the pot away.

He laughed at me. "Not white lead and cinnabar, no, but this will be as if your eyes had grown that way."

"Masou, please, please tell what the Queen is planning for me," I begged. "She won't breathe a word."

He put his finger on his lips and winked. "Mr. Somers himself said we must not tell, and when he said it he was staring straight at me," he whispered.

I sighed. Masou would not cross the leader of the Queen's Troupe.

Then he and Ellie did a ridiculous little dance, while juggling some of Lady Sarah's dozens of face-paint pots. Finally, they replaced the pots, oh, so carefully, and backed out of the door into the passage, where they immediately became serious and well behaved. They do make me laugh.

I hate not knowing what Her Majesty is up to, even though I know she would never be cruel to me as she sometimes is to other courtiers. Oh, Lord, preserve me. I hope I don't have to dance by myself! Or sing!

Now I must sleep.

I should not really be writing this at all. We're in the Queen's Chapel and the Palace Chaplain has been preaching for at least four hours. Maybe not quite that long, but I'm sure it is nearly dinner time. I am pretending to take notes on his sermon (hah!).

When we processed to chapel this morning, we passed by the Great Hall. It seemed all the Household were there, hanging up red silk banners and scurrying to and fro to fetch ladders and hang tinsel hearts for the ball. When I saw the hustle and bustle, I wasn't sure if I was excited or terrified, and my heart beat fast.

The Queen isn't listening to the sermon, either. She's snorting quietly at something in the paper she's reading. She always brings her red boxes with her so she can read during the service—as she told me, it's necessary for her to be there, but the good

Lord knows how busy she is with the idiots of her Council, and will forgive her if she uses the time productively. I'm sure that's right.

I have to stop now. The Chapel Boys are singing— so beautiful, like birds. I must pack my ink away— the service will finish soon.

I am sitting in a window seat with my daybooke and penner and I shouldn't be doing this AT ALL. I am all dressed now in my rose-velvet gown, ready for the ball, and if I got ink on my gown . . . But I feel so scared, my heart is thudding and my palms are like slugs. I have to do something. It's the sleeves I'm worried about: they're white, so any speck of ink will show. I suppose I could get Fran to unlace them and put another pair on, but I don't know which of my pairs of sleeves would match.

After Chapel I had a little food I wasn't hungry for, and then Mrs. Champernowne called me to the Queen's Withdrawing Chamber, where all the closets are, to help me dress. First, I had a bath in the Queen's own tub with rose-water soap from Castile and then, when I was dry, I put on my new smock.

I expect Lady Sarah and Mary Shelton were flurrying around in our chamber, arguing over partlets and false fronts and making accusations about pots of perfume. But it was peaceful in the Queen's Withdrawing Chamber so I had plenty of time to get nervous.

We waited behind a screen while the tub was taken out by some of the Queen's Serving Men, and then Mrs. Champernowne rubbed her hands to make them warm. "Now then," she said to me. "Please do not wriggle, Lady Grace."

When Ellie gets dressed she laces her bodice over her smock, puts on a petticoat and her kirtle, slips her cap, shoes, and wooden pattens on, and there she is.

Well, me getting ready for a feast takes an awful lot longer than that. Mrs. Champernowne brushed my hair, and her own tiring woman brought my new partlet, all covered with embroidered flowers. The linen is transparently fine; I was scared I'd tear it when I put my head through the neck hole. And I hate the feeling of having the tabs tied under my armpits. It tickles! The Queen has given me a new pair of white silk stockings with rose-wool garters and new rose-embroidered dancing slippers. The staymaker had brought my new stays. They're cut French-style, and they're so tight round the waist I can hardly breathe. Even my bumroll is new, though my petticoat and farthingale are altered ones of my mother's. The top petticoat is of white damask, embroidered with roses.

My gown is just *amazing*! It is very heavy, because it's mostly made of rose velvet and all in a piece—so I had to sort of dive in and slide. I popped out with my hair everywhere and my arms waving. It took ages for Mrs. Champernowne and Fran to do all the lacing and tying together. The silver aiglets on the ends of the laces were decorated with roses so I knew they were my mother's. Suddenly my chest felt stuffed full with sadness that she wasn't there to help me dress for my first proper grown-up feast.

"Oh, sweetheart," said Mrs. Champernowne. She gave my shoulders a squeeze, then dabbed my eyes and nose for me. "If you make your nose all red, we will have to paint it with white, look you."

I nodded and tried to direct my thoughts elsewhere.

When they had finished, they turned me round to look in the Queen's own looking glass, which is huge and made of Venetian glass and worth as much as a good horse! It was as if a tall lady had come in and was facing me. While Fran tied a small ruff round my neck, I curtsied to her—the reflection did the same. Well, I knew it was me, really, but I didn't believe it until then.

"There now," said Mrs. Champernowne, sounding satisfied. "A very beautiful Maid of Honour."

"Do you think so?" I thought the strange lady staring at me from the looking glass certainly looked better than I usually do.

"Any man should think himself lucky to have you to wife, my dear," she said. "Of course, *Sir Gerald* will be able to buy you as many gowns as you like."

I smiled to myself. My Lord Worthy had clearly been drumming up support for his nephew. "What about Sir Charles?" I asked, partly because I wanted to put her off the scent of my Lord Robert, who is probably my favourite.

Mrs. Champernowne sniffed. "Sir Charles would more likely give you horses," she answered. "And as for that young fool, Lord Robert, I hope you do not throw yourself away on him. Sir Gerald was putting him right on something the other day, and all Lord Robert could do was gawp at him."

It is true that Lord Robert can be a bit tongue-tied, but at least he isn't old. He is about twenty. I wonder what he was arguing about with Sir Gerald. I didn't ask because Mrs. Champernowne clearly wanted me to. And I don't want any more good advice about how nice Sir Gerald is.

"Off with you now," Mrs. Champernowne said. "And do not so much as speckle your kirtle, Lady Grace, or I will birch you, by God, Queen or no Queen. Her Majesty must dress now."

I slipped my pattens on to protect my slippers and wobbled through the door. As soon as I got into the passage, I found Ellie and Masou peeking round the corner from the back stairs.

Ellie clapped her hands. "You look beautiful, my lady," she said wistfully. "Truly beautiful."

"Oh, fie," I replied. "Anyone could look beautiful in this dress."

Ellie shook her head. She has a bump on the bridge of her nose and quite a lot of spots and her hands are red from the washing soap.

"Anyway, it's very uncomfortable," I added. "It's too tight round my waist and I can't bend my arms properly and my neck's stiff from the ruff and I dare neither breathe nor scratch!"

Masou made an elaborate bow to me, then came

close with his little pot of kohl and dabbed a tiny amount on my eyelids. It tickled and I was scared he'd get my ruff dirty, but Masou is very quick and dextrous. I looked in the side of a polished silver jug which stands on a chest near the window, and it did make my eyes look more . . . mysterious, I suppose. Masou was wearing some for his stage paint already. "You have no necklace," he pointed out.

He was right, I didn't.

"Why would that be?" He bowed again, smiling, and I knew it was the clue to the Queen's riddle that I'd asked for. Then he was off with Ellie because they both had lots to do before the ball.

Very late, this same Day

I am writing this by the watch candle. I'm in my own bedchamber at last. In the other bed, Lady Sarah and Mary Shelton are asleep. Lady Sarah is snoring like a pig, while Mary Shelton is snoring like a badger.

I had to stop quickly earlier and hide everything away because Mrs. Champernowne was coming. (I got Ellie to come and fetch my daybooke and penner to the bedchamber later on.)

Everything in my head is all muddled up—there is so much to tell of this night's events!

Mrs. Champernowne fetched me to the Presence Chamber and I sat there on a cushion with the other Maids of Honour, feeling like a wooden doll and wishing I could run round the Privy Garden half a dozen times. I didn't. I think Mrs. Champernowne really would have birched me, if I'd done that. But I did wriggle a bit because of a fleabite on my back.

"Now stay still, Lady Grace," Mrs. Champernowne scolded. "Remember, the stuff for that gown cost Her Majesty hundreds of pounds, never mind the tailoring!"

I goggled at her.

"You could buy a house in the City of Westminster with that, look you. So none of your hoydenish tricks," she went on.

I was really glad she hadn't spotted me using pen and ink.

After a long while of waiting and talking quietly, it was time to go. I felt sick with nerves. The Queen arrived in her wonderful gown of cloth of silver and black velvet. Everybody else was in white or silver damask to match her—it's quite an honour that I was allowed to wear rose. Lady Bedford, the most favoured Lady-in-Waiting, arranged the Queen's long black damask train and veil and then we all set off, walking two by two down the passages where the Gentlemen of the Guard stood in their red velvet, and all the other courtiers cheered and clapped. I had to walk with Lady Sarah, who was furious about all the special treatment I'd received and wouldn't talk to me.

The Great Hall was festooned with red and purple ribbons and tinsel hearts dangling from the beams. The Maids of Honour don't often go in there because the Queen likes to eat in the Privy Parlour and we usually keep her company. (Last month, the Queen was so busy with paperwork and Council meetings that she had her food brought on a tray, and we had to find our food as best we could. In the end, I gave Ellie some money and sent her out to get pasties for all of us at the nearest cookshop. We all burned our mouths because they were still so hot!)

We lined up behind the top table on the dais, facing all the other tables in the hall. The Queen made some sort of speech of welcome, but I was still feeling sick so I didn't listen. I looked quickly for my suitors, but they were all at the other end of the top table, next to Lord Worthy, ignoring each other. The Queen had kindly arranged things so that they wouldn't be staring at me. I saw Ellie right down the other end of the hall and she waved to me, only I couldn't wave back because of being dignified.

I thought I would run lunatic with all the to-ing and fro-ing. I hate feasting. I hate having to sit around being polite and conversing while my stomach's rumbling like a cart on cobbles as we wait for ages for the food to arrive. This time there was a *really* long wait while the serving men, squires, and pageboys sorted themselves out by the hatch outside. Then I nearly jumped out of my skin when the musicians blared on the trumpets to announce them. They processed in to very loud stately music, carrying beef and venison and swan and suckling pig and some chickens—and a game pie as big as a wellhead. I felt quite sorry for them, having to carry the food above their heads on huge silver platters. Then there was *another* long wait while they took the meat to the carving table for carving.

By this time, my mouth was so dry and my stomach so clenched up about the dancing (and whatever the Queen was going to do), I couldn't eat anything at all except a bit of manchet bread and butter and a few candied carrots and potherbs, like the ones decorating the sallet. So it was wasted.

The only good thing that happened was that when

the serving man brought me the candied carrots, he had a very strained expression on his face. Then, when he leaned over to get the plate of fried-bread sippets, he farted very loudly—which made me and Mary Shelton giggle.

And as for swan-meat—ptui! (Mrs. Champernowne says a lady must only spit discreetly into her handkerchief, but I can spit in writing, if I want.) They only have it because it looks so pretty. It's all put back together after carving and covered with a suit of swan's feathers with a cunningly carved head and neck as well, so it looks as if it's still alive and swimming on the silver platter. But I don't care if it is a royal bird, it tastes fishy and horrible—even worse than turkey!

Lady Sarah would not talk to me at all during the two covers of food; she just kept chatting to Mary Shelton and Carmina, who was next to Mary. It was fine—at least I didn't have to try to chat back with my mouth so dry. Mrs. Champernowne told the page to give me watered wine, which helped a bit. I had to sip it really carefully, though, because I was terrified of spilling any on my gown.

After the first set of dishes, there was a pause. I was just beginning to relax, thanks to the wine, when *bam-bam-da-da-bam-bam!* I nearly fell off the bench with fright.

In came French Louis with a big drum, banging on it like a madman. Behind him were the dwarf twins, Peter and Paul, juggling with red satin hearts, and behind them was Mr. Will Somers, the Queen's Fool, flipping slowly over and over and jumping up to turn over in the air. And then, with the drum going *bam-da-da-bam-da-da-bam* and the trumpets making an even more awful noise than they did to start with, in came Little John, the huge strongman, holding a pole on his head. And at the top of the pole, standing on a little platform about the size of your two hands, was Masou. I stared with my mouth open. I was already tense! I thought this was really too much. Out of the corner of my eye I saw Ellie watching, too, white as a sheet, hands to her mouth.

And as if that weren't dangerous enough, Masou stood on one leg and started juggling with batons. He saw us, grinned, and winked at me. And then he tilted, waved his arms, wobbled, and fell . . .

I couldn't help it—I screamed. Everybody else was screaming, too. But then, in midair, Masou turned a backwards somersault and landed perfectly on his feet like a cat. And then he caught the batons he'd been juggling and carried on—while doing a jig. Everybody whooped and clapped; even the Queen was laughing and clapping.

I clapped, too, but only a bit because my hands were shaking so much. Ellie looked as if she'd nearly fainted. I don't know what gets into Masou when he tumbles for an audience. I think he goes wood-wild in the head.

The Queen spoke to one of the pages and Mr. Somers brought Masou up to the dais to be presented to the Queen. I didn't hear what she said, but when all the tumblers bounced and jumped and cartwheeled off again, Masou turned somersaults in the air and his face was shining.

And then it was time for the banquet course and we all stood up and processed out to the Banqueting House in the garden. They had taken it out of storage and put it up specially, and the rude pictures on the canvas walls of Venus and Cupid had lasted quite well—the paint had hardly cracked and Venus's naked bottom was still quite pink.

I like the banqueting course usually, with all the jellies and sweetmeats and custards—and the beautiful marchpane subtlety in the middle. This one was a sculpture of Venus again, with Cupid aiming an arrow made of liquorice, all made in pink sugar plate and really pretty. Except I could see that there were three blue velvet cushions lying on the table in front of the banquet, and little squares of white silk covered the things that were resting on them.

So that meant I couldn't even enjoy the sweetmeats—like the marmelada of quinces, which is my favourite, or the vanilla egg creams. I was too busy trying not to stare at those cushions. On one was a sort of roundish lump, on the second was a long and pointed shape, and the thing on the third one just looked like a heap of peas!

They had laid a floor of polished wood to dance on and the musicians in the corner began a Burgermeister dance to break the ice. It's such a silly German dance; you can't be dignified when you're wagging fingers and linking arms.

All the Maids of Honour swept off in a long line to face the gentlemen and bow and curtsy. Somehow, Lord Robert had managed to barge into the row facing me, so we partnered and, while I held his hand and did the first bit of dancing, he stared at me and went red and said, "Umm . . . er . . . Lady Grace . . . um . . ."

"What?" I said breathlessly. But by that time it

was his turn to hop and point his toes, and by the time he'd come back to me he'd missed his chance because we had to go back and change partners.

It was like that every time he looked at me, or we took hands in the dance: he was trying to say something he'd clearly made up beforehand, but each time he just stammered and looked sweaty. It was very irritating. I think that a lot of Lord Robert's manly silence is Lord Robert not knowing what to say. Still, at least he's only twenty. That's something. And he has quite good legs. The other girls say he has high birth and low pockets—by which I suppose they mean he has no money and his estates are mortgaged. But I don't care about that as long as he loves me. I've got plenty of money of my own. Though it would be nice if he could say something other than "Um . . ." occasionally.

Next there was a Pavane, otherwise known as the most boring dance in the world. Dances are for jumping about and getting breathless. What's the point of all that stately walking to and fro in lines, holding hands, turning, bowing, curtsying, and stepping backwards and forwards? Yawn! For this one I got Sir Charles, who was looking unusually sour and bad-tempered.

"At least this is a tune we know," I said to him, as he walked me back and forth.

I'd realized that the musicians were playing "Greensleeves."

"Hm?" He looked puzzled. "What do you mean, my lady?"

I nudged him in the ribs. "It's 'Greensleeves,'" I said. "The song you always sing when we go riding?"

He smiled wanly. "Oh yes, how silly of me to forget. 'Greensleeves,' of course . . . *Ta dah, di dah, di dah, dah dah dah* . . ." His voice was flat.

I tutted. "You seem to have a bad throat, Sir Charles," I said. "You really should not sing. And nor should you dance."

Not that he can. A Pavane is about all he can manage, though his knees seemed a bit less stiff.

Next thing, the Master of Ceremonies announced a Volta. We've just done it in dancing class. It's very scandalous because you have to show your knees! But the Queen loves it. I myself don't like the bit where you have to dance while the gentleman stands there, or the bit when he gets to show off. What I like is when the gentleman takes hold of the lower edge of your stays and lifts you up as you jump and bang your feet together. That's great fun. Though last Tuesday morning the dancing master was very upset. "You are supposed to come down like a feather! A *feather*!" he shouted at me, when a painting fell off the wall of the Long Gallery.

As we lined up, ready to go round to our partners, I thought that Sir Gerald was going to partner Lady Sarah (whose bosom was nearly hanging out over her bodice again—honestly, I know not why Mrs. Champernowne doesn't chide her for it). But then Lord Worthy moved next to Sir Gerald and said something in his ear, and he changed places with another gentleman, who looked very pleased.

So for the Volta I got Sir Gerald. He smiled and bowed and looked straight at me. The new gentleman was staring at Lady Sarah's chest, but Sir Gerald was looking at my face. (Well, I've got nothing to see further down, even in a French-cut bodice.) He has one of those very handsome faces, all straight lines and angles, with quizzical black eyebrows. He's tall, so it looks as if he's staring down his nose at me. I've played some Primero with Sir Gerald (I won! Ha ha!) and walked in the Privy Garden for our formal meetings, but that's all. He's quite old—though not as ancient as Sir Charles. I think he had a wife, but she died in childbirth. At least he's neither fat nor tongue-tied.

"Your ladyship is more beautiful than I have ever

seen you," he said. "Rose velvet becomes you, Lady Grace."

I tried to blush, but couldn't. "Thank you, Sir Gerald," I replied.

I'd done my bit of the footwork so he did his. The thing about a Volta is, if you can dance, it gives you a chance to show off. Sir Gerald can certainly dance. I've never seen anything like it, the way he jumped and kicked and moved his feet in time to the fast drumbeats. Then it was time for me to jump and, when he caught hold of my stays and lifted me, I went higher than I ever do with the dancing master, who's always complaining that we've utterly undone his back. I went right up, twirled, and came down quite well, too, because I'd gone up so straight. He steadied me as I landed and lifted me again, so I was breathless by the time the jumping bit was over.

"Do you think Lord Robert could do that, my lady?" he whispered, and he wasn't even breathing hard as we paced around in a circle with others of our set. "Or Sir Charles?"

I know Sir Charles couldn't—he makes heavy weather out of helping me into the saddle. But Lord Robert? He's young and quite skinny but I think he's strong, too. I saw him tossing Mary Shelton into the air without much difficulty. And she's no slender reed.

"Don't throw yourself away on rustics," Sir Gerald went on as we joined up once more. "Lord Robert is poor and Sir Charles will always love horses more than you. Marry me."

And then the dance parted us, leaving me rather annoyed. I really don't like being told what to think. Besides, I knew who I liked more and it certainly wasn't Sir Very-very-sure-of-himself Gerald. Let Lady Sarah have him.

At last the Queen clapped her hands, the dancing music stopped, and she beckoned me forward. "Good friends," she said, while the musicians in the corner played a pretty, soft tune on their viols. "Today is a joyous day for our dear Lady Grace. She has petitioned me to marry her to some gentleman of my choosing . . ."

I hadn't, but I know that's what my father put in his will before he died serving the Queen in France in the first years of her reign.

". . . and I have chosen three goodly nobles, each of whom would be a fine husband for any woman. But which man will kindle our Lady Grace's young heart?"

There was a murmur and then Lord Robert came

forward and dropped to one knee. "Umm . . . I will, Y-your Majesty," he stammered.

Behind him came Sir Gerald, who also kneeled. "Your Gracious Majesty . . . who by offering Lady Grace increases her own grace . . . ," he began. I saw Lord Worthy smile fondly at his nephew's charm. "My Lady Grace needs a *man* to her bridal bed, not a mouse. *I* am the most manly of the suitors," Sir Gerald declared.

At this, the other Maids of Honour giggled a little, and Lord Robert went purply red and looked at the polished floor.

Sir Charles then came forward and put his knee down firmly. "But *I* will be the best husband for Lady Grace, Your Majesty," he said. "Because she and I have friendship in our favour."

I looked at Sir Charles, feeling very uncomfortable. Yes, we were friends—of sorts—but he did look particularly old tonight. And his face looked not nearly as pink and jolly as usual. Perhaps he was nervous, too.

The Queen clapped her hands and smiled. "You offer yourselves, but what of your inmost hearts?" she said. "And what of Grace's young and unschooled heart? We shall try if heart can speak to heart upon this Feast of St. Valentine." She turned to me and beckoned, so I went forward and curtsied to one knee.

She caught my hand and raised me up. "Each of Lady Grace's lovers has presented a gift, unmarked and unknown. Now it is for Lady Grace to select the gift that likes her heart best, and so, the man who will have her heart."

My heart went *thump! lurch!* and I wanted to be sick, which I obviously couldn't, standing next to the Queen like that.

"Come, my dear, make appraisal of the gifts," the Queen commanded.

I went and looked at the cushions, pulling the white silk squares off each gift. One was a small, silver-chased ivory flask with a lid that took off and became a cup—the sort of thing the Queen carries in her sleeve when she hunts, with aqua vitae in it.

The second was a small jewelled knife, set with garnets and pearls, with a pearl Cupid on the end—very pretty. Of course, I have an eating knife, but it just has a bone hilt and a plain leather scabbard, so it isn't pretty enough to wear on special occasions. I liked the knife—I picked it up and drew it to see whether it was just for show. There was a sharp steel blade, so I put it back carefully.

The third cushion bore a pearl necklace with gold

links—quite simple, but very long, so you could wrap it round your neck and have it dangle all the way to your waist, or wear it as a snood round your hair. I touched the pearls. I am very fond of pearls; my mother used to wear them. I always wear a little pearl ring that she gave me. And what was it Masou had said? I glanced across at him, playing a lute in the corner with the musicians. Why wasn't I wearing a necklace? Good question.

Then I stepped back and curtsied to the Queen. "May I explain what I judge from these gifts, Your Majesty?" I asked, and tried to think of something clever to say. "This flask, Your Majesty, is beautifully made for bringing spirits to revive one's spirits when hunting. Perhaps Sir Charles, who has been helping my poor horsemanship, is hoping I will need it soon. From this, I guess a great ability to love, a heart deep enough for anyone to drain, a generous and kindly nature."

Sir Charles bowed.

"But I fear it will be a long time before I can ride well enough to keep up with the Queen's Hunt," I concluded.

I turned to the long necklace of pearls with the gold links. "Here is a rope of pearls. He who gave it knows my favourite jewel is the pearl and has given a long enough length that I will not feel constricted by it. I read sensitivity to my likes in the giver. But, nonetheless, is the rope of pearls meant to bind me tight, my Lord Robert?"

As usual, Lord Robert reddened and bowed. Sir Gerald was looking very smug now.

"And the beautiful dagger. Surely it speaks of a keen intelligence and a cutting wit. I was tempted because I would like so pretty a knife—but who woos with a blade? Surely a knife cuts the knot and does not tie it, Sir Gerald?"

Now Sir Gerald was scowling. It gave an ugly sneer to his mouth. He knocked back another silver cup of wine and held it out for a pageboy to refill.

I turned to the Queen and went down on one knee again. "In conclusion, Your Majesty, I am happy in your service. I yet have no desire to marry."

The Queen shook her head, smiling sadly. "It was my promise to your parents, Grace," she said. "You must have a husband to look after your estates."

"Well, in that case . . ." I stood, sighed, trailed my fingers along the dagger and the flask, and then picked up the lovely pearl necklace and looped it carefully round my neck. "I choose my Lord Robert's gift."

He looked absolutely moonstruck. Quite like a calf with the bellyache, as Masou described him. I had to squash the urge to laugh.

He came forward with his face as red as ever to kiss my hand. "Um . . . Lady Grace . . . I, um . . . Um," he said.

The musicians struck up another dance tune as Sir Gerald rolled his eyes and drank another cup of aqua vitae. Lord Worthy hurried over and whispered in his ear again, which provoked a snarl.

Lord Robert and I danced a passage of the Volta, which got everyone staring, but that's what the musicians were playing. And yes, when Lord Robert lifted me, he felt strong enough and he steadied me when I landed—but he still didn't manage to say anything except "Um" and "Er." I felt quite sorry for him, though at least when I'm married to him *I* shall be able to talk as much as I like.

The other courtiers joined in and other couples went jigging and jumping and whizzing past us. I saw Sir Charles sitting at the side near a bank of candles, watching us rather sourly. Then Sir Gerald came through with a rather stout Lady-in-Waiting, and barged Lord Robert out of the way and trod on his foot. Off he went again.

Nobody else had noticed, but Lord Robert was gripping his sword. "I h-hate him," he sputtered.

I put my hand on his, gripping his sword hilt. "But you won and he lost," I said. "Why not be kind and forgiving?"

"My Lady Grace . . . ," said Lord Robert, "you . . . are . . . so . . . w-wonderful."

Well, it was the longest speech he has ever made me, and it was quite flattering, so I smiled and kissed his cheek.

Dancing makes me thirsty and so, when the music stopped, I fanned myself and asked for something to drink. Lord Robert went to the sideboard where the pages and serving men were pouring wine. He waited patiently for Lord Worthy to get himself some mead, turning to survey the hall before taking a goblet for himself and a little Venetian glass cup of a flower water for me.

Sir Charles and Sir Gerald were collecting the gifts I had turned down. I was sorry I had offended Sir Charles, because usually he really is a nice old thing. Sir Gerald looked furious—pale, eyes glittering, with little patches of colour on his cheeks. He rocked as he swept up the dagger and stuck it in his belt. "Only a silly little chit of a girl chooses a stripling boy over a man grown," he snarled. "Does she think Lord Robert will look after her? She'll be wiping his bum for him."

He glugged back his wine, not noticing some pink spots on his ruff. He held it out to be refilled, but the pages and serving men are given strict orders by the Queen that anyone who looks drunk is not to be served. She won't have scenes at her Court as they do at the King of Scotland's, for instance.

"Oh, for Christ's sake, have we run out of booze already?" Sir Gerald demanded vulgarly.

I took my flower water out of Lord Robert's hand because he was scowling at Sir Gerald, and turning pink at being called a boy. I was very glad I hadn't chosen the dagger now; who wants to be married to a bully?

Then the crowd parted, and there stood the Queen. Those who knew Her Majesty well could see that, inside, she was furious. "If you need wine to drown your sorrows, Sir Gerald, I am sure that the winner of Lady Grace's heart will be magnanimous enough to offer his own," she said lightly.

Lord Robert went a darker red and his fingers clenched on the goblet in his hand.

Lord Worthy hurried forward and took Sir

Gerald's arm. "No need, no need," he said comfortably. "Come, nephew, I think you've had enough already."

"If Sir Gerald is in need of wine, then wine he must have," declared the Queen, in the tone that nobody likes to hear. "Perhaps you won't accept it from your victor, Sir Gerald . . . ," she added, as she glided across the floor and held out her hand for Lord Robert's cup.

I stood on Lord Robert's toe and he bowed jerkily and handed his goblet to the Queen.

"But surely you will accept it from me," she finished.

As she glided back I realized Her Majesty was being very clever, smoothing over the quarrel, perhaps preventing a duel. She handed Lord Robert's cup of wine to Sir Gerald and of course he had to bow to her and then he really did have to drink it.

"From so fair and merciful a hand, what can I do but accept?" he asked, and drank it all down in one go. Then he made to bow again, lost his balance, and fell flat on his nose!

I laughed and the Queen laughed, and so did everybody else, especially Lord Robert. Only Lord Worthy was still upset. He rushed over, pulled Sir Gerald to his feet, and hissed something in his ear.

Sir Gerald bowed again, this time less unsteadily. "Your Majesty, by your leave, I think I had best get to bed," he mumbled.

"Yes," said the Queen pointedly. "I think that would be wise, Sir Gerald. The oblivion of the wine cup is no real cure for a broken heart, but at least there can be the oblivion of sleep, and all shall be forgotten in the morning."

I thought she was being very nice to him; she is normally much sharper with anyone who drinks enough to fall over. Though I was very surprised that Sir Gerald was upset enough at my rejecting him to get so drunk.

"Thank you, Your Majesty," he said.

Lord Worthy went with him to the door, but the Queen summoned him back. "Come, my old friend, my Lord Worthy," she called. "As long as my lord the Earl of Leicester is away, I need a partner. Come dance with me."

He could hardly refuse, but he didn't look very happy about it as he took the Queen's hand, bowed, kissed it, and then led off with her in the French Farandol.

After all that, I was feeling so hot in my rose-velvet gown that I decided if I didn't cool off, I'd melt. So I slipped my pattens on and went out of the

Banqueting House into the Privy Garden, where it was quite cool and dank. I passed several bushes rather full of people, two by two, and one with a young gentleman flat on his back singing to the stars. I walked quickly on past the maze, to the part that gives onto the kitchens and the buttery.

Ellie was there with someone I recognized as Pip, Sir Gerald's manservant, who was flapping his hands about.

"I only wanted to brush it out," he was saying. "Just shake it and brush it and perhaps dust it with rose-leaf powder before hanging it, so it would be fit for the Court another day. But he was in a rage, you know, quite beside himself. . . ."

Ellie tutted and popped into one of the store sheds to emerge with a bucket. "Where did you say he was sick?"

"On the edge of the mat," Pip told her. "I'm sorry, I would do it myself, but . . ."

"Not to worry." Ellie made a wry face. "I'm used to it after feasts."

She caught sight of me and grinned, rolling her eyes. Her sleeves were rolled up and she had her apron on.

". . . so I'm sure the canions will be crumpled and his ruff bent. And when he wakes up tomorrow and finds I haven't undressed him, I'll be the one to get the blame, you know. It'll all be my fault and I shouldn't wonder if he doesn't kick me out then and there and . . ."

Poor Pip was wringing his hands. I'm more pleased than ever that I turned down Sir Gerald's pretty knife—you can tell a lot from the way someone treats their servants and it's *not* a good sign that Pip is so scared of Sir Gerald.

"He's in one of my Lord Worthy's chambers, isn't he?" asked Ellie. "Why don't I knock on the door, go in, and do the floor, and if that doesn't wake him, you'll know it's safe enough to go in yourself and put everything away before you go to bed?"

Pip looked pathetically grateful. "Would you do that? Be careful, he can be violent when he's drunk and angry," he warned.

"Oh, fie!" sniffed Ellie. "If I can't dodge a kick when the kicker's blind drunk, I deserve a bruise on my bum. Don't you worry, Pip, I'll see to it." She gave me a wink and hurried past to the Grace-and-Favour Chambers, lugging the bucket of lye and a floorcloth.

I turned and went back to the Banqueting House, where the light from the banks of candles was shining out through the painted canvas, throwing silhouettes of Venus and Adonis onto the grass. So I stood and looked for a while, although I was getting chilly.

Somebody came near and turned to bow to me, then took my hand. "Who is it?" I asked.

"Robert," came the reply.

I smiled and relaxed and let him hold my hand. In the darkness I could only see the shape of him.

"When may I k-kiss your lips, my Lady Grace?"

Another long speech! Perhaps it was easier for him to talk when no one could see.

"When we're properly handfasted next month," I said primly.

He kissed my hand instead and I let him. It was very romantic and proper. "A long t-time away. W-will you d-dance again, Lady Grace?"

"With you, my lord?" I said. "Of course."

I let him lead me back to the dancing and we joined the line for another Farandol, which I thought was quite brave of Lord Robert, considering how often I had trod on his toes during the Volta.

We danced several more dances together. Sir Charles came up, still looking miserable, and offered to shake Lord Robert's hand, which I thought was quite good of him. He stared at me all the time, though, which worried me. Then I saw Pip, Sir Gerald's man, come back into the hall and speak to

Lord Worthy—who was holding the Queen's fan for her while she watched Sir Christopher Hatton, one of the Queen's favourites, demonstrate a new measure in the Volta. Lord Worthy spoke sharply to him, glancing over at Lord Robert and me once or twice. From the hand gestures, it looked as if Pip was explaining how Sir Gerald had been sick and gone to bed, and Lord Worthy looked a little less worried then.

At last the Queen decided that she had danced enough—and so, naturally, had all her Maids of Honour and Ladies-in-Waiting. We formed up in a line, a little less neat-looking than it had been on our arrival, and processed out, while the musicians played and the men started gathering together and talking about taking a boat down to Paris Garden.

When I went to help the Queen undress she waved me away. "No, my dear, take Fran to your chamber and get yourself to bed. You must be exhausted."

I suddenly noticed how sore my feet were and how my legs ached and how my stomach felt strange from being squashed together by my tight new stays, so I kneeled and kissed her hand.

"Was this St. Valentine's Feast to your liking, my dear?" She smiled at me.

"Oh yes, Your Majesty. I've had a wonderful time," I told her. And it was true—once I'd got the business of the gifts out of the way.

As I took my leave, the Queen added, "Grace, you will find something waiting on your pillow, my dear."

I curtsied again, wondering what it was, and made my way with Fran to my chamber.

Fran unlaced and unhooked me very quickly, and the rose-velvet kirtle and bodice came off. Then the petticoat and farthingale and bumroll and the other petticoat, and then, at last, Fran unlaced the stays and I said, "Oooff!"

It's pleasing to wear stays and know how small your waist is, but it's even better to take them off and let everything sag. And then, of course, your innards start working again, so you really need to be alone, and Fran knew it, so she smiled and gave me a kiss on the cheek.

"You were beautiful this evening, Lady Grace. You outshone them all," she said.

Now I know it isn't true because no one with mousy hair can outshine Sarah Copper-locks Bartelmy, but it was nice of her to say it, so I kissed her back.

She went out, carrying my kirtle and French stays for brushing and hanging up in a closet.

I took off the pearl necklace my Lord Robert had given me and placed it beside my bed, then changed into my ordinary smock that I wear to bed and used the close-stool.

Fran had poured out some fresh rose-water so I could wash my face and I used my new toothcloth for my teeth and fennel-water to rinse out the almond-and-salt paste.

So here I am. There is a fire in the grate and it's not cold, so I have put my dressing gown on to sit in my favourite corner and write everything down.

Perhaps as I am writing all this in my daybooke, my mother will peek down from heaven and read it, too, so it's as if I am writing to her. I know she would have enjoyed me dancing at the feast. I wonder what she would have thought of my suitors? I think she would have approved of my choice. I know she wouldn't have liked Sir Gerald and I'm sure she would have understood about Sir Charles being too old.

I am finding it hard to keep my eyes open now. I must retire to bed.

The early hours

I had intended to sleep, but now cannot. I am all unsettled and must write this down, too.

When I pulled back the bedcovers I saw a small package on the pillow. At first I wondered which gentleman had placed it there, but then I remembered the Queen's words as I left her chamber. I picked it up and held it to the candle—then had to put it down again quickly as I recognized the writing on the front. It was my mother's writing, dated 14 February 1568, the night she died.

Sometimes I wish that when it happened, on that night a year ago, instead of being where I really was, tucked up fast asleep in a truckle bed in my mother's chamber, I was an angel. Then, God willing, I could have saved her.

I shall tell the story properly, as if I were a storyteller at the fair. Then perhaps I'll get through it.

I've heard that making a tale of a terrible matter may tame it, so the memory no longer rises up and fights away sleep.

My mother, Lady Margaret Cavendish, was a Gentlewoman of the Bedchamber and one of the Queen's closest friends. On 13 February 1568, after kissing me goodnight, she was sitting down to a quiet supper with the Queen, when a man came from Mr. Secretary Cecil to say there was an urgent dispatch from Scotland. The Queen told me she kissed my mother, said she would be back in ten minutes, and suggested my mother try a little wine to help her megrim headache. Then she went to hear the news from Scotland.

And my mother poured herself some wine and drank it. . . .

When I think about it, this is where I imagine being an angel. I fly into the room just as my mother takes up her goblet and I shout, "My lady, do not drink the wine!" And as I would have been a very impressive sight, what with the wings and halo and all, my mother drops the goblet on the rush matting, and then one of the Queen's canary birds—the vicious one that pecks your hair—flies down and drinks it and falls over and dies and so she knows that the wine is poisoned. And then the Queen comes back and they call the guards and test the wine and the doctor finds it contains a deadly poison called darkwort. Then everyone bolts the doors and quarters the Court and so they catch the evil Frenchman sent by the Guises to kill the Queen. . . .

But that's not what happened. My mother drank the Queen's wine and took terribly sick.

The first I knew was when Mrs. Champernowne came and woke me up and wrapped her own furry dressing gown round me. I was too sleepy to walk straight, so she gave me a piggyback—I can hardly believe she did it, when she's so sharp and cross, but she did. And then she brought me into the Queen's own bedchamber.

I could see the Queen was putting pen and ink away and she had tear tracks all down her cheeks. There was incense burning in a little dish, but you could still smell a nasty, dusty, bitter scent in the air. Mrs. Champernowne was crying, too, and I started as well, though I was still too sleepy to know why. Then I looked at the Queen's bed, and saw my mother lying there with her stays open. She had been bled, for her arm was bandaged. And I woke up properly.

My mother's eyes were shut, and her face looked

like candle wax. There was a kind of yellow froth at the corners of her mouth.

I rushed to her. "Is it plague?" I whispered.

"No, Grace," the Queen replied gravely. "If only it were, for she might recover. I think she has taken poison meant for me. The doctor has gone to look at the vomitus."

The door opened and my uncle, Dr. Cavendish, hurried in, wrapped in a fur-lined gown. He came to the other side of the Queen's bed, took my mother's pulses again, felt her brow, and opened her mouth and eyes.

I concentrated on holding her limp hand. I knew she was going to die and leave me. Did you know that when your heart breaks, it really feels like that? I thought I had a big crack all down the middle of my chest, it hurt so much.

Uncle Cavendish shook his head at last. "Yes, Your Majesty," he said heavily. "It is poison. From the yellow staining on the mat in the Withdrawing Chamber where she dropped the goblet, I am afraid it is darkwort." His face was quite grey because he had always liked my mother a lot.

"I have a piece of unicorn's horn in my cabinet," said the Queen, "and a bezoar stone."

"Alas, Your Majesty, not even they will help against essence of darkwort. It will not be long now . . ."

"I have called the Chaplain," the Queen told him.

They were speaking quietly but I heard them. I cried and put my arms round my mother as if I could hold her back. "Don't go," I whispered. "Stay with me, Mama. Please, stay . . ."

But she was too deep asleep to hear me.

I felt Uncle Cavendish standing behind me. "She has no pain," he said to me. "She can't feel anything now."

He might be a doctor, but I know that when I took my mother's hand to kiss it, I *know* I felt her grip my fingers to say goodbye. Then I kissed her face.

The Queen came and kneeled next to me and wrapped her arms round me and didn't mind when all my tears made her velvet bodice damp. She rocked me a little, silently, and I felt her crying, too.

My mother died at a little past midnight, St. Valentine's Day, 14 February 1568, the worst day of my whole life. I was only a babe when my father died serving the Queen in France, so I didn't really know about it. But my mother dying . . . I can't describe how terrible it was because I don't know enough long words, and anyway, I'm not a poet. It made a huge hole in the world.

Everyone has been kind to me over this last year, especially the Queen. She comforted me whenever I was really sad and promised me she would never send me away to be brought up by a stranger. Lord Worthy volunteered to be my guardian and administer my estates until I could marry and have a husband to do it for me. My Uncle Cavendish couldn't do it because he was ill, or so they told me. I think he is just drunk most of the time. He was always very fond of my mother and I don't think he has ever recovered from not being able to help her.

Oh yes, they found the poisoner. He was working for the dastardly Guises, who are always plotting the Queen's downfall. He tried to escape from the Queen's pursuivants and they killed him in the fight. The Queen was furious, though I don't think an execution would have made me feel any better.

By drinking Her Majesty's wine with the poison in it, my mother saved the Queen's life—and England from a terrible civil war like they have in France. That's why she is buried in Whitehall Chapel.

And now I shall take the courage to open the package.

Alas, I have made a blot in my daybooke—I'm afraid the package made me cry. As I opened it, a small leather purse fell onto the pillows. I left it there while I read my mother's letter. Half of it is in my mother's writing, with the letters getting bigger and more wobbly. Then it changes to the Queen's handwriting, which is sweeping and beautiful. There are two blots from tears at the end. That must be why Her Majesty was putting pen and ink away when Mrs. Champernowne brought me in that night. I will keep the letter here always, tucked in my daybooke.

My darling Grace,
  I am dying. My heart breaks that I shall not see you grow to womanhood, nor find you a fine man to take care of you and your estates.
  As you approach thirteen years, you must be found a husband soon. The Court, for all the Queen's kindness, is no place for a young maid. Her Majesty agrees and will take on the role of finding you a suitable match, so you may be handfasted and marry at sixteen.
  Rest assured that the Queen will do all that I

64

would have done for you. You shall now have
my pearl ring that came from your father, and
all my gowns and horses. At your betrothal my
pearl earrings shall come to you.

You are the best of daughters, my love, and I
had rather anything than leave you so soon, but
none of us may gainsay God's call. I pray that
you will be happy and virtuous and always as
beloved as you are of me.

Farewell, my heart's delight, and at
Judgement Day be sure we shall meet again.

Until then my love is with you always.

Your mother,
Margaret, Lady Cavendish

I opened the leather purse. Inside were the earrings. They are beautiful pearl ones, with a setting of garnets and diamonds, like a pair the Queen often wears, only not so big.

Taking my candle, I went and looked in Lady Sarah's glass and put the hooks in my ears. As I stared at myself, and watched the garnets and diamonds glistening in the candlelight, I was reminded of my mother wearing them, and laughing.

Oh no, another teardrop blot. Time for bed.

It is still very dark outside. Something woke me up. I am in bed, wearing my mother's earrings for comfort. Her letter is under my pillow. It is only paper but it makes her feel closer, almost as if she's in the room with me like she used to be when we shared a chamber near the Queen's own. I hope I don't get ink on the sheets.

The other two are still asleep in their bed. Lady Sarah is still snoring like a pig, while Mary Shelton is now snoring like a billy goat. But that isn't what woke me. There is some kind of flurry over near the Grace-and-Favour Chambers. I can hear hushed voices, somebody running, lots of nervous whispers. Nobody wants to wake the Queen, of course. She's always bad-tempered in the morning, especially if it was a late night.

There's definitely something interesting happening. I'm going to find out what it is.

Later this morn

I cannot believe it. I've never heard of such a thing. A duel, perhaps—they happen sometimes and then there's a scandal until it all dies down. But this! I can hardly write, my hand is shaking so much.

I have just told my bedfellows, Lady Sarah and Mary Shelton, and they've rushed off to look for themselves. I don't want to go back just yet because I need to think about something.

It seems hours ago that I got up, slipped a dressing gown over my smock, and put on my pattens, then clip-clopped out into the passageway. But it must only be five and twenty minutes or so. I thought the fuss was coming from the Grace-and-Favour Chambers, held by my Lord Worthy as a sign of the Queen's esteem, so I made my way there.

I didn't take a candle, I just crept along the stone floor, down the stairs, and along the passage. A crowd of people, wearing dressing gowns or clothes they'd thrown on hurriedly, were gathered round one of the doorways.

And there was poor Pip, white as a sheet, wringing his hands and stuttering. "I only went into my m-master's chamber so early to put out a bite of bread and beer for when he woke up, and I've n-n-never ever seen such a thing in all my d-days!"

It took a bit of quiet work with elbows and feet to get through—I'm tall enough, and being skinny and flat-chested is sometimes useful. Then I saw what had happened.

I didn't scream. Well, I did, but I had my hands to my mouth so it only made a squeak. At least I didn't swoon. That would be such a Lady Sarah thing to do. But my legs went all wobbly and my stomach turned inside out.

There was Sir Gerald, still in his velvet doublet, face down on the bed with the curtains pulled. And there was a dagger in his back!

In fact, it was the pretty dagger which had been his gift to me. I couldn't take my eyes off him. It wasn't that disgusting—there wasn't even any blood. It was just so shocking. My heart was banging *bam-da-da-bam* like French Louis's drum.

I'm not sure how long I stood and stared before I noticed that Sir Charles was in the room, by the bed, and so was Lord Robert, standing by the wall in his shirt and hose. He looked pale green.

There was a flurry and Lord Worthy arrived with four of his men, ploughing through to the front of the crowd and marching straight in. He stopped dead, staring at the bed. His usually rather grey and boring face was as white as the feathers of that nasty swan we'd eaten at the feast.

Pip kneeled. "My lord, I b-brought Sir Gerald's

breakfast early and s-saw . . ." He trailed off and just waved a hand helplessly.

Lord Worthy didn't seem to be listening properly; he was still staring at the pretty dagger in his nephew's back.

Then he gazed round, collecting his thoughts very slowly, as if somebody had scattered them all over the room and he was having to bend down and pick up each thought separately. After an age he began to speak. "First, double the guard on Her Majesty's bedchamber. When she wakes, please tell her what has occurred. Has Dr. Cavendish been sent for?"

"On his way, m'lord," said one of the men-at-arms of the Queen's Guard. "As this crime took place within the Verge of the Court, we must call my Lord Chamberlain and convene the Board of Green Cloth to hear the inquest."

Lord Worthy's face then crumpled and he held on to the pillar of the bed.

I felt so sorry for him, even though he had little time for me, despite being my guardian. I slid next to him and touched his arm.

He turned his head and looked at me, but I don't think he saw me. His hair was standing straight up and he looked quite exhausted—and quite slovenly for him. He hadn't even changed his shirt, which had a wine stain on the blackworked front and a greenish stain on the cuff.

He blinked at me, then shook his head and turned back to the corpse. "Did anyone see anything suspicious after my nephew left the St. Valentine's Ball?"

Pip started with how he had wanted to attend his master, and how he had gone in and hung up Sir Gerald's doublet but left his hose and canions so he could sleep off the drink, and how he had gone in specially early with bread and beer . . .

I noticed he had left out Ellie cleaning up Sir Gerald's vomit for him. I opened my mouth and took breath to point this out, and then I thought a bit: it might be better if Ellie's being there wasn't mentioned—it was impossible she could have stabbed Sir Gerald, but I was sure that the person who *had* would love to get an unimportant laundrymaid blamed for it!

My uncle Dr. Cavendish arrived then, wrapped in his brocade and marten dressing gown and rocking slightly. His face was puffy and his eyes bloodshot and he looked as if he wished his head would just get on with it and fall off. He even winced at the candle-light. Then he bent to examine Sir Gerald.

As he was doing so, Sir Charles pointed to a little silver shape lying next to Sir Gerald's hand on the pillow. "What is that?" asked Sir Charles sharply.

Dr. Cavendish picked it up and held it close to a candle. "It's an aiglet," he said. "Still with a bit of lace attached. Hmm. The crest . . ."

"That's not my master's," said Pip, peering at it closely. "Looks more like the Radcliffe crest."

"What?" snapped Lord Worthy, and everybody turned to stare at Lord Robert Radcliffe.

He stared back, going red, doing his usual thing of mouth-opening-but-nothing-coming-out.

"By God, you must have dropped it when you stabbed Sir Gerald!" shouted Sir Charles. "It's clear evidence."

"B-b-but . . . ," stammered Lord Robert desperately.

"Don't lie, sir—how else could your own aiglet come to be there?" demanded Sir Charles. "You were jealous of Sir Gerald's affections for your lady love—jealous enough to kill your rival while he slept."

"I . . ." Now Lord Robert grabbed for his sword hilt, but since it was not part of his night attire, he didn't have it with him. Lord Worthy's henchmen moved to either side of him.

"Aha!" said Sir Charles, standing four square in front of Lord Robert, waving his forefinger. "So now you threaten me? How long will it be before you come and stab *me* in *my* bed?"

It was no good, I had to say something. After all, he was my betrothed! "But, sirs," I said, "could not the killer have put the aiglet there on purpose to implicate my Lord Robert?"

They didn't hear me at all. They just went on shouting. Sir Charles and Lord Worthy really didn't like Lord Robert. Both looked delighted that they could blame him for the killing and present the Queen with the culprit as soon as she heard the news. It was so convenient, I knew nobody was going to listen to a young maid in her shift and dressing gown.

So I watched, feeling sick, while Lord Robert's arms were grabbed by Lord Worthy's men. Then he was officially told he was under arrest on suspicion of killing Sir Gerald, most dishonourably, while he slept.

Lord Robert stared back, white-faced. At least he had the sense not to talk. Then there was a pause while Lord Worthy tried to think where to put him. There are no dungeons at Whitehall, every scrap of space being needed by the Court. All the dungeons are downriver at the Tower. In the end they decided to put him in the basement of one of the Court Gate towers, in one of the storerooms there, which has barred windows.

Lord Robert didn't say anything when they took him away. Lord Worthy and Dr. Cavendish conferred to arrange the details of the inquest. It was decided that there didn't need to be an autopsy because it was obvious what had killed Sir Gerald—nobody survives a knife blade stuck deep into their back, even if it is a very pretty one with garnets on the hilt.

Suddenly it occurred to me that the blade could have been mine if I had chosen to marry Sir Gerald. Would I then have been charged with murder instead? That made me feel so sick, I turned and ran all the way back to my chamber.

When I got there Mary Shelton was sitting up in bed with her hair in curling papers and she looked at me curiously. "What are you doing out of bed, Grace?" she asked.

"The most extraordinary thing has happened," I told her excitedly. "There's been a murder at Court!"

Mary let out a little scream and Lady Sarah blinked slowly awake. "Wherefore are you making such a fuss and bother?" she asked irritably. "I'm trying to sleep."

"Oh, Sarah, dear," gasped Mary. "Really, you'll never guess. There's been a murder. Grace knows all about it."

Sarah snapped awake immediately. "Lord preserve us!" she exclaimed. "A murder? Not the Queen?"

"No, no, not the Queen," I assured her quickly, as I pulled my stays on over my head. "Somebody stabbed Sir Gerald in the back."

"How dreadful!" Sarah declared, looking downcast. "He is so charming and he dances well. Will he recover?"

"Unlikely. He is dead. It's very mysterious. They have arrested Lord Robert but I don't think he was the assassin. . . ."

That was that. By now, they weren't listening. I've never seen either of them dress themselves so fast and then they ran out of the door and down the passage. I wonder when Mary noticed she still had her curling papers in.

Poor Sir Gerald, I still can't believe he is really dead. One moment showing off to me in the Volta, the next moment—gone!

And as for my Lord Robert . . . I hate to think of him locked in some storeroom. The Queen will have

him committed to the Tower if nobody does anything to find out the real murderer. I feel so sorry
for him. Of all people who might have stabbed Sir
Gerald, I really don't think it was he. Why should
he? I'd agreed to marry him, hadn't I? Now if Sir
Gerald had stabbed Lord Robert, that would have
made sense. . . .

I must soon dress and make ready to serve the
Queen at her rising. I do find that writing about
things clears the head; if you set it down in black and
white, you must think it through first. The Queen
told me that and she is right—she is very wise. Aha!
That's what I'll do to help Lord Robert. I'll speak to
the Queen for him. At least she never tells me not to
worry my pretty little head about things.

Later this Day—eventide

I am back in bed, writing this to keep myself awake.
I have a plan, and it's very exciting, but I mustn't
fall asleep if it is to work! After dressing this morning, I went along to serve the Queen at her rising,
hoping she would be in a mood to talk. Everyone at
Court knows if you want to talk to the Queen, you
have to pick the right moment.

While I held the Queen's bodice straight for Lady

Bedford to sew the neckline into place, I got up courage to talk to her.

"Your Majesty," I began hesitantly. "May I talk to you about—"

"My Lord Robert?" The Queen had her lips compressed and looked very fierce. "Very well. But please remember that the aiglet lying on Sir Gerald's pillow was his."

"Indeed, Your Majesty!" I agreed. "But it makes no sense for Lord Robert to want to kill Sir Gerald over me, when I'd chosen him anyway! Is it possible that someone planted the aiglet, so that we should think the worst of poor Lord Robert?"

The Queen looked at me for a moment, while Lady Bedford tutted disapproval that I was being so cheeky.

Then the Queen said, "Hmm."

"At least don't commit him to the Tower yet," I begged. I kneeled and took her hand to kiss it. "Please, Your Majesty, may I . . . try and find out the truth of the matter?"

"Well, really, I don't think it's suitable . . . ," began Lady Bedford, but the Queen held up her hand.

"Very well. You may make discreet enquiries, Lady Grace," she said sternly. "But report your findings to me, and to no one else. Lord Robert can stay where he is for a day but after that I must commit him to the Tower, or release him."

"Thank you, Your Majesty. Um . . . may I . . . ?"

"What?" She was starting to sound seriously annoyed now, but I knew she was about to meet the Scottish and French Ambassadors and I couldn't bear the thought of sitting about on a cushion with incomprehensible French and Scotch whizzing about my head.

"Please may I walk the dogs?"

"Oh, go to!" she snapped. "By all means, I had rather have you out with them in the garden than wriggling about on a cushion distracting me."

"Thank you, Your Majesty, thank you!"

"*If* you can go upstairs and change your kirtle without making a thunder to wake the dead."

Honestly! Anyone would think I was made of lead. I ran upstairs as quietly as I could, changed into my hunting kirtle, wrapped a cloak around me, and then carried my boots down the stairs until I got to the door into the Privy Garden—where I astonished the guard there by pulling my boots on and lacing them, standing on one leg. One of the dog-pages brought me the dogs on their lead and we ran out into the garden, Henri in front, barking madly.

I went round the maze twice and then through

the gate into the Orchard, where I let the dogs off the lead and climbed my cherry tree to sit and think in a good sitting place—the crook between two branches. I could see where the buds were coming, but it was still too cold and wet for them to swell yet.

My head felt close to bursting with plans. I knew exactly how to find out the murderer: Uncle Cavendish once told me how much you can tell from a dead body. For instance, if you shine a light into the eyes, you might see an image of the murderer. And if you bring the true murder weapon near it, the body will bleed again. So it was obvious what I had to do—I needed to see Sir Gerald's body again.

I climbed down and went to explore the compost heaps. Ellie and Masou were there, bent over something on the ground. Eric rushed between them and tried to grab whatever it was, but Ellie snatched it up and held it out of reach while he bounced on his haunches, yapping.

"Ellie," I said, "why are you holding a half-skinned rabbit?"

"We are going to spit-roast it over a fire and eat it," Masou answered, as if this were perfectly obvious.

"And I'm going to peg out the skin and scrape it and cure it to make a muff for the winter," Ellie put in.

I tied up the dogs out of reach and squatted down to watch Ellie finish her work. She was very quick and deft. She had already taken off the paws, and she was peeling back the skin as if she was undressing it. It wasn't nearly as disgusting as you'd think because there wasn't any blood. The rabbit was already drawn and gutted.

And that's when the thought suddenly struck me: when I saw poor Sir Gerald with the dagger in his back, there hadn't been any blood around the wound! Which didn't make any sense because only *dead* bodies don't bleed—and surely Sir Gerald was alive when the dagger went in. It was one more mystery and one more reason why I needed another look at Sir Gerald's body.

"One of the kitchen spit-dogs caught it in the yard and broke its neck and I managed to get it off him," Ellie was explaining about the rabbit. "I gave him the guts. There now," she finished, handing the rabbit to Masou.

Masou had a long peeled twig, which he carefully threaded through the rabbit, and then he hung it over the fire, where it started to steam and cook. Ellie sprinkled some breadcrumbs over it while we began to discuss the murder.

There had been plenty of gossip and theories about it, one of which, Masou and Ellie told me, was that armed Scots had burst into the palace and murdered Sir Gerald in his bed in mistake for the Queen. I told them what had really happened and explained why it couldn't have been Lord Robert. I *did* have a moment's doubt, because I suddenly remembered Lord Robert saying that he hated Sir Gerald and reaching for his sword at the St. Valentine's Ball. But then I realized that that was just silly—Lord Robert would never have stabbed Sir Gerald in the back. I'm sure of it.

"Poor man," said Ellie ghoulishly. "He'll hang for a clean bill then."

"No, he won't," I said. "I'm not having my future husband hanged before I can even marry him—that would be stupid."

"But not so bad if it happened after the marriage?" asked Masou teasingly.

"At least then I'd be a proper matron," I sniffed.

"I'll go along and throw lavender and rue on the scaffold," said Ellie. "And I'll tell him how sad you are—that'll comfort him. And then I'll get the ballad-maker to invent a ballad and print it and—"

"Ellie, he's not going to hang because I'm going to find out what really happened," I told her severely.

Masou made a mock bow and turned the rabbit on its spit. "My lady, you are all-wise," he said. "Tell me, how will you do that?"

I punched him on the arm (not hard). "First I want to get a good long look at Sir Gerald's body," I began. "I've heard that it's being kept in St. Margaret's Chapel."

"Ugh," said Ellie. "Why?"

"Because when I saw Sir Gerald's body with the knife in it there wasn't any blood," I said very significantly.

"So?" frowned Masou.

"So, if I stabbed you, blood would come out, wouldn't it?" I explained. "Probably quite a lot if I stabbed deep enough to kill you. But there wasn't any blood around the wound and I remember my uncle, Dr. Cavendish, telling me once that the tides of your blood only stop when you die."

"Oh," murmured Masou thoughtfully.

"So I simply must look at Sir Gerald's body

again. And there's another reason, too." I lowered my voice because it was a frightening idea even if it was a well-known fact. "If we look into his eyes we might even be able to see who the murderer really was!"

"Why didn't the doctor do it when he saw the body?" asked Ellie matter-of-factly, munching on one of the marchpane arms of Venus that Masou had produced from his sleeve.

"Well, my uncle was upset," I said. "And he drinks too much, ever since . . . you know."

They both nodded.

"But I'm sure I've picked enough up from him to spot anything that might help," I went on.

Masou laughed. "So all we need to do is creep out to St. Margaret's Chapel at dead of night—"

"Yes, I was thinking *midnight*," I put in. "Then we take a careful look at Sir Gerald's body, shine a light in his eyes, and we'll have the answer."

"Such simplicity that we must do it and nobody else has," Masou said, grinning.

I scowled at him. "Nobody else has because they all want it to be nice and simple. Lord Robert hasn't got a lot of friends and he owes people money and it would be simple if it were he," I explained.

"Not for the people he owes money to," Ellie pointed out.

"What about Lord Worthy's men, who will be guarding the chapel?" Masou asked quietly.

I hadn't thought about that. "You don't have to come with me," I told them. "I don't want you to get into trouble. I can find St. Margaret's Chapel on my own, you know."

"Oh, fie!" said Ellie. "I owe you one for not telling anybody that I cleaned up after Sir Gerald." She made a face. "Not a penny did I get for it, and his sick smelled horrible."

"And I," said Masou, "am a warrior and afraid of nothing—*and* I'm the best boy acrobat in Mr. Somers's troupe. They will require much worse of me before they turn me off, and if they do, why, I'll go to Paris Garden or the theatre and make my fortune."

"I'll go to the apothecary and get a sleeping draught," said Ellie, winking at me. "Maybe it will find its way into the guards' beer."

I kissed them both—Masou rubbed quickly at the side of his head where my kiss had landed. Then I gave Ellie some coins for the sleeping draught and rushed off to round up the dogs and take them back in for rubbing down by one of the dog-pages.

Which is why I happened to be at the stables talking to a groom when Sir Charles came wandering along, as he always does at that time of day. "Ah! Lady Grace," he said.

"Did we have a riding lesson today?" I asked, conscience-stricken that I might have forgotten it.

He looked bewildered and then said, "No, I think not. With all that has happened . . ."

"Well, at least let's go and say hello to Doucette," I suggested, because I didn't want him to be disappointed. "I'm sure she misses you, if not me."

"Hmm," he replied. He still seemed very uncertain, so I led him to Doucette's stable and unlatched the upper door. She put her pretty head out—I think she has some Welsh pony in her—and nickered to me. I patted her velvety nose and she blew.

Sir Charles reached out suddenly to pat her neck, and she jerked away, snorting and showing her teeth. He pulled back. "Good God, what's wrong with the nag?"

I stared with astonishment. Never ever in all my many (fairly dull) riding lessons with Sir Charles have I heard him talk of a horse that way, or indeed seen a horse react to him like that. It was astonishing.

I was going to ask what was wrong with *him*. How

could he forget everything he had told me about moving softly and slowly with horses? But then a dog-page came trotting up with the newly brushed dogs.

"My lady," he said breathlessly, "the Queen has called for you to take the dogs to her."

I guessed Her Majesty's Council meeting had tried her patience. She likes to play with the dogs when she's annoyed. I took the leads, said a hurried goodbye to Sir Charles, and rushed back to the Privy Gallery.

Just in time, I remembered to take my boots off before I went upstairs to change again (it is hellishly hard work to look smart and fitting for the Queen's magnificence). Then I lifted my skirts and raced up the stairs. As I reached the top, Mrs. Champernowne pounced.

"What are you doing, Lady Grace?"

"I'm going to change my kirtle again so I can attend Her Majesty properly attired," I said, quite sickly and sweet.

"Your stockings, child, look at your stockings!"

I looked down at where I was still holding up my skirts. Well, they had been a very nice pair of knitted white silk stockings but they were now a bit blackish around the feet and there was a hole in the toe of one and the knee of the other.

"Oh," I said, hastily dropping my hem to hide the offending garments. "I was trying not to make so much noise, Mrs. Champernowne, like you told me, and . . ."

She shut her eyes for a second, then looked up to the ceiling. "Lady Grace, boots are for— Wear your slippers while you— Oh, for goodness' sake, give me the stockings and go and put your woollen ones on. You cannot possibly attend the Queen with filthy stockings, look you . . ."

Very quickly, for she seemed near to bursting with annoyance at me, I stripped off the offending stockings, gave her the whole lot, along with garters, and ran barefoot along the passageway to my chamber to change again! Woollen stockings are a penance! They itch like mad! Why not go barelegged? Who can see your legs under all the petticoats and the farthingale and so on? Ellie doesn't even own a pair of stockings and it doesn't seem to be killing her.

The Queen was in a terrible mood that afternoon. I sat near her while she petted the dogs and threw balls for them, and did some embroidery. Mary Shelton was then lunatic enough to slap crossly at Henri when he bounced over to lick her face.

"Out of my sight!" Her Majesty roared. I've left out her swearing because it's too rude to write down. "How dare you beat my dog? Out, you, and your sour, yellow looks . . ." And a hairbrush and a pot of lip balm whizzed past Mary's head as she ran for the door, ducking as she went.

I whispered to Lady Bedford, suggesting that maybe the tumblers might amuse. So they were sent for and we all watched Masou and a little old dwarf man and a strongman do somersaults and handstands and juggle with their feet. Masou then did a trick where he kept pretending to drop his balls and clubs and then caught them with his feet or his knees or his teeth and kept it all going, and that, at last, cheered the Queen up.

Since she felt sorry for him, Her Majesty invited Lord Worthy to share supper with her. And then she bade me join them, too. I really didn't want to—I was too nervous about the midnight plans to have much appetite for pheasant and salt beef and venison pasties. But I didn't have any choice.

Lord Worthy arrived late, looking flustered and still upset, and he still hadn't changed his shirt. Normally the Queen would have thrown a slipper at him for that, but she was being gentle with him because of his bereavement.

Lord Worthy decided to talk only to the Queen and only about terribly boring things like Scottish politics and French politics—it was all Guises and Maxwells and if so and so did this, then such and such would do the other thing. How anybody can keep it straight in their head is a mystery. I didn't mind. I was thinking about what we were going to do later in the night, wondering what I would wear and whether Ellie would manage to get the sleeping draught. I sat there looking as interested as I could, fighting the urge to yawn. At least there were some new Seville orange suckets, which I really love.

At last Lord Worthy ground to a halt.

Her Majesty put her hand out and touched his. "My lord, you will now have the estates belonging to Sir Gerald to administer as well as your own and Lady Grace's," she said softly.

Lord Worthy looked bleakly at her. "I have a very good steward, Your Majesty," he replied. "We shall manage."

"Of course," Her Majesty agreed. "And of yourself, my lord?" she continued gently. "I know how highly you rated your nephew."

"I did, Your Majesty. He was a fine young man—

with a young man's faults, true. He was hasty-tempered, inclined to sarcasm when crossed, certainly arrogant, but I believe time would have mended those faults as it normally does."

"Well," said the Queen, blinking at the dullness of Lord Worthy's voice, "we shall commit young Lord Robert to trial in a day or two."

Lord Worthy nodded sadly, still staring at the candle flame.

I watched him curiously. It had suddenly occurred to me that he might be almost as sad about his nephew dying as I was about my mother dying. My eyes suddenly prickled.

The Queen could see there was no cheering him up, and so she went over to her virginals, which stood in the corner of her Withdrawing Room, lifted the lid, and began tuning them. The Queen is very musical. She played some beautiful Italian music which made me feel much better—I really like listening to her play. Even ambassadors do; you can see them tense up as she gets ready to start and then smile and relax because they can actually tell the truth and be complimentary at the same time.

Lord Worthy sat politely and I got the impression he was waiting to talk to the Queen on his own, so as another song came to an end, I rose and curtsied and asked to be excused to go to my bed. The Queen kissed me goodnight on the cheek and I went upstairs quite slowly, feeling sorry for Lord Worthy.

The other girls weren't there yet, they were playing cards in the Presence Chamber, but Ellie was sitting on my bed looking very perky.

"How did it go?" I asked her. "Did you get the sleeping draught?"

"Yes. You gave me lots of money—look, I got a whole bottle of laudanum for it." She held up a small green bottle. "I got all wrapped up in a striped cloak and went to an apothecary in Westminster."

I looked sideways at her. "Where did you get a striped cloak?" (Only harlots wear them—it's a sort of uniform for them. The City Fathers make them do it.)

"Oh, we do a little extra laundry on the side," Ellie said casually, "and one of the strumpets at the Falcon got a new one when we were washing hers, so she didn't bother to collect it, said we could keep it. It comes in quite useful sometimes."

I nodded.

"Here's the change." Ellie dropped the coins on my bed. "Now remember not to drink any of the wine on the sideboard there—I've put several drops of laudanum in it so the two twitter-heads will sleep well."

Ellie can't bear most of the Maids of Honour, which is hardly surprising, considering how rude they are to her when she collects their dirty linen.

"Me and Masou will meet you by the kitchen," she continued, "an' if you don't turn up by the time the moon is over the trees in the Orchard, we'll go and 'ave a look at Sir Gerald ourselves. He's already in St. Margaret's Chapel but I don't think he's laid out yet—they need to do the inquest first."

Ellie hopped off the bed, gathered up a couple of smocks lying in a twist on the floor and one ruff that had been stamped on, stuffed them in her bag, and headed off down the passageway. So I cleaned my teeth, changed into my hunting kirtle, pulled a smock on over the top of it, and here I am. And now, at last, I can hear Lady Sarah and Mary approaching. Soon I will set off on my midnight adventure.

For now, I will pretend to be asleep.

*Eventide, just past five of
the clock from the chimes*

Lord preserve me, I am in the most terrible trouble. I hardly dare think how angry the Queen was. At least, as I am sent to my bedchamber in disgrace, I can write this.

To begin where I left off. Last evening, the two twitter-heads came back quite late, about ten of the clock. They had been playing Primero and were arguing over who had given her point-score wrong. Olwen, their tiring woman, helped them out of their gowns. They glugged some of the drugged wine after they'd cleaned their teeth and got into their beds, still arguing about the Primero game. I gathered they'd lost to Mrs. Champernowne.

Olwen bustled about hanging things up and brushing things and folding things until I wanted to shake her, and then she left, at last. Very soon, I could hear the twitter-heads snoring.

I waited impatiently for the guard to change at midnight outside the Queen's Privy Gallery. When I'd heard the changeover I slid out of bed, leaving the curtains closed, and pulled off my smock. I'd already left my horrible wool stockings off. Then I crept out of the door and down the passageway, dodging into a doorway when a cat came past with a mouse in her mouth.

The first frightening part was climbing out of a window into the Privy Garden. That bit over, I slunk through the gate into the Orchard: it was kept locked, but I knew that the gentleman who held the key hid it under a stone next to the gate so he didn't lose it. I went through the Orchard to the compost heaps, where Ellie and Masou were waiting for me.

Ellie was already wearing boy's clothes—borrowed from one of the women at the laundry whose son had died of plague the year before, she said, which made me shiver. She'd brought another set for me, but I refused to wear them. Only people like Ellie, who've already had plague and got better, aren't scared of it, because you can't get it twice.

Masou shrugged. "If we are caught, my lady, it

will go better for us if they can see you are one of the Queen's women," he said.

I didn't really want to hear about that because I think half the fun of a midnight adventure is getting disguised. I frowned. "I'll have to wear my kirtle then," I concluded. There was nothing else for it. I could hardly climb the Orchard wall in my shift.

We climbed over the compost heap and the old bean staves covered in bindweed, and found the bit of wall that's crumbling. Masou had brought a rope to help us and we scrambled over.

The next courtyard was behind a row of houses that were rented by the room to the young gentlemen of the Court. It was a mess of brambles, beer barrels, broken horn mugs, broken clay pipes, tables, a broken lute, half a dozen chairs that must have been in a fight, and a piece of petticoat caught on a nail halfway up a wall.

We crept through the clutter, with Masou muttering in his own language when he caught himself on a thorn; then we slid along an alleyway that gave into New Palace Yard. Westminster Abbey loomed over us as we passed through the gate leading to the chapel where Sir Gerald's body lay.

Masou crept ahead noiselessly to see if any of Lord Worthy's men were still awake.

"They'll be snoring," whispered Ellie behind me. "I found 'em hanging about waiting for his lordship to finish supping with the Queen, so I took their flasks down to the buttery for 'em. Aqua vitae and laudanum. Wasn't that kind and serviceable of me?" She grinned.

Masou crept back, his white teeth shining in the moonlight. "Sleeping like babes."

We picked our way past them—they were rather sweetly propped up against each other on a bench inside the church porch—and carefully, carefully opened the heavy wooden door into the chapel.

There were six black corpse candles around the body, which had been wrapped in a shroud and was laid on a trestle table covered with damask. No doubt a very special elaborate coffin was on order but it hadn't arrived yet.

It was very cold and very frightening. The moon was shining through the old Papist stained-glass windows, making pale blues and yellows on the shroud, and there was a nasty smell. Ellie shivered and crossed herself, while Masou clutched a little amulet he wears round his neck and muttered in his own language.

I gulped, stepped forward, and nearly tripped on a step. Heart beating fast, I then went right up to the body. Up close, the smell was truly awful, a bit like an unemptied close-stool. But there was something else as well: another, much fainter odour—dusty and bitter, it caught inside my nose. Curiously, it made me want to cry. Why? I didn't understand it. Although it's sad when someone dies, I certainly hadn't loved Sir Gerald.

He was lying on his back—they'd taken the knife out of the wound, of course. I held my breath and slowly drew the shroud back from his face.

There were pennies on the eyes to hold them shut. I took them off. The lids were half opened. His eyes were like jelly. I held a candle close, but I could see no reflection of a murderer in Sir Gerald's eyes. I wanted to look at the dagger wound again, but I didn't want to actually touch the corpse in case I was cursed. I reasoned with myself that Sir Gerald's ghost should be pleased we were trying to discover his murderer. But then I remembered that Sir Gerald wasn't a very nice man in life, so you could hardly expect his ghost to be. And then I noticed a slight yellow crusting at the corners of his mouth.

I blinked in surprise. My heart began to thud. That same yellow crusting had been on my mother's lips when she died. Now I knew where I'd smelled the dusty bitter odour on Sir Gerald. I had smelled it at my mother's deathbed. The smell of darkwort poisoning.

I stood for a moment, trying to understand. It seemed lunatic, but what if Sir Gerald had already been killed by darkwort poison when he was stabbed with the dagger? That would account for his not bleeding when stabbed, would it not? For if he was already dead, the tides in his blood would have stopped, and thus no blood would have streamed from the dagger wound.

Suddenly there was the sound of voices and heavy footsteps. Masou and Ellie and I froze, staring at each other. There was a scrape at the church porch, an angry shout. The door latch rattled. They were coming in.

I felt so sick I thought I was actually going to vomit, and my legs felt as if they would bend sideways like a rag doll's. Ellie had her hands to her mouth. Masou looked grey. Both of them would get really badly beaten if anybody saw them—especially Masou. Lord save us, they might even flog him properly! Both of them might be dismissed from the Queen's service, they would probably starve—whatever Masou said about making his fortune in Paris Garden. Whereas if I got caught . . .

"Hide," I whispered. "I'll manage this."

They hesitated, then slipped into one of the box pews. I could hear scraping as they hid under the bench.

I stayed exactly where I was near the body of Sir Gerald and started to cry. I don't find it easy to cry when I want (though Lady Sarah and Mary Shelton seem to find it so. They often grizzle to win sympathy and favour). But as soon as I thought about getting birched, or the Queen telling me off (which would be worse), the tears came. I helped them along by sniffing hard and sobbing and pinching my fingers on the middle of my nose.

The chapel door was thrust open and the guards marched in, along with Lord Worthy. They all looked very fierce—but, as I'd hoped, they came to a halt in the aisle when they saw me, sobbing by the body of my dead suitor.

Lord Worthy hurried forward looking flustered, and perhaps a little suspicious. "Well . . . well . . . Why did you not just *ask* to pay your respects, my lady? And why at night? It would have been far more . . . fitting . . . for you to come during the day, properly attended . . ."

"I . . . I wanted . . . to be alone with him," I

gulped, giving the performance my all. "I didn't want people flapping handkerchiefs at me."

"But how did you get here? Did someone help you?" Lord Worthy demanded.

"No, no!" I shrieked, terrified in case he searched the chapel. "I came all by myself, and it was very frightening."

Lord Worthy paused, staring blankly at Sir Gerald's corpse. I stood there, thinking how very hard-hearted of Lord Worthy not to try to comfort me. He is supposed to be my guardian, after all!

"Come, now, my lady," he said at last. "This is all highly unsuitable. With no escort . . . It is really very improper. I shall have to accompany you back to Court myself and hand you into Mrs. Champernowne's care."

Oh no! I thought. I hung my head and sobbed quite genuinely now.

"Come along," he said. He took my arm, pinching a bit, and led me out of the chapel by the other door, followed by his henchmen, who were gawking at me as if I had grown a bear's head. They clearly didn't know what to make of it all.

We walked through the churchyard and up through another gate into King's Street. On we went through King's Street Gate, and entered the palace at the end of the Privy Gallery. There, Lord Worthy spoke to the two gentlemen on guard. One of them walked off, looking highly amused.

We stood there, Lord Worthy tutting to himself and playing with a handkerchief in his pocket, me changing from one leg to the other. My heart would have been in my boots if I'd been wearing any. But I wasn't. I was wearing an old pair of dancing slippers. I really hoped Masou and Ellie had had a chance to get away from the chapel. I thought I'd seen a dark shape flit behind us as we went through the court-yard, but I wasn't sure.

After what seemed like ages, Mrs. Champernowne appeared in the door, her hair in curling papers, dressing gown wrapped around her against the cold. There was a mixture of astonishment and fury on her face, which would have been very funny if it had been aimed at somebody else.

"What is the meaning of this, Lady Grace?" she snapped.

I just muttered and stared at the ground.

"Out of bed, at this time of night . . . Was there any sign of a young man?" Mrs. Champernowne demanded of Lord Worthy suspiciously.

"No, there wasn't!" I shouted. "I was visiting the corpse of my—"

"That's enough," snapped Mrs. Champernowne. "When I wish to hear your lies, my lady, I shall ask for them."

"Mrs. Champernowne, I can vouch that there was no young man," said Lord Worthy. "There was no one else in the chapel."

"Hmph," said Mrs. Champernowne. Then she turned to Lord Worthy. "Thank you so much, my lord, for rescuing Lady Grace from her silliness . . ." She simpered disgustingly.

"Hmph," I said.

Lord Worthy bowed, Mrs. Champernowne curtsied. He and all his men went off towards the Grace-and-Favour Chambers while she grabbed my arm and pulled me upstairs behind her, pinching nastily as she went. "If I find out there *was* a young gentleman . . ."

"You can use a strap on my bare bum, Mrs. Champernowne!" I said hotly, furious that they thought I was no better than any other twitter-head. "Do you think I'm as stupid as Lady Sarah?"

"Lady Sarah has not been found in St. Margaret's Chapel at three in the morning where she had no business to be," Mrs. Champernowne pointed out.

"Not yet," I muttered; luckily, Mrs. Champernowne didn't hear. "I know it was foolish but I wanted to . . . um . . . say goodbye to Sir Gerald and I didn't want to be surrounded by chattering fools when I did and so I climbed a couple of walls and went to do it privately, and there most certainly wasn't any young gentleman anywhere near"—there was Masou, of course, but he's not a gentleman, so this was quite true—"and I didn't do anything wrong."

"You were not in your bed when you should have been, and you were where you should not have been," snapped Mrs. Champernowne—rather confusingly, I thought. "How dare you abuse Her Majesty's trust in you, how dare you sneak around like . . ." Then she took hold of herself. "Well now," she finished, "we will not bandy words like a couple of fishwives . . ."

Bit late for that, I thought. You must have woken half the Court with all that burbling, you old dragon.

At the top passageway she decided it was too late for me to retire to bed again and too early to tell the Queen, so she locked me in her little dressing room.

It was very dark and very stuffy and smelled rather

strongly of Mrs. Champernowne and rose-water and lavender water and a very expensive jasmine oil she gets from the east, which made the air almost too thick to breathe. I think she was hoping I would stand there stewing over what was going to happen in the morning, but I was really too exhausted. So I sat down on the rush matting, leaned my head in a corner, and went to sleep.

Hell's teeth! I must go and find more ink.

Later this Day, with new ink

Lady Sarah always keeps some ink new-made in her dressing table so I took that. She'll never notice.

In the morning I was shaken awake by Mrs. Champernowne, who seemed just as furious. I didn't get any breakfast and was told that Her Majesty would see me in the Presence Chamber, so I had to trot along behind Mrs. Champernowne in my grubby old hunting kirtle, all muddy from climbing walls. I kept thinking about Ellie and Masou. I really hoped they got away.

In the Presence Chamber the other Maids of Honour were sitting in a row on cushions, sewing— Lady Sarah I'm-so-pretty Bartelmy was mending a tear in one of her petticoats.

The Queen wasn't on her throne, but the chair she was sitting in by the window had a cloth of estate over it, so it was sort of official. I went towards her when she beckoned me, and then stopped three paces away and went down on both knees.

Her Majesty has pale skin but very dark brown eyes which sometimes seem to be able to reach out and dig right into your head. They were doing that now. I looked down, trying not to feel grubby and insignificant. She let me kneel there in silence for a long time and then . . .

"*What* in the name of *God* happened last night?" she shouted. "Have you run wood-wild? God's blood, I never heard the like!" And so on, swearing shockingly—which I have left out to save her reputation. Finally she ran out of ways of repeating that I'd been found in that cursed chapel by Lord Worthy. "Well, Lady Grace?" Her fingers rapped the arm of her chair. "What is your explanation?"

I sighed, feeling very tired. I also had a crick in my neck. But at least there was no sign that Masou or Ellie had been caught. If they had been, they would have been there in the Presence Chamber, too. That made me feel a lot better.

"We are waiting for an answer," said Her Majesty coldly.

"Um . . . I wanted to . . . um . . . well, look at Sir Gerald one last time," I offered.

"Why?" Her Majesty demanded rightly.

"I'm so sorry, Your Majesty, I just did." I looked up.

"And did you at least pray?" the Queen enquired.

"No, Your Majesty, I didn't have time. Lord Worthy came."

"Hmph." There seemed to be frustration in every inch of the Queen's body. "Lord Worthy tells me that there was nobody else in the chapel and that he feels sure you were not there for any immoral reason . . . But for the sake of your reputation, Lady Grace, you must *not* behave like this. It is not seemly in any young heiress and most certainly not in anyone in my service."

"No, Your Majesty," I replied quietly.

Finally the Queen said, "You will return to your chamber, Lady Grace, and remain there until I send for you. Perhaps you are overwrought with the strain of the St. Valentine's Ball and what took place afterwards. I shall ask Dr. Cavendish to attend you there and be sure that you are not sickening for anything."

I kept my head down, wondering if the Queen was really as angry as she appeared. And then I heard Her Majesty sigh and she leaned forwards to speak quietly in my ear. I saw some of the Ladies-in-Waiting looking over at us curiously, but they couldn't hear what she said.

"See now, Grace, you have put me in a most trying position. I cannot be seen to countenance such wild behaviour," she whispered. "You must try to be a little more discreet in your investigations." Then she called for Mrs. Champernowne to take me back upstairs to my chamber.

Back in my room, I sat on the bed, hugely relieved that I still had Her Majesty's support. Though, sadly, she seemed to have forgotten that I had not breakfasted. I sat listening to my stomach gurgle and wondered what to do next.

Thankfully, one of the tiring women brought me some bread and cheese and beer at midday. By that time I had washed off the mud, changed into my third-best kirtle, and was doing some embroidery by the little window. I started off hating needlework when my mama began to teach me. The sampler I first practised on seemed boring and pointless. But as I got better at it, I found I was able to draw pictures onto the white linen and then colour them in with silken threads. I find embroidering wonderful peacocks and singing birds and snakes and bears and horses a great comfort.

As the afternoon light faded, I had to stop because I couldn't see well enough. I stamped around the room, feeling that awful itchiness under my ribs that you get when you're bored. I would even have been quite pleased to see Lady Sarah and Mary Shelton. Then I thought of my daybooke and so I lit a candle and I have spent all this time writing and not caused very much mess. I'd better stop. There's someone at the door.

Later this Day, not long gone seven of the clock from the chimes

It was Masou and Ellie! We hugged each other. Masou kept shaking his head and saying something in his own language so Ellie tutted at him.

"Did they birch you?" asked Ellie anxiously. "Is your bum sore? I brought some comfrey ointment in case . . ."

"No, no," I told her, smiling. "It's all right. I didn't get any kind of beating. I've just been sent to my room until the Queen asks for me."

"Did you see anything in Sir Gerald's eyes?" asked Masou eagerly.

"No, but I did see something else," I told them. "There was a yellow stain on Sir Gerald's lips and a nasty bitter smell about him and I remember that . . ." I stopped. I hated what came into my mind when I said that. "I remember it from . . . from when my . . ." I stopped again and swallowed hard. "That's what killed my mother. Poison that made yellow froth on her mouth, that smelled bitter."

"Yes," said Ellie slowly. "And there was the same stuff in the sick I cleaned up from the mat in his chamber. A nasty yellow stain—I couldn't get it out by candlelight and I tried ten-day-old urine on it yesterday, and it still wouldn't come out."

They use disgusting things to clean with at the laundry—I sometimes can hardly believe what Ellie tells me. For bad stains? Dog dirt so old it goes white, for instance!

"They had to put a new piece of matting in where my mother dropped the wine cup," I said heavily, "because they couldn't get the stain out."

"But if he was dead by the poison, why stab him with the knife?" asked Masou.

He and Ellie both looked at me. "To confuse everybody? To make sure?" I suggested.

None of us could work it out. I told them I was probably not supposed to have any visitors and they should go, so Ellie picked up a very dirty shift of

Lady Sarah's and they went out again. What I think is that

This same Day,
nine of the clock from the chimes

I had to stop again and put my pillow over everything, as my uncle, Dr. Cavendish, arrived. I hope it isn't too blurred. There's a little ink on the pillowcase, though.

Since my mother died, I have only ever seen my father's brother in one of two states: drunk or hung over. He was hung over now—bloodshot eyes, grey face, miserable. He sighed and told me to sit on the bed and then he looked into my eyes and ears and mouth, put his ear to my chest, and then sat there quietly taking my pulses. There are twelve pulses, apparently.

Then he asked me questions, some of them very embarrassing, and when I told him "no" to all of them, he looked very puzzled.

"I would have said you were too young for the green sickness," he said. "There's no sign of fever, no sign of too much bile."

"That's because I'm not ill," I told him. And nor

did I want to be ill—I hate being bled—and as for purging . . . Lord preserve me!

"Then what possessed you to do such a foolish thing, Grace?" he asked. "If you were some silly minx like Lady Sarah then I would not even need to ask, but you are normally such a sensible, level-headed girl."

Am I? How boring, I thought. "I'm sorry that you should have seen so ugly a sight as a man killed with a dagger in his back while he slept," Uncle Cavendish went on, "and more than sorry that it should have been done by your own betrothed. But you cannot let this sad business turn your head, Grace—"

"But, Uncle, Sir Gerald wasn't killed by that knife," I interrupted.

He gave me a weary smile. "And what makes you say that, Dr. Grace, eh?"

"Uncle, there was no blood," I explained. "If you get stabbed by a knife, blood comes out."

My uncle just stared at me.

"Don't you remember telling me, Uncle?" I asked patiently. "You said that the heart is the body's furnace and the lungs are the bellows for the furnace. And the blood—the sanguine humour, you called it—carries the vital heat from the furnace to every part of the body, ebbing back and forth like tides."

"That's right," my uncle agreed.

"But if the tides had stopped because the man was dead, there would be no waves of blood to flow from the wound," I pointed out. "And I saw the dagger in Sir Gerald's back and there was *no blood,* was there? You saw it, too," I urged.

My uncle nodded.

"So that's why I wanted to go to the chapel," I hurried on. "To see if I could see the murderer's reflection in Sir Gerald's eyes and solve the mystery. I did not. But, Uncle, when I was in the chapel I noticed something else about the body." My voice shook. "There was a faint spot of yellow scum in the corner of his mouth and a bitter smell."

"You mean . . ." He blinked hard, swallowed. "Grace, just because your mother . . ." He felt absent-mindedly in his doublet, no doubt for his flask, which goes everywhere with him. I put my hand on his to stop him.

He stared at me for so long I thought he was angry, but then he spoke very softly. "I'm sorry, Grace, I should have noticed these things myself."

"Go and look, you'll see," I pressed him. "You've not had a surgeon open the body—you could if you asked. . . ."

"On the contrary, I asked and my Lord Worthy refused. . . ." My uncle spoke slowly and thoughtfully. "But I will go now and take a closer look at the body." He kissed me on the cheek, smelling rather sour himself, and then hurried from the room.

Lady Sarah and Mary Shelton have just returned. I am very tired, probably from not getting enough sleep last night; saving an innocent man is exhausting work! I shall stop writing now and prepare for bed.

I am writing this hurriedly, before I am summoned
to attend the Queen at supper. I have had the most
exciting day! And what we discovered! I can hardly
believe it, though I heard it with my own ears. I
should probably write this in orange juice—it's very
secret—only I can't because of the marmelada. Also
I need more ink and a new quill—mine is quite worn
down with all my writing and it won't sharpen properly any more.

When Lady Sarah and Mary Shelton came back
last night there was a lot of tutting and sighing over a
couple of broken pots and a small tear in the curtain.
Well, what was I supposed to do? It was so *dull* being
in my chamber all evening, and I just wondered if I
could get all the way round without touching the
floor, which led to a slight accident with Lady Sarah's
pots of face paint and Mary's bed curtains.

This morning the Queen sent for me. She told

me privately that she would have to commit Lord Robert to the Fleet Prison. It's supposed to be a bit better than the Tower, so I hope he won't be too miserable there. She also said that I might now leave my room and continue my investigation, as long as I was present to attend her at supper.

Relieved, I returned to my chamber and changed into my hunting kirtle. Then I went in search of Ellie, taking with me a spare pork pasty I had saved her from my supper.

Mrs. Twiste, who's in charge of the laundry, had set her scrubbing out the huge boiling bucks at the back of the laundry and she was just finishing when I found her.

"I've got an errand next," she said to me as I sat on the wall and watched her gobble the pasty in two bites. It was a cold frosty morning and her cheeks and nose were bright red. She gulped down the last crumbs and added, "I've got to take a pile of sheets to Mrs. Twynhoe. Would you like to help?"

Officially, Mrs. Twynhoe's married to the Naper's Deputy, who looks after the household linen, so she's in charge of all the bedlinen. But really she's a midwife and a wise-woman. I'd always wanted to meet her. "Is she really a witch?" I asked eagerly.

"No, she ain't a witch," Ellie replied. "She's a

114

lovely person and she knows all there is to know about herbs and potions. So we can ask her where somebody could have got darkwort from."

It was a pity about her not being a witch—I'd always wanted to ask one if they can really fly. But I was still very curious to meet Mrs. Twynhoe, so I went with Ellie to deliver the sheets.

Well, Mrs. Twynhoe was a real disappointment. She didn't even have any warts! She was a short, round person with a beaming face and soft grey curls under her cap and she had arms like a sailor's. She took the baskets from us as if they didn't weigh anything and put them on the long wooden rollers they use to help smooth out the linen.

"Mrs. Twiste said I should stay to help you if you needed it, Mrs. Twynhoe," said Ellie with a little bob.

Mrs. Twynhoe beamed even wider. "Oh, there now, of course you can, my dear. And call me Mrs. Bea—Twynhoe is such a mouthful, I couldn't even say it properly meself on my wedding day. If you could help me roll the sheets once I have the steam working, perhaps your friend could hem a sheet for me—I've just put it sides-to-middle and it needs a good needlewoman."

She gave me a thimble and a needle and a skein of

thread and an enormous linen sheet already pinned and then she and Ellie set to work stretching the sheets over the rollers using hot-metal irons from a small brazier. It looked very difficult and skilled and Ellie was impressively efficient. The big airing room soon got hot and steamy. I was sitting by the window stitching at the sheet as nicely as I could. I wondered how she knew to give me that job and then I thought she had probably seen me often enough, following the Queen in procession, and I just hadn't noticed her.

Ellie was chatting away to her about herbs and I listened carefully. "Half the soapwort in the kitchen garden got eaten by some nasty fly," she said. "We're having to buy it in from my Lord Worthy's gardens on the Strand."

"Oh, that's a nuisance. Did they plant it in among garlic and carrots?" asked Mrs. Bea.

Ellie shook her head. "The new Head Gardener likes things in straight rows and squares and he hates mixing plants in the same bed."

"More fool him then," said Mrs. Bea wisely. "Garlic is a charm to protect against blackfly."

"Mrs. Bea, Lady Grace wanted you to tell her what you know about darkwort," said Ellie finally.

Mrs. Bea's jolly red face suddenly looked serious. "That's nasty stuff, my dear. No good is ever done with darkwort." Mrs. Bea's eyes suddenly became like the Queen's—sharp enough to make a hole in your head. "And why are you so curious about darkwort?" Then she suddenly remembered my mother. "Oh, my dear . . ."

"Mrs. Bea, I've reason to believe that Sir Gerald Worthy died of it the day before yesterday," I put in.

Mrs. Bea stopped smoothing the linen sheet. "Do you now?"

"Yes. I know because I recognized the faint yellow froth on his lips and that bitter smell," I replied.

"Hmm." Mrs. Bea stared very hard at me and then at Ellie and then took the newly-smooth sheet off the rollers and folded it up with Ellie's help, speaking as she did so. "Darkwort is a herb, related to belladonna or deadly nightshade. It's very rare. If dried and pounded, it makes a poisonous powder with no taste, though when mixed with certain substances—wine, for instance—it stains yellow."

"Where might somebody get hold of darkwort?" I enquired.

Looking thoughtful, Mrs. Bea went and poured herself some mild ale out of a jug on the table by the door, offering us some as well. Ellie has never been known to turn down food and drink, and I had some because the heat in the room had made me thirsty. It was very good, better than I'd expected, flavoured with preserved lemon peel.

"Now then," Mrs. Bea said, sitting down and smoothing out her apron. "Perhaps four apothecaries in London might sell it. It is very expensive. At least ten shillings for a scruple."

"Which apothecaries are they?" I asked.

Mrs. Bea smiled at me. "I think I should not give you reason to run gallivanting around London town asking what villain has bought darkwort recently, even to save your future husband," she said.

I sighed. "How can I do it then?"

"Marry, I shall go and ask them myself," said Mrs. Bea stoutly. "And they're more likely to tell me the truth than you, my dear, since they know me. And then I shall tell you."

She was being so helpful I decided to risk it. "Thank you, Mrs. Bea," I said carefully. "And what's also really needed is for someone to look around the chambers of people like my Lord Robert, quietly, without alarming them . . ."

"And find if there's darkwort powder?" Mrs.

Bea's bright eyes were considering me. "Hmm. How is the sheet coming along?"

"Hm? Oh, I've finished. It was only plain sewing," I replied.

She took the sheet from me and looked at the hem very critically, then nodded her approval. "I think you and Ellie might have a little free time now. I'll tell Mrs. Twiste I sent you in search of some pillow-slips and sheets that are missing." She dug in a chest. "Here's a white cap and apron so you look the part, my dear."

Ellie smiled and curtsied and so did I because she was kind and she didn't have to help us, did she? Then we took the linen bag and rushed out and down the passage.

I was glad of the cap and apron—they would be a useful disguise in case we met anyone who knew me. I put them on. Ellie explained that when fetching things from the courtiers' chambers she was always sent with someone, partly to prevent any pilfering, partly to make sure no one treated her badly. Both Mrs. Twiste and Mrs. Bea had dim views of the average gentleman.

We made our way down to the next floor, which is the Long Gallery, above the Queen's Apartments. It sounded as if elephants were galloping about in there. Ellie stopped me going in and we hid at the bend of the stairs to listen to the musicians playing the drum and viol while the Maids of Honour practised their dancing. The Dancing Master was wailing as usual, "And two and one and leap . . ." There was a thunderous series of thuds. "Like a feather!" shrieked the dancing master. "On the toes! *Mon Dieu, ce sont les vaches . . . vraiment . . .*"

Ellie giggled and so did I. After a minute the music stopped and there was a rush of footsteps on the stairs, followed more slowly by the Dancing Master and one of the musicians, both drinking from little flasks.

When they had all gone we entered and found Masou standing gravely on his hands and walking up and down—he had been roped in to provide a partner for girls who needed to practise.

"No, I cannot come," he said to us when we told him what we were going to do. "Mr. Somers wants me to be able to walk on my hands and juggle with my feet and I must practise for a new tumble he has made." He went up and down again, looking as if he could walk to York like that. "And also, laundrymaids may poke about in chambers but if I should be found there, they'll think I was thieving."

So we left him and made our way to the Grace-and-Favour Chambers to begin our search. The first place we went was my Lord Robert's chamber. I had to be sure, before we looked elsewhere. One of his men was sitting by the door, playing a game of cards. He looked very depressed.

Ellie marched right up to him. "Mrs. Twynhoe wants me to find some sheets and pillowslips," she said.

The man shrugged and opened the door. I slipped in quickly, carefully hiding my face, and Ellie followed. We found quite a small, odd-shaped chamber, with a bed with four tall carved corner posts, and a truckle bed, and more mess than you would believe possible. The floor was covered with chicken leg bones, half-chewed sausages, bits of paper, and dirty hose. I was fascinated. It was nearly as bad as a Maid of Honour's chamber.

We discovered pots of ointment, with prescriptions from my Uncle Cavendish stating that they would prevent skin blemishes. Our hearts thudded when we found packets of herbs secreted in a chest amongst Lord Robert's hose. Ellie picked up a note that was with them and handed it to me to read. It was in my uncle's writing. He had prescribed a potion to cure a stammer. *"Boil marigolds, agrimony, and borage in posset drink, sweeten it with sugar, and let* the patient drink it going to bed," I read out loud. Poor Lord Robert. It clearly hadn't worked.

Nowhere did we find a yellow powder that might be darkwort. I did discover, however, why Lord Robert was so poor. It seemed he was always losing money at cards to other courtiers, and losing more at dice in the City inns. One small chest was almost full of bills and letters about debts. He seemed to owe money to everybody I'd ever heard of, and plenty I hadn't.

There was also a letter, written but not finished, from Lord Robert to his Lady Dowager mother, dated 14 February:

Dearest Mother,

You will be pleased to know that I have at last managed to make a good match, thanks to the Queen's kind offices, and your good advice. I expect to be out of debt as soon as I am handfasted to the heiress of the Cavendishes. As you predicted, beloved Mother, she liked pearls better than any of the other gifts on offer, they being a flask and a knife. Luckily, I find her not too foul-visaged, although hardly begun to own womanly curves, being rather skinny. She seems virtuous and

cheerful and her worst vice is that she talks
constantly. No doubt time will improve her greatly.

"Huh!" I said, feeling very hurt. I'd thought the pearls meant Lord Robert had found out what jewels I like best; but no, he'd asked his mother what girls like. And worse, much worse, he'd only been interested in my estates. How disgustingly unromantic. And who was he to say I was "not too foul-visaged" and talked too much? Better than not being able to talk at all, *I* think.

I didn't tear the letter up, although I wanted to. I read the important bits to Ellie, who clearly didn't know whether to be shocked or amused, and then I put it back in the chest. Since it was perfectly obvious Lord Robert didn't deserve me, he could have his pearls back and tell his conniving mother it had all gone wrong!

But still, no yellow powder anywhere.

Ellie had found one pillowslip that didn't belong there and put it in her bag. Then she looked at me. "Well?" she said.

"I'm still going to help him get out of the Fleet," I told her. "But I certainly won't marry him. Now, Lady Sarah next, I think."

Ellie raised her eyebrows. "Why her?" she asked curiously.

"Lady Sarah was after Sir Gerald at the ball," I explained. "Maybe she hated him because he was chasing me." Then I added bitterly, "Though I know for a fact he was only doing what his uncle, Lord Worthy, told him. After my inheritance too, no doubt."

"Well, of course he was," said Ellie tartly. "They all were, except Sir Charles, who is surely rich enough."

We came out of Lord Robert's chamber and Ellie thanked the man, who went on playing with his cards. We walked on quickly down the Stone Gallery, across the little bridge, and into the upper story of the Privy Gallery to the chambers of the Maids of Honour and Ladies-in-Waiting.

In my chamber, Ellie sorted through the many pots and potions belonging to Lady Sarah. Not one of them was sulphur-yellow, though several were purple and more than one looked and smelled like dung. There were the usual white lead and cinnabar to make a red colour, and ground lapis lazuli and malachite for colouring eyelids blue or green, and some sticks of kohl. One bottle held something which Ellie sniffed and announced was probably a tincture of tansy and pennyroyal mint, and another was labelled FOR THE ALLUREMENT OF ALL KINDS OF LOVE, which made me laugh.

There was also a miniature of Sarah, which made her face much more heart-shaped than it really is and her chest even bigger. We also found dozens and dozens of love letters from moonstruck courtiers, including several each from Sir Charles, Lord Robert, and Sir Gerald! I scowled. They were supposed to be courting me; how dare they write rubbish to Lady Sarah, too? Surely having a big chest isn't *that* important?

"Yes, it is," said Ellie, when I put this to her.

I couldn't resist poking my nose round the door of Mrs. Champernowne's chamber, which was tidy and clean, with a big pile of books next to the bed, including two with nothing except boring sermons in them. No yellow powder.

We decided to look in Lord Worthy's chambers as well—it was only fair to search everyone's room. There was more paper piled up there than I have ever seen in my life. Ellie poked around, found a sheet with a nasty stain on it under the bed, and put it in her bag. I discovered a recipe to cure baldness together with a screw of green powder and several pots of ointment. I took the lid off one of the pots, but it smelled so strongly of horse dung that Ellie screwed up her face in disgust—though she was on the other side of the room—and I was nearly overcome! I quickly put the lid back on.

Then off we went to look at Sir Charles's room. Ellie protested at this. "Sir Charles is a kind old thing. He left me a lovely gift on Christmas day with two mince pies—and he made sure I got them," she said, with her hands on her hips.

"Well, we've got to investigate everybody who's even vaguely possible, Ellie—nobody's beyond suspicion except the Queen," I said firmly.

Sir Charles's Grace-and-Favour Chamber was near to the Court Gate, close to one of the small staging stables.

There was a servant there, fast asleep on the truckle bed, so Ellie and I had to creep about. We did have the excuse of looking for Mrs. Twynhoe's pillowslips. We checked the few pots on the table, looked under the bed and in the clothes chest. No yellow powder.

It wasn't until we were about to go out of the door again that I realized a funny thing about Sir Charles's shoes. They were lined up at the foot of the bed—two pairs of smart shoes to wear at Court, one pair of riding boots, all quite new. And then there were other pairs of shoes under the bed, and another pair of riding boots, rather more worn. But these looked smaller, and when I put one of the old shoes next to one of the new ones, I could see clearly that the old ones were quite a lot smaller. "Look at that," I whispered to Ellie. "Isn't it odd?"

"What?" said Ellie.

"His shoes. Look, the new ones are big and the old ones under the bed are small. It's as if Sir Charles's feet grew suddenly, like mine did last year. But he's too old to have growing feet."

Ellie looked and frowned in puzzlement.

Suddenly I heard footsteps in the passage. Sir Charles's voice called out, "Stevens, are you there?"

Ellie and I looked at each other in horror, and then Ellie scuttled under the bed and I went with her. We hid in a nest of footwear and old hose as Sir Charles came into the room.

I looked at his feet. He had another pair of boots on, very smart, brand new, and his feet were very big. I tried to remember Sir Charles's feet when I'd seen them before. Had they changed?

Sir Charles went over to the manservant on the truckle bed and shook him awake.

"Wuzzat?" muttered the man. Then he woke up properly and we heard him scrambling to his feet. "Um. Yes, Mr. Amesbury."

Ellie and I looked at each other. *Mr.* Amesbury?

"Go and check on my brother. Make sure he has water and can't get out," said the man who I had thought was Sir Charles.

"Yes, sir, if you say so," replied Stevens sullenly.

"I do say so, Stevens." The voice was cold and nasty, nothing like Sir Charles's friendly rumble.

I felt my jaw dropping open. Sir Charles wasn't Sir Charles—he was somebody else entirely! With the same face, maybe, but bigger feet and . . . A thought popped into my head. Didn't Sir Charles have a brother? I screwed up my eyes, trying to remember. A brother who had died in France . . .

If he'd died! What was his name? Harry? No. Hector.

"Best put a knife in him, sir, then drop him in the Thames," said Stevens, who was pulling on his jerkin. "That way—"

"Thank you for your advice, Stevens. I am perfectly well aware of what's best," snapped the impostor. "However, I cannot possibly do it until I know all his business dealings—and where he has hidden the deeds to his house."

"Don't think he'll tell you, sir," said Stevens. "Not wivout some better persuading."

"I know my brother, Stevens. He'll tell eventually rather than starve."

What a horrible way to talk about your brother! Ellie's eyes were like saucers. I was having to hold my hand over my mouth because the smell of stale cheese from the old hose was making me want to cough.

"And then once I'm safe I think I shall become ill for a while, so I can get rid of this padding," the impostor continued. He clearly was the not-so-Honourable Hector Amesbury, brother to Sir Charles.

Hector sat on his bed and changed into his riding boots with help from Stevens.

"First I must make an appearance at the stables," he said, "or somebody will wonder why my horse-mad fool of a brother has suddenly gone off the beasts. But then I shall come and . . . talk . . . to him again. Tell him that."

"Yes, sir." Stevens was by the door. "Couldn't I just . . . rough him up a bit—give him a taster, sir?"

"Very well. But don't do too much damage," Hector told him, still in that nasty cold voice.

"No, sir."

I still had my hand over my mouth, fighting not to cough. I really hoped Hector would go soon so I could get away from the hose. Ellie didn't seem to mind the smell but she was shaking. What kind of brother was Hector Amesbury? He'd imprisoned Sir Charles and was starving him! It was outrageous. Especially as Sir Charles was so fond of his food.

As the door shut behind them I scrambled out as quick as I could. Ellie followed more slowly, still trembling.

"Lord save us!" I said. "Perhaps *he* murdered Sir Gerald."

"He must have done! If he could imprison and starve his own brother . . ." Ellie shook her head. "And poor Sir Charles loving his food, and all."

"Exactly," I agreed. "And that's why Doucette didn't like him," I added thoughtfully. "Doucette *knew* it wasn't Sir Charles, the clever animal. And that's why he couldn't sing 'Greensleeves' properly at the ball! But why? Why would anybody do this to their own brother?"

We rushed back up to the Long Gallery to tell Masou. He was carefully flipping himself over from walking on his hands to standing upright, doing a somersault on the way.

He soon stopped as he listened to our story, though.

"We have to rescue Sir Charles," I said firmly. The other two just gawped at me.

"How?" demanded Ellie.

"It's obvious—we have to find out where he is and go there to free him," I told her. "Somebody has to follow Hector Amesbury and find out where he goes."

Masou looked at the two of us, then looked theatrically round the room, and then put his finger to his own chest.

I smiled sweetly at him and nodded.

Masou started putting on his shoes and pattens and clopped to the door of the gallery.

"He should be at the stables now," I said. "He said he'd go and see his brother afterwards."

Masou nodded and ran down the stairs. Then he ran back up again to ask, "What if he takes a boat?"

I felt in my petticoat and found some pennies, which I tossed to Masou. "If he catches you, pretend that you were about to ask him for a job," I suggested. Masou grinned, then went back downstairs again.

Ellie and I went back to Sir Charles's chamber and searched it more thoroughly, starting at one corner and going all the way round to the other. Nothing. Not the faintest smallest smidgeon of powder of any colour, let alone yellow, nor any staining. So Ellie took a couple of dirty shirts and we went back to Mrs. Bea, who received the pillowslips and shirts, checked them, and told Ellie to take them all down to the laundry and get back to work.

Then Mrs. Bea looked shrewdly at me. "Did you find anything interesting?" she asked.

For a moment I wanted to tell her all about Sir Charles and Hector, but there was a risk she might tell Mrs. Champernowne and then where would we be? So I shook my head and tried not to look as excited as I felt.

"No darkwort anywhere." I tried to look disappointed and I think I managed it quite well.

"Hmph. Come back to me tomorrow, my dear, and I shall tell you if any apothecaries have sold it recently—they may not remember, mind, or they might have been paid to keep quiet. But I'll ask for you. It would be a sad thing if Lord Robert were to lose his head over this."

"Wouldn't he hang?" asked Ellie ghoulishly, still hovering at the doorway. She hated to miss out on any gossip. "I thought that's what happened to murderers."

"That's right, Ellie, but being a nobleman, he can ask for the mercy of an axe," Mrs. Bea explained.

It didn't sound like much of a mercy to me. But still it was nice of her to help us and I said so. That made her laugh a lot, which made her pink face quite wobbly.

"Lord above, Lady Grace," she said, "I don't want anyone who owes me money to be executed."

"Does he owe you money, too?" I asked.

"Certainly," she replied. "For three wart-charmings and a spell against tongue-tie. And a spell to enchant cards in his favour, but I only get that if it works, and I don't suppose it has."

I scowled. "He owes everybody money—that's why he wanted to marry me."

"Of course he did, dear—you didn't think he loved you, did you? Did you love him?"

"Certainly not," I said, tossing my head. "He hasn't exactly done anything very lovable for me and he hasn't a word to say for himself. Besides, it's undignified to fall in love; that's for men to do."

Mrs. Bea chuckled. "Quite right. A well-born lady like you has no business falling in love and I'm glad to hear you've got your head well sewn on."

"Unlike Lord Robert," put in Ellie, and snickered.

I gave Mrs. Bea back her cap and apron and went

to my chamber to find that my dinner had been left outside the door for me. There was manchet bread, salt beef and potherbs, and a hard cheese with pickled eringo root against the scurvy. I gobbled it all down and I have been scribbling away at my daybooke ever since, but now someone is coming.

Midday

God's bones! There's so much to tell. I hardly know
where to start and I'm so tired from being up all
night again. But I must write this down no matter
how much my head is whirling because otherwise I
won't sleep at all. And besides, this was a most wondrous midnight adventure!

Last time I was interrupted it was Mrs.
Champernowne bustling in.

"Wherever did you go, child?" she wanted to
know. "The Queen was asking for you."

"I . . . went for a walk," I said, hoping it didn't
sound as silly to her as it did to me, "around the
palace. The Queen did say I could—"

"I think you have been treated very gently, Lady
Grace," said Mrs. Champernowne severely. "There

had better be no more trouble from you. Now get your kirtle on and attend Her Majesty at supper."

Lord Worthy was dining with the Queen again but this time I wasn't invited. I just brought the Queen's wine when she beckoned me and held a napkin for her to dry her fingers after she rinsed them. The Queen was quite distant to me, and I was desperate to let her know what I'd discovered. I wondered how Masou was getting on. Was he back yet? Was he safe? I chewed a fingernail nervously, and Her Majesty told me off.

The tumblers came in and, thank the Lord, Masou was among them, walking in on his hands and backwards somersaulting onto his feet. He stared at me and winked, so I could hardly wait until I had an excuse to leave the Queen's side. At last I had to go down to the buttery to refill a pitcher with ale. The jugglers and tumblers were there, drinking thirstily. Masou made a great flourish of taking the pitcher and filling it at the barrel for me. Then we went into a little alcove and Masou told me the story.

"I followed Sir Charles . . . ," Masou said, and mimed tiptoeing after him, dodging from tree to tree.

"It's really his brother Hector," I corrected him.

Masou rolled his eyes. "Who is telling this story?" he demanded. I smiled and gestured to him and he made an elaborate bow. "So I followed the Evil Brother to the Palace of Horses, praying to Allah that he would not take a horse to visit the Unfortunate One. Allah be praised, he did not. He scowled about at the grooms for a while and then went down to the watersteps and shouted, 'Oars!' A black ship with black sails, rowed by a green serpent, came. He stepped aboard and the snake rowed him away towards London town.

"After the black ship had departed, I shouted, too, and lo! a golden barque with a ruby sail appeared, rowed by a yellow serpent, who said, 'What is your desire, O Prince of Acrobats?' I jumped aboard and beseeched the serpent to follow the Evil Brother's boat, at which he transformed to an ugly djinni and said, 'Then pay sixpence for it.' Alas, nothing would do but that I must pay, and so he rowed and followed the Evil Brother to some steps which shone with silver and gold and led to a fair garden and little stone houses. Here I paid the djinni and crept ashore. I hid in a wondrous bush that covered me like a Cloak of Invisibility while the Evil Brother went to one of the houses and knocked on the door. It was opened by another evil one, with blood on his knuckles. I did not see the Unfortunate One but he was there, for so I heard Evil Brother say. And then, in great fear lest he find me, I went back down the steps and looked for a boat. At last I came across a little cockleshell with a cobweb sail steered by a monkey, who took me aboard when I begged him. And so I came back unto the Court just in time to tumble for the Queen."

Masou swept another bow and then stood with his arms folded looking very stern. I clapped. "What a wonderful story!" I said. "Is any of it true?"

"Certainly, in essence," said Masou, grinning. "I think the Unfortunate One is imprisoned in one of the little cottages of St. Mary Rounceval churchyard."

"We will have to go there tonight," I decided. My heart was sinking at what the Queen might say, but what else could we do? "Is there any way we could get in without the guard knowing?"

Masou thought hard. "There are windows—I think they are glass, quite small, but I think I could pass. Yes, it can be done. But, my lady, it would be very dangerous—"

"Then we'll do it," I said. "Can you arrange for a boat?"

Masou bowed with his two hands crossed on his

chest. "I am my lady's to command," he said, and cartwheeled away.

I hurried back to the Withdrawing Room with the pitcher and then put my hand to my head and curtsied to the Queen, explaining in front of everyone that I had a megrim from the excitement of the last few days and asking if I could go to my bed.

Her Majesty didn't quite believe me, I could see that, but she let me go.

Once again I had to wait, lying stiff as a board with fright and excitement with a smock over my hunting kirtle, until Mary and Lady Sarah were back from attending the Queen—except Mary came back but there was no sign of Lady Sarah at all. Oh, well, I thought, I can tell on her if she tells on me.

I crept out while Mary snored, and tiptoed down the passageway to the Orchard door, where Masou and Ellie were waiting.

"Did you bring money?" asked Masou. "We must pay for the boat."

I had a few pennies. We threaded through the palace, dodging serving men and night-wandering courtiers, to the watersteps. Masou whistled softly, and a boat rowed close. It wasn't a normal Thames wherry; it was tiny, with a little sail and a scrawny boy about Masou's age rowing it.

"Who's he?" I hissed. "Is that the monkey in the cockleshell?"

"My lady, may I present my friend Kersey," said Masou with a flourish. "Kersey, this is the Lady Grace I told you about."

"What did you tell him?" I whispered.

Masou shrugged innocently.

The boy in the boat drew the oars in, snatched off his greasy cap, and made a bow. "Honoured, lady," he said. "Sorry I din't believe you, Masou. Come aboard, ladies," he added, winking at Ellie.

Ellie sniffed. "Don't you go calling me a lady," she said sternly as she hopped in and I followed. "I'm here for to attend on my lady and save her reputation."

Masou elbowed me, and I pulled out my purse and gave Kersey all my pennies. He grunted and put them away in his sleeve, then coughed and looked embarrassed. "See, lady, Masou told me you was one of the Queen's Ladies-in-Waiting . . ."

"I'm a Maid of Honour," I said, wishing Masou could have kept his mouth shut.

"Right, Maid of Honour, and wot he said is that you get to see the Queen every day and she speaks to you."

"Yes, that's true," I admitted.

"I met the Queen once," Kersey said. "She was wearing all silver and black velvet and with diamonds in her hair and I held the boat for her when she went on her barge—'cos me dad's one of the relief bargemen—and squashed me thumb and she gave me her kerchief to bind it up and said she hoped as it would be better soon. She's wonderful, isn't she? Just gave me her own kerchief and said—"

"She's very kind to people who look after her," I agreed.

Kersey was rowing us along the northern bank of the Thames, dodging some of the dangerous eddies. He seemed more interested in talking than rowing, though, which worried me. "I wish I could see her every day like you." His face was shining with adoration. "How do you get to be a courtier?" he asked.

"Well, you have to be rich, or rich enough to pretend to be rich," I replied.

Kersey nodded. "How rich is that?"

"A velvet suit costs a hundred pounds, for a cheap one," I told him. He gasped, and shut up.

Masou tapped the side of the boat and Kersey rowed it close up to the shining, slimy wall of some houses near the water's edge. There was a row of windows overlooking the water, and watersteps going up to a gate.

"That is the cottage where Sir Charles is being held," whispered Masou, pointing to a house at the far end of the row. "There's a man guarding the door, so I will have to break in at the back."

Kersey was tying his craft up tight to the wall by a ring.

"I want to get up to that ledge there," said Masou, gesturing towards the windows. "And I need a diamond ring."

"Why?" asked Ellie.

Masou grinned, with a flash of white teeth. "For the reason that only diamond is of enough hardness to cut glass," he explained.

"Hmph," said Ellie.

There were diamonds in the pearl ring my mother gave me. I hesitated and then gave it to Masou.

He smiled at me because I could have said no, it was too valuable. "Now, it's fine that you are tall," he said to me. "But I hope you are strong, too. You must give me a lift up."

"Standing on the boat?" I asked.

"Yes. I could not use a ladder—too rigid," Masou explained.

Kersey was tying the other end of the boat to another ring.

"But—" I began.

"Kersey and Ellie will hold you steady. All you need do is stand firm and I shall climb you like a living tree."

Firm? On a boat? I saw a bit of stone sticking out and I leaned over and grabbed it.

"Good," Masou said, and sprang onto my back. He is quite small and very lithe, but he is also heavy. I went "Ooof!" and nearly fell down.

"I told you it should be me," sniffed Ellie. "I'm stronger."

"But not tall enough," said Masou, fitting one foot onto my shoulder. "There, it's just enough."

The boat creaked and tilted sideways. Masou climbed on my other shoulder and balanced. It hurt! My shoulders felt like they would break; there was a sort of bounce and then the weight was off.

Masou was crouched on the ledge, peering through the window. He muttered in disappointment, reached round a piece of wall, and slid onto the next windowsill. Another grunt. Ellie and I were staring at him, really scared that all the adventure was for nothing. I noticed that Masou had something long wrapped in cloth and slung across his back, and I wondered what it was.

He slid along and reached for the next window, peered through, and said, "Hah! Allah be praised."

He crouched there for what seemed a long time and there was a dreadful scraping screeching noise, which must have been the diamond cutting glass, then a tapping. A big piece of window came out, held by Masou with his fingers and a knife, and he threw it down into the Thames. Then he reached in, found a latch, and opened the window. He uncoiled a rope from round his waist and tied one end to the window post. "Climb up by the rope now, Lady Grace," he called softly down to me.

I wasn't sure how to do it, but Masou told me to wrap it round my waist and pull myself up by my arms, putting my toes into the cracks in the wall. It was very slimy and slippery. I nearly went in the water twice, but I managed to get up on the ledge and crouch there, my heart going *bam-da-da-bam!* like a drum at a dance.

Masou moved the rope so it hung into the room, then dropped down. I followed. There was soft straw, a dreadful smell of damp, an unemptied chamberpot, and a rather fat man lying huddled up in a cloak in the corner.

I went over to him and touched him on the shoulder. He snorted, and jumped awake with his fists up. I backed into the corner.

"Who? What?" he shouted angrily.

"Sir Charles?" I asked, because I wasn't sure. Masou was busy with a tinder box. He lit a candle and then I saw it definitely was Sir Charles, though he looked terrible. His beard was untrimmed and his hair was standing on end. He was in his shirt-sleeves with the cloak wrapped around him and he had a nasty black eye as well.

"Good heavens, Lady Grace, what in the name of God . . . ?" His eyes narrowed with suspicion. "Did my brother bring you?"

"No." I scowled at that. "I don't know what sort of brother he is, but *we've* come to rescue you."

I practically gabbled as I told him what we'd found out and how we came to help, and he shook his head as if bewildered. Meanwhile, Masou had unslung the thing on his back and was unwrapping it.

Masou bowed. "Sir, I think the window is too small for you, but I brought this." He handed Sir Charles the long poignard dagger he had brought with him.

Sir Charles gripped the hilt, tested the blade, then

shook his head. "I can't leave. Look." He lifted one of his feet and we saw there was a manacle round his ankle and a short chain stapled to the wall.

Masou smiled again and brought out a little wallet which had hooks and files in it. He checked the ring around Sir Charles's ankle while I listened at the locked door to make sure the man guarding it hadn't heard anything. There was a series of scraping noises and then a brisk sound of filing. At last I heard a click, and next moment Sir Charles was standing up with the poignard in his hand. Even though he was a fat old man, he looked very angry and quite frightening. "Pray, now, climb back out of the window," he ordered.

"But, Sir Charles, we can help you . . . ," I began.

"Lady Grace, this is not a sight for you. I will meet you at the watersteps," he replied firmly.

Masou bowed to Sir Charles and held the rope for me to climb up, which was even more difficult the second time because my hands were so sore.

We dropped back into the boat and waited.

Suddenly we heard banging and screaming from Sir Charles. "Help! Help! I'm choking . . . arghh . . ."

It didn't sound very realistic but there was the sound of a door being unlocked and then Stevens's voice. "Didn't you learn your lesson the first time, you—"

There was a thud, a scuffle, a horrible sort of crunching noise, a short cry—and then silence. A few minutes later we could hear Sir Charles breathing hard on the watersteps and see his broad silhouette there.

He got down carefully into the boat, which was distinctly overloaded with all of us, and washed the poignard and his hands in the water. Then he offered the blade back to Masou, who shook his head. Nobody said anything. In truth, I felt a bit sick.

Kersey rowed us all slowly and carefully back upriver to Whitehall, which took longer because the current was against him.

"What happened to you, Sir Charles?" I asked, so I wouldn't think about my queasy stomach and how close the water was as we struggled slowly upstream.

Sir Charles turned to me. "My lady, all I know is that I went for a nap after our ride on the day of the St. Valentine's Feast and woke up in that foul place with a chain on my leg," he said. "I could scarce believe it possible, and yet my twin brother was there, demanding to know where my papers were and what my business dealings were at the Royal Exchange." Sir Charles wiped his brow—he was sweating heavily, even though there was a chill in the air. "My twin brother, Hector, always hated me—even though I gave him money whenever he asked for it—I thought he was in France fighting the Papists. And then I had word that he was dead, as I told you. But there he was, threatening me with starvation and worse if I did not do as he demanded. Of course, I did not, as I *knew* I would then be a dead man for certain. But then he sent his henchman to threaten me and strike me—"

"What happened to Stevens?" I asked.

Sir Charles looked away. "Honour is satisfied for the blows he gave me. He is dead."

"Oh." That was all I could manage to say. It was hard to imagine plump, jolly Sir Charles, who took me riding and sang "Greensleeves" for me, killing someone with his own hands. Even with good reason.

"Good," said Ellie. "Serves 'im right."

I looked at the sky and saw it was nearly dawn. My heart went into my boots. We'd rescued Sir Charles but, oh, I was going to be in so much trouble.

Sir Charles saw my face and said very kindly,

"Never fear, Lady Grace, Her Majesty will be delighted with you presently. Let me but speak to her and she shall be reconciled." Then his face went back to being rather bleak.

Nobody said anything more as we struggled back up to Whitehall, with all of us paddling eventually against the tide. We reached the steps and climbed up them to find a bemused Yeoman of the Guard barring our path.

Kersey let us off and then rowed away to the kitchen steps as fast as he could.

I recognized the Yeoman, who sometimes guarded the Queen. "Good morning, Mitchell," I said. "Will you send to Her Majesty to say that I have rescued the real Sir Charles Amesbury from imprisonment by his brother and brought him back to her?" I did my best to sound as imperious and commanding as the Queen, though I fear my stained, green-wool, third-best kirtle did not help.

That put the cat among the pigeons! What a lot of fuss and flurrying around, while Her Majesty was awoken and prepared for an audience. Eventually we were all brought into the Presence Chamber, where the Queen was sitting on her throne looking absolutely furious, Lord Worthy at her side. Mary Shelton and Lady Sarah were peeping round the side of the dais, faces alight with curiosity. They must have come in to arrange the Queen's train and then managed not to be dismissed by pretending to be very intent on their embroidery.

The Queen didn't even look at me. I just hoped her fury was for the benefit of appearances. If she had truly tired of my adventures, I really was in trouble! Sir Charles stepped forwards, kneeled, and told her what he had told us on the boat. The Queen listened silently. Then, without comment, she sent for the man calling himself Sir Charles.

Hector Amesbury arrived, looking nervous. Sir Charles stood to face him, his hand on the poignard. At first glance, they were like two peas in a pod, save for Sir Charles being half-dressed and unshaven. But side by side I could see that Hector was an inch or so taller.

"I see my poor mad brother Hector Amesbury has escaped," sneered the pretend Sir Charles. "The poor fellow believes that he is really me. He's very convincing, I grant you."

"How could you do this, Hector?" said the real Sir Charles, sounding very sad. "I gave you a good income, I helped you to go to France—how could you do it?"

Hector shrugged. "His insanity is flamboyant, as

you see, Your Majesty. It is not surprising that your innocent Maid of Honour, Lady Grace, has been fooled by it."

The Queen looked from the real Sir Charles to the false one and back, then frowned. "How shall this be resolved, gentlemen?" she asked.

I was too excited to remember to kneel. I just burst out with: "Your Majesty, I know a way!"

After I'd said that there was a nasty silence.

"Well?" the Queen enquired. She didn't sound at all encouraging.

I swallowed and curtsied again. "We could ask one of Sir Charles's best friends," I said. "Doucette!"

And so we all went in a very odd sort of procession to the loose box where Doucette was stabled. Sir Charles smiled for the first time as he heard Doucette nicker.

"Here, horsey," said Hector Amesbury, looking scared. "Here!"

Doucette was led out of her loose box by one of the stableboys. As she approached Hector, she looked sulky, her head down. Then her head came up when she smelled Sir Charles and she whickered happily. She dragged her stableboy straight over to the real Sir Charles, who patted her neck and let her nuzzle him. For the first time his battered face relaxed and he looked like the jolly person I knew.

"See?" I said. "Have you ever known any horse that didn't love Sir Charles?"

Hector advanced on Doucette, looking very tense. "Now then, horsey, you know me," he said sternly, reaching for her bridle.

Doucette turned her head, put her ears back, made a disapproving snort, and nipped his arm where he'd stuck it out towards her.

He jerked it back, looked desperately from the horse to his brother to the Queen. By now everybody was scowling at him.

That was when he realized he was as good as dead. Suddenly he punched the man standing next to him and started running for the Court Gate.

Two of the Queen's Guard went after him and one made a huge flying leap onto his back, while the other grabbed his doublet and swung him down. He went over, yelling that it wasn't fair, in a pile of crimson velvet and fists, and all the padding came out of his doublet.

The guards brought him back to where the Queen was standing, with Sir Charles by her side. She stared at Hector with her eyes like chips of ice and her lips so tight they had almost disappeared. She looked terrifying.

"Mr. Amesbury, you have one minute to avoid a trial for high treason by confessing everything." Her voice was like ice, too.

Hector had lost his nerve. He fell to his knees and put his face in his hands. "It's not my fault— you can't blame me for trying to do something to better my life, when that maggot stole my rightful inheritance. He struts around claiming to be the elder but it's me: *I'm* the elder twin, *I* should have inherited the estates and lived in luxury while he should have gone to France to fight for starveling Huguenots!"

Since half the stableboys and dog-pages in the place were leaning out of loose boxes and windows to eavesdrop on this, the Queen announced that we would return to her Presence Chamber and so back we all processed, Hector surrounded by the Queen's Guard and Sir Charles gallantly offering the Queen his arm—which she politely refused. (I don't blame her. A most unpleasant smell surrounded Sir Charles due to his having been imprisoned for days.)

In the Presence Chamber, Masou, Ellie, and I all sat by the wall while the Queen sent for a clerk to take everything down, and my uncle, Dr. Cavendish. Mary Shelton and Lady Sarah had picked up their embroidery again and were sitting quietly in the corner, hoping the Queen wouldn't notice them and send them away.

Sir Charles stood and told of his and Hector's dramatic birth, so long ago it was before the Queen was born! There had been twin sons born to the Amesbury household and a scarlet thread was tied about the wrist of the first-born twin. But it was the depths of winter and Mother Corbett, the midwife, had built up the fire in the lying-in chamber.

"Alas, some swaddling bands, hung before the fire to warm, caught alight," said Sir Charles. "In seconds the whole lying-in chamber, with all the hangings, was roaring with flame. My father ran in and carried my mother out. The midwife caught up the babies and saved them. All the men from the village came up to make a bucket-chain and out the flames, and at last the fire was stopped, though that part of the house was almost destroyed. But in all the confusion the scarlet thread upon my wrist was lost. Only Mother Corbett said I was the elder twin because she remembered carrying the first-born on her right arm and the younger one on her left."

Hector snorted. "The word of a drunken old witch . . ."

"She remembered clearly and never wavered—" began Sir Charles.

"How dare you!" shrieked Hector, who seemed to have taken all leave of his senses. "It was *I* who was the elder twin and *you* the pretender. I have known it ever since old Mother Corbett told me the tale when I was nine. I have known it and you have always denied it."

"I deny it because it is not true," said Sir Charles levelly.

"And so," said the Queen, "what did you do to right what you conceived as an injustice, Mr. Amesbury?"

Hector looked at the rush matting, his face working, and I noticed that there was spittle on his chin. "I was near enough blown to pieces on a French battlefield," he said. "I took my survival as a sign. Wherefore should I struggle through war and bloodshed when my rightful inheritance waited in England? I had my commander write to my brother to say I was dead, and then I returned, in secrecy, to England." He looked up, his broad Charles-ish face sour and ugly with spite. "Sir Charles's pageboy took a shilling to put laudanum in his wine and I smuggled him unconscious out of the Court in one of the carts bringing hay for the horses. I had already rented the abandoned cottages at St. Mary Rounceval. I took my brother's place—I only needed to have new footwear made that fitted me, and wear his clothes with a little padding stuffed inside. And so I fooled everyone."

He laughed and wagged a finger. "You were all so blind, it was almost laughable. All you see are the clothes. I decided I must marry the Cavendish girl to secure a fortune of my own. And to do it, I first needed to—"

"Kill Sir Gerald?" asked the Queen flintily.

"Yes," Hector agreed enthusiastically. "And likewise be sure that Lord Robert was accused of the murder, so I would be the last suitor and could be sure of marrying the girl. That way, no matter if someone discovered my true identity, I would still be her husband and still have her estates."

He laughed more loudly, sounding slightly hysterical now. "I fooled you all again with my genius and cunning! I simply went to Lord Robert's chamber and cut an aiglet from one of his doublets; then I hurried to Sir Gerald's chamber, where I found him so sottish with drink that he made no stir when I crept in.

And so I took the dagger that lay on the chest, stabbed it into Sir Gerald's back where he lay, and left Lord Robert's aiglet on the pillow. Thus I rid myself of all competition at a single stroke!"

"And then you came back to the Banqueting House to dance and feign kindness to Lord Robert?" demanded the Queen.

Hector nodded, looking very proud of himself.

"Was it so light a thing for you then, to kill a man who was helpless?" The Queen's voice was soft but cut like steel.

Hector shrugged.

"But Hector, for God's sake," broke in Sir Charles. "Why in God's name did you think such a mad plan would work?"

"Of course it would have worked. Why shouldn't it? Nobody would suspect dear old Charles Amesbury of killing Sir Gerald—he's got plenty of enemies, especially Lord Robert. . . . And once I was married to the Cavendish heiress, none of that would have mattered anyway. I would have been safe—rich like you. No more struggling to find a living, no more fighting in France . . ." Hector seemed to have forgotten completely that there were other people listening, especially the Queen. He pointed his finger at me. "Nothing went wrong until that interfering girl poked her nose in where it wasn't wanted."

I sniffed. I dare say he would have called anyone who found him out "interfering."

"*Lady* Grace," Sir Charles said severely to Hector, "was good enough to rescue me from the vile dungeon you put me in."

"Well, Lord Robert should think twice about marrying some girl who might take it into her head to run off one night and rescue somebody!"

The Queen's eyebrows went right up her forehead at this. Hector saw her and stopped talking, his face twitching.

After a long and impressive silence, the Queen spoke. "Mr. Hector Amesbury, you shall be committed to the Fleet, and of course my Lord Robert shall be released. We shall then see to it that you are arraigned for the murder of Sir Gerald Worthy—"

I coughed. I had to. You're not supposed to interrupt the Queen.

She looked in my direction and sighed. "Yes, Lady Grace. What have you to add?" she asked.

I stood up, wishing that I didn't have big stains all over my poor hunting kirtle. I had to say it, though, because somebody who has once killed with poison might do it again . . . and again.

"Well, you see, Your Majesty, I don't think Hector Amesbury *did* kill Sir Gerald, even if he thought he did. He was so anxious to get rid of him, he didn't realize that Sir Gerald was already dead."

"*What?*" exclaimed Hector, whose eyes looked as though they might pop out of his head.

"What are you talking about, Grace?" the Queen enquired patiently.

"Someone had been there before, Your Majesty. You see, my uncle, Dr. Cavendish, noticed that the wound in Sir Gerald's back hadn't bled, and he deduced that this must be because Sir Gerald was already dead when he was stabbed," I explained.

My uncle threw me a grateful look.

"And then, when I . . . um . . . when I went to visit Sir Gerald in the chapel, I noticed that he had a sulphur-yellow staining on his lips and there was a nasty bitter smell."

The Queen's expression hardened. Clearly, she knew what I was talking about. "Darkwort," she said grimly.

"Yes, Your Majesty," said Dr. Cavendish, sounding dolefully hung over again, "I'm afraid so. It is my intention to obtain a Court order to open the body. I suspect we shall find that the liver is quite blackened."

Lord Worthy went grey at this talk of opening his nephew's body. I felt quite sorry for him. Looking pale and drawn, he leaned forward to speak to the Queen. "Your Majesty," he said, hoarsely, "I find myself rather overcome. Would you be so good as to allow me to withdraw?"

The Queen looked at him with concern. "Of course, my Lord Worthy," she replied kindly. "Do you require the services of Dr. Cavendish?"

"No, no, not at all," Lord Worthy said hurriedly. "Dr. Cavendish is needed here. A brief rest and I am sure I shall be quite recovered." He hurried from the Presence Chamber and the Queen turned back to the doctor.

"So when Mr. Amesbury stabbed Sir Gerald, he was stabbing a corpse!" she declared.

Hector was giggling like a small child. "That's not murder, is it? Tell her, Charles!" he pleaded, and Charles shook his head. "You can't hang me for stabbing a corpse, can you?" Hector pursued.

"It was attempted murder," said the Queen coldly, "and shall be tried as such. You shall also be tried for kidnapping and false imprisonment of your own brother, and the *wicked* imposture you attempted on ourselves. And if the jury does not decide you should hang, then I should think it's likely you shall spend the rest of your days in Bedlam, since it seems you are quite mad."

Her Majesty signalled for Hector Amesbury to be taken away. He went, still giggling and shaking his head, seeming to have retreated into his own world.

"Sir Charles, I am pleased that Dr. Cavendish has declared you not to have taken any great hurt from your brother's wicked practices."

Turning even ruddier than usual, Sir Charles went nearer and bent onto one knee. "Your Majesty, you are too kind," he puffed. His intention was clearly to kiss the Queen's hand. But Her Majesty hastily held a lace handkerchief to her nose and bade Sir Charles rise to go and take his rest, saying that of course he could remain in his Grace-and-Favour Chamber as long as he needed to.

After Sir Charles had left, the Queen looked serious again. "So we still have a poisoner abroad at Court," she said gravely.

I stepped forward. "Yes, I'm afraid so, Your Majesty. I knew that if news spread that a darkwort poisoning was suspected, the villain who had it would get rid of any remains. So I helped Ellie in her laundry round and we secretly searched all the chambers for darkwort. But we found none. It was while we were searching Sir Charles's chamber that we overheard Hector talking of how he had imprisoned his brother."

"I see," said Her Majesty. She nodded to Ellie, and then beckoned her and Masou forward.

They kneeled down in front of her.

Ellie was now as white as one of the sheets she helps to iron. I was surprised she was so overawed. I knew she had collected the Queen's dirty shifts for washing hundreds of times. But I suppose it's not the same as actually meeting the person who wears them.

Masou just went a bit grey. But he managed to flourish off his cap in quite a good bow.

"Masou got us downriver and did all the hard work of climbing up to the window and getting through it," I explained.

The Queen nodded graciously. "Oh, I recognize you," she said to Masou. "Will Somers thinks very highly of you—though he complains you are sometimes hard to find. And now we know why. . . ."

Masou looked rather sheepish, and I had to try not to laugh.

"Well, Ellie and Masou, you appear to be loyal and supportive friends to my Lady Grace," Her

Majesty observed. "Thank you. You may leave us now."

Both of them scurried out, looking very relieved. At least Masou remembered to back the last few steps, though Ellie tripped on her petticoat when she tried to copy him.

I guessed they would wait outside, trying to eavesdrop, if they weren't shooed away. They passed Mrs. Twynhoe on their way out.

"Is it urgent, Bea?" asked the Queen rather crossly.

Mrs. Bea curtsied and fanned herself. "I'm afraid it is, Your Majesty," she replied. "Lady Grace here told me of the dastardly doings with darkwort in Court. And I must tell you what I found."

"Ah . . . ," said the Queen. "This is very timely, Bea. We are all listening."

Mrs. Bea curtsied again. "Now then, I went myself about the apothecaries in Westminster and London town. I know 'em all, and most would talk only to those they know about their dealings with darkwort. Only one of 'em—my old contact in Cheapside—had sold darkwort in recent weeks."

"And did you find out the purchaser?" the Queen demanded grimly.

"Why, Your Majesty, that's why I had to hurry myself and tell you," Mrs. Bea replied. "Please believe me when I say I would never do nothing to hurt you, Your Grace, never in all the world."

"I know that, Bea," said the Queen softly, because Mrs. Bea looked very upset and was twisting her hands round about each other.

"Well, but . . . it's a terrible thing, Your Majesty," Mrs. Bea went on. "I couldn't believe it when I heard it. In fact, I told the man he was a liar, which annoyed him. . . ."

The Queen tapped her fingers on the arm of her chair of state and Mrs. Bea collected up her thoughts. "He told me that a skinny serving man bought the darkwort from him. He was wrapped up in a cloak. But when he took out his purse to pay, the cloak slipped open—enough for the apothecary to recognize the servant's livery. It was Lord Worthy's," Mrs. Bea finished dramatically.

There was a stunned silence.

The Queen broke it. "Impossible!" she shouted. "Besides," she added, "Lady Grace and that good wench Ellie searched all the Court chambers for evidence of darkwort—including Lord Worthy's—and found none."

"That's true, Mrs. Bea," I confirmed. "We found no yellow powder anywhere—"

At this, my Uncle Cavendish started. "But Grace," he said urgently, "darkwort powder . . . it is not yellow, my dear, it is green."

I stood there open-mouthed.

Mrs. Bea nodded vigorously at me. "Yes, my love—pure darkwort is green. It's the mixing with wine that turns it yellow and makes it stain such that not even ten-day-old urine will shift it."

Ellie and I *had* found green powder in Lord Worthy's chamber. And I had seen green staining on his cuff. Heart thudding, I told the Queen.

Her Majesty became as still as a statue, her face hard like marble. "Mr. Hatton!" she roared.

One of her Gentlemen put his head round a door. I caught a glimpse of Ellie on the other side, trying not to be noticed so she wouldn't get sent away and miss everything. I was sure now that Masou must be eavesdropping as well.

"Send for my Lord Worthy to come to the Presence Chamber at once!" the Queen commanded.

Mr. Hatton disappeared at a run. We stood awkwardly and waited—me, Mrs. Bea, and Uncle Cavendish. My hands were clenched and my mind was racing. Yes, it fitted . . . But why had he done it? Why would Lord Worthy want to poison Sir Gerald—his own nephew? It just didn't make sense.

At last Mr. Hatton returned and announced my Lord Worthy, who looked tired and strained.

"My lord," said the Queen formally, "I have it on good authority that one of your servants purchased darkwort recently. And that it was seen in your chamber."

Lord Worthy turned pale, his eyelids fluttering. For a moment he couldn't speak. Then he croaked, "Your Majesty?"

"Darkwort, my lord!" the Queen rapped out. "You deny it?"

"Of a certainty, I do, Your Majesty. It is out of all reason. How dare anyone put forth such foul lies . . . that I, Lord Worthy, should have dealings with such terrible poison . . . what villainous mischief . . ." By now Lord Worthy was gabbling.

"Your Majesty, may I ask Lord Worthy a question?" I put in hesitantly.

The Queen nodded.

Lord Worthy looked at me. "What? What are you doing here? This is no business for a Maid of Honour."

"She has made it her business, my lord," the Queen snapped, "and so have I!"

"My lord, I believe that you have a green stain that may be darkwort on your shirt-cuff. Would you please show us?" I asked nervously.

Lord Worthy's face became closed and haughty. He lifted both his hands. "By all means. See? There is no darkwort staining on my cuffs."

My heart sank. Lord Worthy must have changed into a clean shirt—the evidence was now lost in the wash.

Just then there was a timid knock on the door.

"What is it? We are busy!" the Queen bellowed.

Ellie sidled awkwardly into the room, curtsying and bobbing her head like a pigeon. "Ahem . . . ," she began. "I couldn't help overhearing, earlier . . . And I thought I should confess that, as I've been . . . otherwise occupied, as you might say . . . I'm runnin' a bit behind on me laundry duties. . . ." With that, Ellie brought out from behind her back a rather grimy-looking man's shirt.

My heart leaped. "Is that whose I think it is, Ellie?" I asked. "My Lord Worthy's?"

Ellie nodded, with a respectful curtsy.

"This is preposterous!" burst out Lord Worthy.

"Am I to be accused by a maid and a servant?" But by now his complexion was almost grey.

"My lord, please be quiet," said the Queen in a very frightening voice.

The mood was extremely heavy. It even silenced the songbirds. None of them so much as peeped.

Still bobbing, Ellie came closer and held out the sleeves of the shirt for all to see.

One shirt-cuff was stained with green.

"Well, my lord?" the Queen demanded.

"Hmph . . . ," said Lord Worthy. "Spinach from yesterday's dinner."

Mrs. Bea shook her head solemnly. "I'd stake my life on that not being spinach," she said. She went to the table and brought the wine jug, then dripped a little onto the cuff. The red of the wine spread over the green—becoming edged with yellow as it did so.

"Darkwort, Your Majesty," she said firmly.

"Am I to be accused by a witch now?" Lord Worthy blustered. "Where is your sworn justice, Your Majesty?"

"Darkwort," my Uncle Cavendish confirmed. "No doubt about it."

"Have a care, my Lord Worthy," warned the Queen, standing up. "You have served me faithfully and I had thought you my friend." Her voice was rising. "Either you stop lying to me now—immediately!—and tell me exactly and truthfully what has happened, or I will put you in the Tower, by God, and have you examined by Mr. Rackmaster Norton. *Do you understand, my lord?*" The last words were at a full-throated roar.

Everyone winced at the thought of Rackmaster Norton.

Lord Worthy stared at her and then something seemed to melt or crumble inside him. He got down stiffly onto his knees and bowed his head. Into the silence we heard his voice whisper, "Yes. It is dark-wort."

I couldn't breathe. Could he . . . ? Had he . . . ?

"Your own nephew, Lord Worthy?" said the Queen.

"No!" Lord Worthy exclaimed. "That was never the intention . . ." He sighed, then continued, his voice flat and dull. "The darkwort was intended for Lord Robert . . . and the blame for Sir Charles. . . .

"It was clear my Lady Grace favoured Lord Robert—and that she also made time for Sir Charles. But I could not possibly allow her to marry anyone except my nephew. So I put the darkwort into Lord

Robert's wine at the ball, and intended to put the remains of the powder amongst Sir Charles's belongings. All would have been well . . ." Lord Worthy put his face into his hands. "But then Gerald had to go and make a fool of himself at the ball, and you insisted he drink from Lord Robert's own cup. I was horrified, but how could I tell him to go against Your Majesty's orders?"

Lord Worthy laughed. A horrible, hollow, defeated sound. "Imagine my shock when the alarm was raised that poor Gerald had been *stabbed*, not poisoned—and moreover, that Lord Robert had done the deed!"

He turned his gaze on me, his eyes burning. "Of course, with a stabbing, rather than a poisoning, being recorded, I refrained from planting the remaining darkwort in Sir Charles's chamber. . . ."

Feeling very sad about the whole mess, I looked away.

"But Lord Worthy," said the Queen, "*why* was it so imperative that Lady Grace marry your nephew?"

"So that neither she, nor anyone else, would find out . . . ," Lord Worthy whispered brokenly.

"Find out what?" The Queen's tone of voice was steely and cold. I think she knew what was coming next, though I didn't.

"That Lady Grace has no estates, no fortune at all."

I felt as if somebody had stabbed me in the stomach. I couldn't even gasp. My guardian, Lord Worthy, was supposed to be my friend and my helper!

"Explain!" the Queen snapped.

"When I was appointed guardian to Lady Grace a year ago, I was in some debt," Lord Worthy began. "So I took the opportunity to mortgage Lady Grace's estate. But my financial situation grew worse rather than better. Within months, the moneylenders foreclosed and Lady Grace's estate was lost.

"It was unthinkable for either Lord Robert or Sir Charles to marry Lady Grace and discover this," Lord Worthy continued. "Only Gerald could be trusted not to disgrace me. . . ." He hung his head.

I felt sick and my stomach was whirling. Lord Worthy had stolen the inheritance my parents left me and then tried to get me to marry his nephew to cover it up? I could not believe it. Nor could Mary and Lady Sarah. They were staring at me, and Mary had tears of sympathy in her eyes. Suddenly their faces seemed to spin like a cartwheel in front of me. . . .

Mrs. Bea caught my arm. "Sit down, my dear."

I sat down with a bump on a cushion and she

pushed my head down. Some of the spinning in my stomach faded. Had I nearly fainted? How disgustingly like Lady Sarah! I gulped twice and sipped some of the wine Mrs. Bea brought me.

"Please, Your Majesty, I beg you, I had to do it, I couldn't let anyone find out, I—" Lord Worthy's voice had taken on a pathetic whining note.

"You *had* to try and poison my Lord Robert so you could hide your robbery from Lady Grace?" snapped the Queen. "You *had* to, my lord?"

"I . . ."

"You did not have to." The Queen shook her head. "You could have come to me when you first found yourself in financial difficulties, and I would have helped you. The money you needed could have come to you openly and honestly. There was no need of more murder in the Court."

"Please, Your Majesty . . ."

"Mr. Hatton, call the Gentlemen of the Guard. My Lord Worthy is to be committed to the Tower on charges of murder, corruption, falsehood, and endangering my life."

The Gentlemen of the Guard arrived and took Lord Worthy away, looking puzzled and frightened.

I was still sitting sideways on a cushion, waiting for my head to stop spinning.

Suddenly I started to cry, which was very embarrassing and I didn't want to, but I couldn't help it. It
had all been such a shock.

Ellie came running over and put her arms round
me. Mary Shelton was there, too, putting a clean
handkerchief into my hand so I could blow my nose.

I thought of another awful thing and my stomach
gave a swoop. "Your Grace, now I'm not rich any
more, do I have to leave you?" I asked, feeling as if
my heart would break again.

The Queen came to me in a rustle of damask and
pulled me to her, crushing my cheek against a jewel
on her bodice. "Of course not, Grace! You are my
dearest god-daughter and Maid of Honour. You
shall stay at Court as long as you like."

"Well then, at least you can marry your Lord
Robert now," said Mrs. Bea in a sprightly there-
there voice.

"I shall not," I sniffled. "He only wants my
money. Besides, I've decided he's an idiot."

The Queen smiled. "I do believe I agree with
you," she said.

That cheered me up so much that I kissed her on
the cheek. "So I do not have to marry?"

"No, Grace, not for now," the Queen replied.
"Though in due course, perhaps you will wish to. . . ."

In all the commotion, Masou had slipped into the room, too. "And if anyone does propose marriage to you now, it will surely be for love, not money," he said. "Mayhap it is a blessing that you are no longer rich, Lady Grace!"

"Precisely," said the Queen. "Well put, Masou."

She smiled at us all, and it's true what they say about the Queen, her smile *is* like magic. It makes you feel warm and safe.

She clasped my hand to hers. "Lady Grace, I owe you a great debt of gratitude for all your work these past few days," she said. "Here you are, only a Maid of Honour and not yet of age. Yet, with the help of your good friends here, you have saved Sir Charles's life, unearthed the wickedness of his brother, and discovered the poisoner of Sir Gerald. There are many men in my employ who have done far less and with less difficulty in their path. Be sure I shall make a good grant to you and find a more worthy guardian to take care of it."

I nodded. "I could help you if there were any more mysteries at Court, too," I whispered.

The Queen laughed. The she whispered back in my ear, "You shall be my first Lady Pursuivant. Let wrongdoers beware!"

I was thrilled! A pursuivant is someone who pursues wrongdoers for the Crown, though most pursuivants mainly pursue spies and assassins. It was all so exciting!

"But have a care, Grace," warned the Queen with a tiny frown. "I still expect my Maid of Honour to behave as befits her blood. I will have no more wild trips down the river at night . . . unless *absolutely* necessary. . . ."

"No, Your Majesty," I said meekly.

Then she smiled again, and clasped me, and sent me to my chamber while Mrs. Bea made me a hot posset to help me sleep (which I haven't drunk yet and it's gone cold). Mary Shelton brought it for me and gave me some of her delicious almond bisket bread. I never realized before how kind she is. And even Lady Sarah is being less trying than usual. I feel very strange about being poor all of a sudden, but I had to stop again. It was Sir Charles and Dr. Cavendish come to visit me.

Sir Charles was looking, and smelling, much better—he was clean and had shaved and his black eye had ointment on it. "Lady Grace," he said, "is it true what I hear of how Lord Worthy wasted your estates?"

I nodded a little dolefully. "But the Queen will help me and she said she would never send me away."

"My dear Lady Greensleeves," said Sir Charles, "were you aware that when there has been a murder, all the murderer's money and property goes to the nearest relative of the victim?"

I nodded. Yes, I'd heard that. But why did that concern me?

"Well," Sir Charles continued, "I am Sir Gerald's heir. His father was my mother's cousin. Which means that I shall inherit Lord Worthy's estates."

I stared. I was really too tired to follow this. "You?"

"Yes," Sir Charles confirmed. "And Lord Worthy's estates are, I am sure, worth more than yours ever were—despite his being a poor manager of his affairs. I, however, am not and I am already wealthy enough for my needs." He took a deep breath. "I shall see my lawyer tomorrow and when all the necessary paperwork has been done, I shall make all I get from Lord Worthy over to you, in recompense for what Lord Worthy misused."

"You will?" I gasped.

He nodded, looking very bright-eyed.

"But why?" I burst out.

Sir Charles smiled fondly at me. "My dear, I know you do not love me, yet for justice's sake you saved my very life. How can I do other than see you do not lose by it?"

So there it is. Sir Charles Amesbury will give me Lord Worthy's estates and even redeem what he can of my own lands. And he said he would petition the Queen to be my guardian and keep good care of them. So from being poor as a church mouse, I am rich again!

Maybe one day I *shall* marry—but it will be for love. My mother always said she loved my father and it was the best of marriages, though it was cut short.

For now? I remain Lady Grace Cavendish, Maid of Honour—and secret Lady Pursuivant! I know that my mother would be proud of that. And *I* cannot think of anything that could make me happier!

addled—confused, muddled, spoiled

agrimony—an herb

aiglet—the metal tip of a lace on a garment, which you thread through holes

Allah—the Muslim name for God

apothecary—an Elizabethan chemist

aqua vitae—brandy

Bedlam—the major asylum for the insane in London during Elizabethan times—the name came from the Hospital of St. Mary of Bethlehem

bezoar stone—a hard, stonelike object from a goat's stomach, used by Elizabethans (unsuccessfully) to cure poisoning

birch—to beat (birch twigs were often used)

blackwork—black embroidery on white linen

Board of Green Cloth—the main administrative body for the Court. It dealt with an inquest if anyone died within one mile of the Queen's person.

bodice—the top part of a woman's dress

borage—an herb

Boy King—King Edward VI, Elizabeth's brother, who died young

brocade—a rich, gold-embroidered fabric

bum—bottom

bumroll—a sausage-shaped piece of padding worn round the hips to make them look bigger

canions—showy fabric leggings, a little like shorts, worn by men

casket—a small decorative box

cinnabar—a red compound of mercury and sulfur, used as red coloring for lips, cheeks, painting, etc.

City Fathers—the rulers of the City of London

close-stool—a portable toilet comprising a seat with a hole in it on top of a box with a chamber pot inside

cloth of estate—a kind of awning that went over the Queen's chair to indicate that she was the monarch

cloth of silver/gold—cloth woven from silk thread that had been wrapped in fine gold or silver wire

commoner—anyone who did not hold the rank of gentleman or higher and therefore did not have a coat of arms *crayfish*—a shellfish a little like a lobster but smaller

damask—a beautiful, self-patterned silk cloth woven in Flanders. It originally came from Damascus—hence the name.

daybooke—a book in which you would record your sins each day so that you could pray about them. The idea of keeping a diary or journal grew out of this. Grace uses her daybooke as a journal.

djinni—an Arabic word for a mischievous spirit—also known as a djinn or genie

doublet—a close-fitting padded jacket worn by men

dugs—breasts

eringo—sea holly, a plant that grows by the sea. It was eaten pickled or candied and thought to have some medicinal properties as well as being a food.

false front—a pretty piece of material sewn to the front of a plain petticoat so that it would show under the kirtle

farthingale—a bell- or barrel-shaped petticoat held out with hoops of whalebone

Grace-and-Favour Chambers—rooms provided to important courtiers by the Queen

Guise—the House of Guise, which was the royal family of France

handfasted—formally engaged to be married

harlot—a prostitute

hose—tight-fitting cloth trousers worn by men

hoyden—a tomboy

Huguenots—French Christians who followed the Protestant, rather than the Roman Catholic, Church

kirtle—the skirt of an Elizabethan dress

kohl—black eye makeup

Lady Dowager mother—a widow who retains the title "Lady" even though her husband's title has passed to his son and heir

Lady Hoby—one of the Queen's favorite Ladies-in-Waiting

Lady-in-Waiting—one of the ladies who helped to look after the Queen and kept her company

laudanum—an opium tincture in alcohol used to aid sleep

Lord Chamberlain—the man in charge of security and entertainment at court

lye—an ingredient in soap. It is strongly alkaline and was used for cleaning.

lying at—sleeping at

lying-in chamber—a room where a woman would give birth

madrigals—beautiful part-songs, which were very fashionable

Maid of Honour—a younger girl who helped to look after the Queen like a Lady-in-Waiting

manchet rolls—whole wheat bread

marchpane subtlety—a sculpture made out of marzipan and then colored

marmelada—a very thick jammy sweet often made from quinces

marten—fur from a marten, a small carnivorous animal

Mary Shelton—one of Queen Elizabeth's Maids of Honor (a Maid of Honor of this name really did exist; see below). Most Maids of Honor were not officially "Ladies" (like Lady Grace), but they had to be born of gentry.

mead—an alcoholic drink made with honey

megrim—a migraine headache

Mr. Rackmaster Norton—the torturer

Papist—a rude word for a Catholic

Paris Garden—an Elizabethan leisure garden beside the Thames that featured all kinds of entertainments

partlet—a very fine embroidered false top that covered just the shoulders and the upper chest

pate—head

pattens—wooden clogs worn to keep fine shoes out of the mud *penner*—a small leather case that would attach to a belt. It was used for holding quills, ink, knife, and any other equipment needed for writing.

pennyroyal mint—an herb

plague—a virulent disease that killed thousands

poignard—an extremely sharp, long, thin blade sometimes used for dueling

posset—a hot drink made from sweetened and spiced milk curdled with ale or wine

potherbs—vegetables

Presence Chamber—the room where Queen Elizabeth would receive people

Privy Garden—Queen Elizabeth's private garden

Privy Parlour—Queen Elizabeth's private parlor

pulses—the beats of the heart

pursuivant—a follower or attendant who pursues someone else

Queen's Guard—more commonly known as the Gentlemen Pensioners—young noblemen who guarded the Queen from physical attacks

religious wars—conflicts arising from religious differences

sallet—salad

scurvy—an affliction brought on by lack of vitamin C in the diet

Secretary Cecil—William Cecil, an administrator for the Queen (later made Lord Burghley)

Shaitan—the Islamic word for Satan, though it means a trickster and a liar rather than the ultimate evil

shift—a polite name for a smock

sippet—a piece of bread, buttered and lightly grilled, from which meat was eaten. The sippet soaked up the meat juices.

smallpox—a nasty, often fatal disease, whose pustules healed and left scars

smock—a neck-to-ankles linen shirt worn by women

staging stable—a stable where horses were kept temporarily when on the way to somewhere else

stays—the boned, laced bodice worn around the body under the clothes. Victorians called the stays a corset.

stews—public baths

Stone Gallery—a passageway at the Palace of Whitehall that led to the Queen's chambers

strumpet—a prostitute

sucket—a sweet

sugar plate—sugar candy that could be molded like modeling clay, then dried and colored

sweetmeats—sweets

tansy—an herb

tides of the blood—the Elizabethans believed that the blood flowed in tides in the body, like the sea.

Tilting Yard—an area where knights in armor would joust or tilt (i.e., ride at each other on horseback with lances)

tincture—a solution of a substance in alcohol

tinder box—a small box containing some quick-burning tinder, a piece of flint, a piece of steel, and a candle for making fire and thus light

tiring woman—a woman who helped a lady to dress

toothcloth—a coarse cloth, often beautifully embroidered, used for rubbing teeth clean

truckle bed—a small bed on wheels stored under the main bed

tumbler—an acrobat

Verge of the Court—anywhere within a mile of the Queen's person

virginals—an instrument, similar to a harpsichord, played by Queen Elizabeth

vomitus—vomit (noun)

watch candle—a night-light

watersteps—steps leading down to the river Thames

wherry—a Thames boat

white lead—lead carbonate, used for white paint and makeup

Withdrawing Chamber—the Queen's private rooms

Betrayal

To the real Jim Woolley—he knows who he is

Eventide

Now I am beginning my daybooke the second
the other is quite filled up. Today was very dull, sitting about winding wool for the Mistress of the
Maids, Mrs. Champernowne. At least there is something happening tomorrow—we accompany the
Queen to the docks at Tilbury. Very exciting! That
is why I am scribbling away and getting ink on my
smock, for I cannot sleep at all. Lady Sarah can't
sleep, either. She is writing a letter to her parents
bemoaning how poorly she is clad and how all her
raiment is utterly out of fashion.

At least the Queen sent me to walk the dogs this
afternoon. She has often given me that task since my
mother, the Queen's best friend, died a year ago,
God rest her soul, leaving me in Her Majesty's

1

care. I think she knows how much I enjoy playing with the dogs and spending time in the gardens, which I do, for that is where I find I am most reminded of my dear mother.

I changed into my horrible old hunting kirtle and then ran on tiptoes downstairs and along the painted passage to the door to the Privy Garden, where Mary Shelton was waiting with the dogs.

Now, I may like Mary Shelton better than I did—she has been very kind to me since my mother's passing. But I didn't want her getting nosy about what I do in the gardens—for I have a secret—so I invited her out with me. We raced up and down, with the dogs yapping away, and fairly soon she was red as an apple and puffing for breath.

"Oh Lord," she said, "I must go in and sit down."

"Are you sure?" I asked, putting my hand on her arm. "We could kick the ball for them again—"

"No, I need a rest," she insisted, fanning herself with her hand.

"Well, I'll run the dogs down to the Orchard," I told her. "I'll see you later."

Mary went inside, mopping her face. I can be quite cunning when necessary—not for nothing has the Queen appointed me her own Lady Pursuivant (for the pursuit and apprehension of all miscreants who trouble the Queen's peace at Court)!

I did run the dogs—throwing a stick for Henri, who is the chief of them despite being the smallest—and they all yelped madly. Then, when I was sure Mary couldn't see me, I slipped through the little gate into the Herb Garden. We have just moved to the Palace of Placentia at Greenwich, which is one of the Queen's most favourite residences. The palace gardens give right onto the river, and you can see the ducks and the swans and sometimes the pages and young henchmen fishing for salmon.

My friends Masou the tumbler and Ellie the laundrymaid have made a hidden place to sit inside the big yew hedge that surrounds the Herb Garden. And that's where I found Masou, who was sitting looking worried, but there was no sign of Ellie at all.

"She said she might be late," Masou explained. "The Deputy Laundress has her running about like a hunted rabbit."

Mrs. Twiste at the Whitehall laundry is a kind lady, but Mrs. Fadget, her deputy at Greenwich, is a nasty hag who loves to order poor Ellie about when we are at Placentia.

I settled down and watched Masou, who was idly

tossing red and green leather balls up and about his head. A bit of wood from the ground joined them, then a stone. It's amazing what Masou can do—turning somersaults in midair, juggling, and balancing. He's getting very big-headed because Mr. Somers—who's in charge of the tumblers—says he's so good. So I don't ever tell him, but I still like to watch.

We heard her cough first, then poor Ellie came dragging herself into the little hide and collapsed onto the ground next to me. She was coughing violently and her cheeks were flushed. I put my hand to her head as my mother used to do and it was all hot and dry.

"Ellie, you have a fever," I said.

"It's just that cold I had last week gone to my neck," she replied. Her throat sounded as if she had been eating sandpaper. "And that Mrs. Fadget"— she turned her head and spat—"I hate her. She had me up till past midnight wringing out sheets, and then up again at dawn to grate the soap. Then I was putting shirts on the hedge and I missed dinner. . . ."

I felt terrible. I usually bring Ellie something to eat and I'd forgotten. She saw me patting my pockets.

"It's all right," she said. "I ain't hungry a bit."

Masou and I looked at each other, feeling very worried now. Ellie! Not hungry? This was bad.

"You should be in bed, Ellie!" I told her. "You should be drinking horrible willow-bark tinctures and sniffing the smoke of henbane of Peru."

Ellie laughed. "Tell Mrs. Fadget," she said. "What's 'appening tomorrow? The Queen's watermen were moaning down at the buttery about how early they've got to get up."

"The Queen's going to Tilbury," I explained. "And we're going with her to see the Royal Dockyards."

"Oh. And will you put it in your daybooke?" Ellie asked curiously.

"Of course," I replied.

"Wish I could do that. Write, I mean," Ellie went on wistfully.

"Well, you can read," I pointed out.

"Only my name. But all the things I see—and the stories I hear in the laundry," she croaked. "I wish I could write them down."

"You could tell me and I could write them in my tongue," suggested Masou helpfully.

"No good to me, I can't read that, neither," Ellie

said, and sighed. "I wish I could read them ballad sheets. Or I could save up all my pennies and maybe, one day, even buy a book and read it!"

My chest felt all tight and heavy. Ellie's voice sounded so sad, as if actually *buying* a book was a mountain she could never hope to climb—and the Queen *gives* them to me! I put my arm round Ellie. "I wish I could have you as my tiring woman instead of sharing Olwen or Fran with the other girls, but the Queen keeps forgetting."

"What I really want is a good sleep," muttered Ellie, and coughed and wrapped her thin arms around herself. Masou took his jerkin off and bundled it up for a pillow to her head. She lay down with a sigh and Masou very softly sang her one of his funny wailing little songs.

Poor Ellie, it is so unfair—she has to keep working even when she's ill, while I have the Queen's own physician to tend me if I so much as sniffle! And I hardly ever get ill anyway. Mind, I don't have to forage around for food, or work till midnight on cold, wet sheets—I'm sure that has something to do with it.

I left them there and came back to the Privy Garden, where I found Mary Shelton wandering about looking all upset.

"Where did you go?" she demanded. "I was looking for you in the Orchard but you weren't there."

"Yes I was," I said quickly. "I was up a tree."

"Oh," she replied, and stopped looking so nosy— Mary doesn't like climbing trees. "Well, the Queen wants you."

When I reached the Queen, I found that she wanted me to help brush her hair this evening— which I like doing despite having to be so careful of the tangles in her curls. She snaps and swears if you pull even slightly and her hair is naturally quite frizzy, so it knots. She is talking about having the whole lot cut off and wearing a wig instead!

I'd better get to bed now. Writing this has made me sleepy—and we've got an early start tomorrow.

Dark before dawn . . .

Now I have but a few moments to write a little—
there! A first blot, too. I can't help it, the sun is not
yet up and my candle is small.

We have all arisen early to accompany Her
Majesty on her visit to Tilbury—where King
Henry's old naval yards are. Her Majesty has been
entreated to visit the yards by Mr. John Hawkins, a
most notable seafarer and merchant to the New
World, whose passion for all things naval seems to
know no bounds! He is making suit for the office of
Secretary to the Admiralty as he has great plans for
the Navy. The Queen finds him charming and has
agreed to hear him. And he has assured her that we
shall have no need to be afeared of bawdy sailors
during our visit. Fie!

I am not sure where Tilbury is, but we are travelling there by boat, which is exciting, except I will be wearing my third-best gown—the russet woollen one with the velvet trimmings—and pray it is not splashed too much.

Lady Sarah's tiring woman, Olwen, has almost finished squeezing Lady Sarah into her white Court damask. We have been told to wear our third-best clothes, but Lady Sarah is insisting on her best kirtle.

Mary Shelton has just whispered to me, "Somebody hopes for a handsome sailor."

Lady Sarah heard us giggling and has just told us to shut up. She is still moaning about having to rise so early. Hell's teeth! She is applying more of that foul-smelling ointment to the spot on her chin— Clown's All-Heal and woodlice mashed together, I think. I wish I had a stopper for my nose.

Time to end—Olwen is coming over to help me with my stays.

Later this Day—eventide

What a day this has been! *So* exciting and unusual. I shall carry on where I left off:

Once Olwen had laced me into my stays, I pulled on my outdoor boots and struggled to get my kirtle straight over my bumroll—I didn't bother with a farthingale because I thought I might have a chance to explore a ship or something, and anyway, the kirtle's a bit short for me and it shows less if I don't wear a farthingale. Olwen then tackled my hair, which, as she is first to say, is hardly my best feature, being rather fine and mousy. She decided to hide as much of it as she could under a sweet green velvet hat with a feather.

I then rushed into the passageway, where Mrs. Champernowne was standing tapping her foot and sighing, as we were all late.

Lady Sarah emerged resplendent in her gown, and Mrs. Champernowne tutted.

"Did you not hear my message, Lady Sarah?" she asked. "We will be taking the Queen's galley down to Tilbury and the damask is sure to be splashed by the water, look you, and be all spoiled and spotted and spattered."

Lady Sarah only tossed her head and said, "I am in need of new apparel. This English-cut bodice is last year's fashion, so of no great moment."

It's all French cut and doublet-style this year—but

I don't call a year particularly old for a whole kirtle and bodice. And I know for a fact that Lady Sarah has five kirtles and any number of stomachers and sleeves and false fronts and petticoats. In fact, most of the mess in our bedchamber consists of Lady Sarah's clothes. Who needs five kirtles? I know the Queen has hundreds but she's the Queen. The Wardrobe is a Department of State, after all!

We'd already eaten breakfast in our chambers, so Mrs. Champernowne led us down the stairs and along the Painted Passage, all holding candles and yawning fit to burst.

The Queen was just leaving her Withdrawing Chamber, with the Chamberers still pinning her bodice. She had chosen brocade-trimmed black wool, so everyone who was wearing silk or velvet looked worried, and serve them right: silk or velvet shows water splashes even more than good wool, and any fool should know better than to out-dress the Queen.

We passed through the palace and into the garden. Torches were burning all the way down the watersteps to where the Queen's galley was waiting. The harbingers and trumpeters were already in rowing boats and wherries, while the Gentlemen of the

Guard, in their red velvet, were climbing into gigs. It was funny to watch them cursing each other: they were having trouble fitting their long halberds into the narrow boats that were to carry them.

The Queen's galley is very handsome—all silver-gilt and red paint—and rowed by the Queen's Boatmen, ten of them, who wear red and black livery and a badge. Some of the other Maids of Honour were nudging each other and pointing out the good-looking ones.

We all had to climb in before the Queen. It wasn't easy getting into a boat that wobbled underneath me, especially when I couldn't see my feet for my petticoats and I couldn't really bend in the middle because of my stays. The Chief Boatman steadied each of us with his arm, and at last we were all sitting down, two by two, along the middle of the boat.

As usual, the Queen had asked one of her favourite gentlemen, Mr. Christopher Hatton, to accompany her. He helped Her Majesty to board, and once the Queen was settled on the cushions under her canopy, the oarsmen pushed off and started to row.

The sun was just coming up and turning the river silver-grey and gold. Every bit of the Thames was full of boats, and wherries with red lateen sails, and gigs, and Thames ferryboats—and little private craft, all overloaded with people. The courtiers still on the watersteps were politely fighting over the few remaining craft, and the boatmen were asking shocking amounts to take them.

I loved it. There was quite a strong wind so I had to hold onto my hat, but it was so exciting to be skimming the water and rocking a bit as the oarsmen bent to the stroke. I always love going by boat. I wanted to trail my fingers in the water, feel how cold it was, but I couldn't reach past the gilded carving on the side, and Mrs. Champernowne was glaring at me something horrid. A swan flapped its wings and honked at her, probably because it didn't like the look on her face, either.

Lady Jane Coningsby and Lady Sarah ignored each other pointedly for the whole journey. Lady Jane has only lately come to Court. Another Maid of Honour, Katharine Broke, went home in disgrace after a scandal with the Duke of Norfolk's nephew, and so Lady Jane arrived to make the number of Maids of Honour up to six again. It's as good as a play to watch her with Lady Sarah because the two of them hate each other so. Lady Sarah has beautiful red hair—like the Queen's, but less inclined to frizz—whereas Lady Jane has wonderful blond curls "foaming down her back," as one of the dafter Court gentlemen wrote in a poem. Lady Sarah has more womanly curves than Lady Jane, but Lady Jane is taller and more elegant. The worst of it is that they always like exactly the same gentlemen!

When we reached Tilbury there was a strong smell of paint. Most of the houses had been newly whitewashed in honour of the Queen's visit—rather badly, as they all had splatters on their shutters. A crowd had gathered at the side of the muddy road, and litters were ready and waiting next to the Gentlemen of the Guard, who were all lined up.

As we climbed laboriously out of the galley and up the steps, Lady Sarah nearly tripped on a bit of rope.

"Do try and watch where you're going, Lady Sarah," sniffed Lady Jane.

Oh, how pink Lady Sarah's cheeks went! And her "rosebud lips" tightened into a thin line.

Then, as Lady Jane was herself being helped ashore, a wave from a nearby boat, overloaded with courtiers, made the galley dip suddenly. She would have fallen in the water if the Queen's Oarsman had not caught her!

"Dear, dear," said Lady Sarah loudly from the

quay. "*Somebody* had a bit too much beer at breakfast."

"I bet you sixpence that Jane slaps Sarah first," whispered Mary Shelton at my elbow, her eyes shining.

I thought about this. Lady Sarah has fiery red hair and a temper to match. "Done!" I declared. "Sixpence on it." We shook hands.

The Queen often rides side-saddle in processions, but today she had ordered a litter with a canopy over it to shade her from the sun or keep the rain off her (far more likely!). I was praying we wouldn't have to ride and, thank goodness, there were litters for us as well. We climbed in, arguing over who should sit in front. But while the rest of us were quarrelling, Lady Sarah had pushed her way to the front of one litter, and Lady Jane established herself at the front of the other, looking very elegant and aloof. Grumbling, the rest of us crammed in behind, then the littermen hoisted us up, and off we went.

As is usual when the Queen goes anywhere, it was quite a procession. The harbingers and trumpeters led the way with the Royal Standard, blasting away on their trumpets, banging drums and shouting, "The Queen! The Queen! Make way for the

Queen's Majesty!" It wasn't really necessary, because the people looked as if they had been camping out all night to see the Queen, but it did serve to wake a couple who were still asleep, wrapped in blankets, as we went past.

After the trumpeters marched half the Gentlemen of the Guard in their red velvet, carrying their halberds and looking miserable because their smart red hose was getting badly splashed with mud. Then came the Queen in her litter, then more Gentlemen of the Guard, then us, then the courtiers, and, at the very back, boys and dogs running along, shouting and barking.

Everybody was waving and cheering, and the Queen was smiling and waving back and blowing kisses. It's wonderful to watch her whenever she processes anywhere. She lights up and seems somehow bigger and more Queenly—and she never minds how muddy the road is or how smelly the people might be (though she might complain about it afterwards).

A little girl ran out with a posy of flowers for her. But as Mr. Hatton reached out to take it from her, the Queen stopped him and gave an order for the procession to stop. Mr. Hatton then dismounted and lifted the little girl up for the Queen herself to take flowers from her sticky, outstretched paw. The Queen then gave the little girl a kiss. All the people roared at that. The Queen pinned the posy to her bodice with a flourish.

I watched Mr. Hatton put the little girl back down on the ground. She curtsied and then, with a shining face, rushed back to tell her mamma and grand-mamma all about it.

Her Majesty then smiled and waved and bowed as the procession moved on.

Mrs. Champernowne sighed. She was uncomfortably squashed in next to me at the back of the litter. "Tut. We'll be needing to burn a stick of incense inside that bodice to have all the fleas and lice and nits out of it now," she moaned.

We eventually arrived at the dockyards, where they build merchantmen to sail to Spain and New Spain and the Netherlands, and France and Muscovy. All the workmen were lined up in front of the ships, wearing their Sunday best to meet the Queen.

Mr. Hatton helped the Queen down from her litter. Mr. John Hawkins was there to greet her. I recognized him from the time he had come to Court to ask the Queen, personally, to visit her Royal Dockyards.

"Oh!" Lady Sarah gasped in front.

Mary Shelton and I craned our necks to see if anybody was slapping anybody.

Typical Lady Sarah: she was simpering and batting her eyelashes because there were two handsome young men standing behind Mr. Hawkins. One was tall with fair hair and a slightly receding chin. The other was shorter and broader, with a cheerful round face and disarmingly bright blue eyes. They looked to be good friends for I caught the shorter one exchanging appreciative looks with the taller one, who winked back.

"Your Majesty," said Mr. Hawkins, "may I present Captain Hugh Derby?" The tall man bowed low. "And Captain Francis Drake." It was the stockier one's turn.

The Queen let them kiss her hand and then stepped onto the planks they had put down to preserve her from the mud. She walked along the line of workmen as they all doffed their blue statute caps and bowed. Mr. Hawkins moved along beside the Queen, introducing and explaining.

Mrs. Champernowne beckoned Mary and me forward to help with the Queen's train, which was wider than the walkway she was standing on.

"Hold it high, the mud is terrible!" growled the Queen. Then she glanced at Lady Sarah and Lady Jane. "Whatever are those two ninnies at now?" she snapped, frowning at them.

I looked at the two ninnies. Lady Jane had a very haughty expression on her face, in spite of the fact that she had her foot in a muddy puddle. It was a pity she was wearing such a pretty pair of high-heeled shoes with pompoms on the front, because one heel now appeared to be stuck. And Lady Sarah had somehow caught her petticoat on a bit of wood. Captain Drake and Captain Derby were practically bumping heads as they tried to unsnag it, both of them quite ignoring Lady Jane.

We walked on through a very battered and splintered gate. It had the Royal Coat of Arms carved above it, but the paint and gilt was all cracked and peeling. We were entering a dockyard. There were no ships, just empty pits where they would have been built and which would then have been filled with Thames water to launch them. Some old bits of wood lay scattered about, and a coil of rope was being used as a nest by seagulls.

The Queen stopped dead and looked around, her hands on her hips. "Good God! What a desolation. Why has this happened?"

"No money, Your Majesty," burred Mr. Hawkins. "No money and no interest. And what's more, all the ships your Royal Father built are near ready to sink from shipworm."

The Queen was frowning. "I had no idea. And I pay thousands of pounds every year to the Royal Dockyards for the fitting out of my warships."

Mr. Hawkins didn't say anything to this, only stared into space.

The Queen's frown became positively menacing. I would hate to be whoever is Secretary of the Navy at the moment.

Mary Shelton nudged me. I looked to where she was pointing and saw that Lady Jane now had her muddy foot firmly on the back of Lady Sarah's damask kirtle, where it would leave a nice clear imprint. Her face was pure innocence, of course.

"I'm going to win when Sarah sees that," I whispered to Mary. "Hope you've got sixpence to pay me."

"Lady Jane will snap first," Mary insisted. "Look at her face."

It was true that Lady Jane was looking very sour,

but I know how fussy Sarah is over her gowns. "We shall see," I replied.

We moved on, with Mr. Hawkins still talking and talking. Mary and I had to hurry forward because the Queen was walking briskly and we had to make sure her train didn't fall in the mud. As we passed Lady Sarah I saw her staring at the muddy footprint on her white damask.

Next thing, Lady Sarah "accidentally" gave Lady Jane a shove with her bumroll, and Lady Jane stepped off the walkway, getting her other pretty high-heeled shoe stuck in the mud.

By now Mr. Hawkins had the crook of his arm held out for Her Majesty to lean on. Mr. Hatton followed behind, looking as if his nose was thoroughly put out of joint.

"Well, you see, Your Majesty," Hawkins was saying enthusiastically, "what we need is a new kind of ship altogether—a lower ship, with no castles and smooth hulls, built for speed—"

"Mr. Hawkins," the Queen interrupted, putting out her white kid-gloved hand to stop him.

Hawkins, Drake, and Derby blinked at her.

She smiled. "Gentlemen, I speak excellent French, Italian, and Latin, not to mention English, but alas, I have absolutely no Sailorish." Then she pointed at a docked galleon. "Those are the castles?" she asked, pointing at the raised ends of the ship.

"Aye," Mr. Hawkins confirmed. "They're used for boarding, Ma'am," he explained. "Being higher than an enemy ship makes it easier to board from them. One can just drop down onto the deck of another ship."

"Ah. I see," the Queen acknowledged. "Then should not our ships have higher castles than the enemy's—else what happens if the enemy boards from his high castles?"

Hawkins grinned and winked down at her. "He'm got to catch us first, Ma'am, which he won't if we have the fastest ships."

"But how do you know your new lower ships will be faster?" the Queen inquired.

"I know it because God made fish for to swim fast and I learned the shape from Him," declared Mr. Hawkins simply.

"The argument is sound," agreed the Queen, nodding. "But can you prove it?"

"Aye, Your Majesty," Hawkins said. "Captain Drake has an amusement for you and your Court if you'll come this way." His expression reminded me of my friend Masou when he is about to pull off a spectacular trick.

We all processed along a walkway covered with canvas to a pool like a big rectangular fishpond. There were two winches with handles at one end and two rollers at the other. Floating on the water, held by ropes that went round the rollers and back to the winches, were two beautifully made model ships.

A chair stood on a dais under an awning for the Queen to take her ease upon, which she did, while Mary and I arranged her train.

Captain Drake stepped forward and his sharp blue eyes sparkled as he talked about the models. "This one here is the exact shape of a Spanish galleon, Your Majesty. Do you see how high her castles are and how round her hull? We based her on a ship I took two summers ago." He moved to the other model ship, which looked much less magnificent. "Now, this one here is a kind of ship that does not even exist yet, although my own ship, the *Judith,* has a hull not so very unlike it. This is what you might call a race-built galleon and the trick's in her hull, which is long and narrow and smooth like a dolphin."

The Queen nodded. "And the winches?" she asked.

"Ah, that's for the wager." He waved forward two sturdy young men. "Now, here are Jem and Michael that are 'prenticed shipwrights and built strong, as you can see. Do you think they could turn the winch quickly?"

Everybody nodded, fascinated to know what he would say next. "Well, I say that the English race-built galleon can beat the Spanish galleon, even if two of the Queen's own gentlewomen are turning the winch for it! In fact I'll wager ten shillings on it. Who'll take my bet?"

Well, the Court gentlemen thought this hysterically funny and, to be truthful, so did we, because the two young shipwrights looked as if they knew a thing or two about turning a winch. Mr. Hatton stepped forward at once to take Captain Drake's bet and so did some of the other gentlemen. But I noticed that Captain Derby simply grinned at his friend and made no move to gamble. The Queen watched and smiled.

"Now, ladies, who shall turn the English galleon's winch?" asked Captain Drake of all of us.

Nobody said anything at first because we were all still giggling and murmuring amongst ourselves. But then I decided to step forward, because it certainly looked an interesting activity. To my astonishment, Lady Sarah stepped forward, too, dropped a curtsy, and said, "I'll do it, too."

The Queen blinked in surprise and then gestured us over. Lady Jane smirked at the girl next to her—and then looked sour when she saw the rapt expression on Drake's face, as he stared at Lady Sarah. I thought Captain Derby looked fairly stupid as well. And the two shipwrights seemed as stunned as rabbits facing a fox at the sight of a damask-clad, red-curled lady of the Court advancing on them, pulling on her gloves.

I hurried after her, only I'd forgotten my gloves so I had to manage without.

"Ready, steady, go!" cried Captain Derby.

The shipwrights started turning their winch, which gradually wound in the rope attached to the Spanish galleon model and pulled their ship through the water.

Sarah and I had a bit of trouble because Sarah was trying to turn the winch one way and I was turning the other, but once we sorted that out, and the English race-built galleon started being pulled through the water, too, it was easy. We even caught up with the Spanish galleon because our ship moved more easily through the water—then fell back a bit because we were still arguing. But then, with everyone spurring us on, we stopped talking, turned the winch together, and our ship got to the other side of the pond first!

Everyone cheered and clapped, and Lady Sarah curtsied prettily, standing in front of me so that Captain Drake would get the full benefit of her breathlessness as he settled up with Mr. Hatton.

"Very impressive indeed, Captain Drake," said the Queen, still laughing and dabbing her eyes with a handkerchief. "And I lost a shilling to Mr. Hawkins, backing your strong young shipwrights—I should have had more faith."

We then continued to another quay, where a very narrow two-masted ship was moored. We went up the gangplank, handed along by pigtailed sailors, and there on the deck was a table laid with a magnificent feast! A big, sullen-looking boy was sitting in the ropes above, waving a rattle to keep the seagulls away.

I could feel the ship rocking gently on the water. I thought it was quite a pleasant, soothing motion but some of the other girls looked a little queasy. The Queen didn't mind, though. She sat in a chair with the Cloth of Estate over it and the rest of us sat wherever we liked. Lady Sarah laughed as prettily as a silver bell when Captain Drake brought her a plate of little pies and carven potherbs. I looked away—it was quite sick-making.

That was when I noticed a mouse pottering gently along the deck beside the rail, its little nose quivering at the smell of all the food laid on the table. Nobody likes rats, but I don't mind mice—although I'm probably the only Maid of Honour *ever* who isn't terrified of them. I elbowed Mary to look because I didn't want her to miss the fun.

Sure enough, as Lady Sarah caught sight of the mouse she let out a terrible shriek, jumped up, and stood teetering on her bench, squealing like a stuck pig.

Lady Jane sneered; then, when she saw what Sarah was staring at, she screamed as well. Everybody else shrieked for all they were worth, except me and Mary—who doesn't like mice but has some sense. And the Queen and the men, of course.

Captain Drake spun on his heel, his hand flying to his sword. Then he took in Lady Sarah perched on the bench, pulling her skirts around her, and the mouse looking curiously up at her, whiskers twitching. In one movement he swept off his velvet cap and threw it over the mouse.

"What in God's name . . . !" bellowed the Queen.

"Only a little waif, Your Majesty," said Drake. He went over and picked up his hat with its little captive and showed the mouse to the Queen. Then he turned to Lady Sarah and said in his soft Devon burr, "Will I kill it for you, my lady, or let it go?"

Lady Sarah's cheeks were very pink. "Thank you for rescuing me, Captain," she gasped. "But please don't kill it."

Drake bowed, went to the side of the ship nearest the dock, and emptied out the mouse and its droppings onto dry land.

The Queen smiled and clapped, so we all did, too. "Well thrown, Captain!" she declared. "What excellent aim. Do you play at bowls?"

"I like a game now and then, Your Majesty," Drake replied, smiling.

"Then you must teach *me* to throw straight," said the Queen. "Alas, it is an art I have never yet mastered."

"Which is just as well when she's throwing a slipper at us!" I muttered to Mary, who snickered.

"If it can be done, Your Majesty, I will do it," said Drake tactfully, and he bowed to the Queen and again to Lady Sarah, who had sat down gracefully on her bench once more.

Neither Captain Drake nor Captain Derby seemed to mind Sarah's being such a ninny. Drake fetched her more food while Derby fetched her more wine. Drake called on the minstrels at the back of the ship to play a tune she liked, while Derby showed her a brilliantly coloured bird with a big beak that came from New Spain, and liked to sit on his shoulder and eat nuts. He called it a popinjay. Then Drake started pointing to bits of the ship, like the ropes and the mast, telling her the proper names.

Lady Jane was watching all this and scowling. Suddenly she gulped and ran to the side of the ship, looking quite green. Then she leaned over and was sick.

"Oh dear," moaned Mary, stumbling to the side herself and doing the same.

"They say an eel's tail eaten raw and no beer for a week will settle an ailing stomach, dear Lady Jane," Sarah said happily. Then she turned to Captain Drake. "I love ships," she said, simpering. "My uncle took me on one of his merchant venturers when I was small and I even climbed up those rope ladders there to the little platform thing. My father was quite shocked when he found out."

"Ah, you climbed the ratlines to the fighting top," murmured Drake, seeming fascinated by Sarah's revelation. "How clever of you!"

Sarah looked delighted. "The Ship's Master

offered to take me as a cabin boy, when I was older—until my uncle explained who I was," she confided. "I was quite a tomboy back then."

I nudged Mary at this because I couldn't imagine it at all. And seeing Captain Drake's eyes stray back down to Sarah's chest, I could see he was having trouble imagining it, too. But poor Mary didn't smile. She was holding her stomach and looking unhappy. In fact, I think me and Lady Sarah and the sailors were the only ones who really enjoyed that meal.

Afterwards, it was time for us to go back ashore, which felt very strange for a minute. Now that the tide was high enough, they had brought the galley round to collect the Queen from the dockside, so we went straight over from the quay to the main watersteps.

The crowd was waiting to wave us goodbye as we climbed into the galley. Her Majesty was already under her awning, waving and smiling again when it happened: as Lady Sarah picked up her skirts, ready to climb aboard, a rope that had been lying on the ground suddenly tightened against her leg. She swayed, wobbled, waved her arms like a Dutch windmill—and fell over the side of the watersteps, right into the Thames!

There was pandemonium. Everyone ran about. Sarah threshed her arms in the water and screamed like a banshee. I observed that Lady Jane was staring innocently into space—right next to the other end of the rope. But nobody else had noticed because they were all either squalling or shouting advice.

Next moment, there was the sound of running feet. Captain Drake pounded by, stripping off his doublet and sword belt as he went, then he jumped into the muddy water in his shirt and hose.

Sarah's skirts were dragging her down and she was screaming and spluttering dreadfully. She grabbed Captain Drake when he reached her and they both went under. When they surfaced, Sarah seemed a bit dazed. Drake had her caught from behind, with his arm around her neck. He pulled her steadily over to the dock wall. Hawkins was there, passing down a rope on a pulley. Drake quickly tied it in a complicated way around Lady Sarah's waist and shoulders and then shouted to the shipwrights on the quay to haul on the rope. Up came Sarah out of the water, covered in weed and looking like a drowned rat. Captain Drake shouted something else, caught another rope, and used it to walk up the wall in a rather dashing way, so that he was on shore, ready to catch the half-fainting Lady Sarah in his arms, as the men winched her down again.

Mrs. Champernowne was there, too, with a shawl and a pair of snips to cut Lady Sarah's stay laces so she could breathe properly.

I gave Lady Jane another hard stare, but by then she was nowhere near the rope that had tripped Sarah, so I couldn't say anything. Lady Sarah was in a terrible state, and though she does exaggerate, I think being half-drowned is enough to upset anyone! Her damask gown and her stays were ruined of course, and, while she had taken no real hurt from the muddy water, she was very cold and wet.

Captain Drake carried Sarah aboard the Queen's galley, where he laid her on some cushions. Mrs. Champernowne chafed Sarah's hands and thanked him very graciously. The Queen, who had witnessed the drama, summoned the Captain. As he kneeled before her, she said, "Thank you for saving the life of our Maid of Honour, Captain Drake. Devon must breed very quick-thinking men."

"Aye, Your Majesty," Captain Drake responded. "If we are not quick of thought, the sea takes us. And it was an honour to assist one of your ladies."

The Queen smiled, pleased with the answer, and held out her hand so he could kiss it.

"Please, Ma'am," ventured Drake, "may I have the greater honour of attending Your Majesty even unto Greenwich?"

The Queen nodded her assent. "To be sure, Captain, you are all most welcome to return to Court with us," she said, "for I have more to discuss with Mr. Hawkins."

We could not leave at once because there was still more fuss to be made over Lady Sarah. A boy from the ship was called and sent running to fetch aqua vitae and a blanket from the Captain's own bed. By the time Sarah was settled, Captain Drake had returned in dry clothes, with only his hair still wet. He looked very dashing, and after his impressive rescue of Lady Sarah, several of the other girls were looking at her quite enviously.

We finally set off. As the oarsmen rowed upstream, Hawkins carried on telling the Queen his plans for the Navy. Captain Derby sat astern, staring thoughtfully at his friend, while Captain Drake sat next to Lady Sarah, agreeing with Mrs. Champernowne that a hot toddy of aqua vitae, honey, citron, and water—with a good sprinkling of nutmeg and cinnamon—would be the best medicine for her.

Mary and I had a bit of an argument about our

bet, but as Lady Jane hadn't actually *slapped* Sarah, nobody had won.

When we arrived at the Greenwich Palace water-steps, Captain Drake swept Sarah up in his arms and carried her all the way to the Queen's own bathroom, where she could have a hot bath. My uncle, Dr. Cavendish, was also called to open the vein in Sarah's left arm in order to guard against infection.

She seems much happier now, and Captain Drake will be staying at Court tonight to see how she is in the morning.

What an exciting day! Everybody is gossiping about Captain Drake and Lady Sarah. I can't wait to see what happens tomorrow.

Morning, at Greenwich

I truly think Captain Drake is in love with Lady
Sarah! He is certainly paying court to her. This very
morning he sent her a posy of flowers tied up by a
pearl bracelet—and a note with it that made her
pink. As I write, Sarah is holding up her hand to
admire the jewel and singing the praises of the
Captain. She really seems quite smitten!

But Hell's teeth! I can scarcely think of a worse
match for her. Everyone knows he is no rich lord,
but a Devon pirate who has made some money on a
voyage lately, and is spending it on his ship faster
than a Spaniard home from the New World. Her
parents will surely beat her if they find out she is dal-
lying with anyone but a rich courtier. Lady Sarah
may think she is safe enough with them a hundred
miles away in the north at Bartelmy Hall, but

someone will surely be nosy enough to write and tell them. And no parents in the world would countenance a fifteen-year-old heiress's flirting with a sea captain! They are seeking a good match for her now.

Mrs. Champernowne has just come in and, seeing Lady Sarah so lively, she said, "Well now, I think you are as fit as a fiddle, so out of bed with you, and back to your duties." And for a wonder, Sarah has not moaned at how hard-hearted she is.

Fie! Mrs. Champernowne has just told me to stop my scribbling as well. I am to change into my second-best kirtle—the white damask. I expect we are wanted to sit in the Presence Chamber and wind wool for Mrs. Champernowne while Her Majesty talks to tedious Scottish ambassadors and the like.

Later This Day

Well, this morning has been far more interesting than I thought it would be. (It's a good thing I carry my daybooke in my embroidery workbag, along with a penner full of pens and ink. Mrs. Champernowne thinks it would be more improving for me to sew in odd moments than scribble, but the Queen allows it.)

It took an age to ready myself for the Queen's Presence Chamber, as my hair simply refused to cooperate. No sooner had one lock been pinned up than another fell down. Why does hair do that some days? For once, even Lady Sarah was ready before me. Finally, I had my damask on and my hair dressed with my rope of pearls through it, and I rushed to the Presence Chamber.

Thank the Lord, the Queen was not there when I puffed in and sat down. Lady Sarah had already arrived and taken my favourite cushion, so I had to have the small hard one. She is clearly quite recovered! I noticed that she had Captain Drake's posy pinned to her bodice and the pearl bracelet on her right wrist. She and Lady Jane were sitting with their backs to each other like sulking cats, as usual.

"Where is the Queen?" I asked, squeezing in next to plump Mary Shelton. "What did I miss?" I could see her face was pink with the effort of not laughing.

"Her Majesty has withdrawn before she gives audience to Mr. Hawkins. She is very annoyed with Lady Sarah and Lady Jane," Mary whispered. "Lady Sarah came in and accidentally on purpose trod on the edge of Lady Jane's kirtle and it ripped a bit. . . . And Sarah said, 'Oh dear, not very well-made, is it? Perhaps I could recommend you a good tailor?' And then Lady Jane said, 'I know you can't help your clumsiness, dear Lady Sarah, because you can't see where your feet are going . . .' And then the Queen threw one shoe at Lady Jane and one at Lady Sarah and told them to stop squabbling like a pair of geese!"

Just then, there was a flourish of trumpets and four of the Gentlemen of the Queen's Guard came in and stood there looking handsome with their halberds, which is their job. The Queen swept in, wearing black velvet and white samite, and we saw that Mr. Hawkins was with her, attended by the two Captains.

As he passed, Captain Drake nodded and smiled at Lady Sarah, and she looked very pleased with herself. Unlike Lady Jane, who looked like she had sucked a lemon.

"My dear Mr. Hawkins," said the Queen in the sort of ringing voice she uses for public announcements that are pretending to be private, "we are so grateful to you for showing us the state of our Royal Father's naval yards and docks. For otherwise we might have gone on for years being cozened out of our Navy, whereas now we most truly intend to make repair and rebuild all that has gone to rack and ruin."

Right on cue, Hawkins, Drake, and Derby kneeled.

"Now, it would be against all right dealing, and clean contrary to precedent, for us to make the sweeping changes that you have been urging, but we can at least make a start. We shall cause to have painted a portrait of our Royal Self, with ships and docks in the background, as it were in signal of our loving watchfulness for the Navy."

I caught Drake and Derby exchanging glances, looking very disappointed. In fact, Drake rolled his eyes. Luckily the Queen didn't see.

"We shall also begin to reform the docks themselves. Or rather, you shall, Mr. Hawkins. For by this patent I hereby make you Counsel Extraordinary to the Navy until the post of Secretary becomes vacant."

Mr. Hawkins bowed low. "Your Majesty shall find me the best adviser—"

"All in good time, Mr. Hawkins," the Queen interrupted impatiently. "For the moment, please continue as you have done, and by all means make friends among the shipwrights. But wait until you have the Secretaryship before you make changes, do you understand?"

"I am certain to have the Secretaryship?" Mr. Hawkins asked, sounding delighted.

"As soon as the greedy idle fat pudding of a man

who has it now consents to die or step down," said the Queen with a ferocious smile. "But all must be done smoothly and politically or the Royal Docks will end up the worse for it."

Hawkins smiled back and nodded. "Aye, Your Majesty, it shall be as you say."

"Excellent. That is all for now." And Her Majesty dismissed Mr. Hawkins and the two Captains.

I have finished my recording just in time—it is midday, and the Maids of Honour are to eat dinner with the Queen in the Parlour.

Later this Day

Hell's teeth! Lady Sarah too is surely in love! There she was at dinner time, sighing and picking at her food because *Somebody* was having to eat in the Great Hall and wasn't there! But she soon perked up when Her Majesty decided to invite Mr. Hawkins and the two Captains to partake of some afternoon air with us in the Privy Garden.

As we walked, Mr. Hawkins continued to expound on ships to Her Majesty. I could see she was listening with interest, but I'm not sure she understood all he was saying because there were so many Sailorish words mixed up in it. I certainly didn't! So I decided to listen in on some easier conversation.

Lady Sarah had, rather rudely, drawn Mary Shelton's attention from Lady Jane to moan to her about the disaster that had happened to her gown the day before. "What I need is a sixteen-yard dress-length of that lovely white samite and some pearls to put with it," she said. Mary nodded politely. "The damask is utterly ruined—it's too bad even to give to Olwen," Sarah went on. "And I *desperately* need a French-cut bodice and a new ruff and some black-worked sleeves and a new petticoat, and even my bumroll smells of river water now so I must throw it away. . ."

"If I can take a fat Flemish merchanter, shall I bring you the booty to make you a new gown?" asked Captain Drake, who had overheard this, as he was supposed to.

Sarah blushed—and I knew why: it would have been more seemly for him to beg the Queen to give Lady Sarah the samite, like a proper courtier, than to go round capturing ships for it! But he didn't seem to know that—and his offer was very romantic. Lady Sarah looked quite charmed by this blatant display of his regard.

"I could do that, too," put in Captain Derby hopefully.

Sarah ignored him. "But I thought only the Spaniards had treasure," she said, simpering up at Drake and fluttering her eyelashes.

"The Flemish are Spanish Netherlanders," Drake explained, "and worth the spoiling, for they carry bolts and bolts of silk and velvet."

"Oh, Captain Drake, then could you capture me a Flemish merchanter with plenty of samite and velvet? And then could you capture me a big Spanish galleon loaded with pearls—like the ones in my lovely bracelet?" Sarah wheedled, with her head on one side and her jewelled wrist held up prettily— quite disgusting to see, really.

"Aye, with a glad heart." Drake laughed and bowed. "Anything my lady desires."

Mary Shelton, who had of course overheard this exchange, elbowed me and made a sick face at all this romantic talk.

The Queen called Sarah over to her then, and the Captains walked off, oh so casually, in the same direction.

I am almost beginning to feel sorry for Captain Derby: he will persist—but clearly Lady Sarah has eyes for no one but Drake.

Later this Day—eventide

I have just had the most terrible shock!

I was first to bed this even. Mary Shelton and Lady Sarah were yet to retire to our chamber. As I was about to climb in, I tripped on something bony. It was Ellie's foot! She was curled up under my bed, shivering and shaking and coughing—not at all well!

She explained to me that Mrs. Fadget has taken no notice of her illness and had cruelly insisted she carry on with her duties. She had sent Ellie to bring all the smocks back from the ladies' bedchambers. But having been washing bedlinen all day, Ellie was exhausted, and she'd fallen asleep under my bed. Poor thing! Her skin was burning up and her breath foul, and she kept saying she was wretched cold.

I decided that I would seek out my Uncle Cavendish, the Court Physician—dearly hoping that, as a favour to me, he would tend to Ellie.

Mary Shelton came in just as I was dressing to fetch my uncle.

"Who is that?" she asked. She didn't sound haughty, as most of the other Maids of Honour might do on seeing me nursing Ellie in our chamber. She sounded kind and concerned.

"It's my friend Ellie from the laundry," I

explained. After all, Mary wouldn't have noticed Ellie even if she had seen her about the palace. "She's very sick. And she has no mother to look after her. And Mrs. Fadget, the Deputy Laundress, has been horrible to her!"

Any of the other Maids of Honour might still have fetched Mrs. Champernowne, who would probably have sent Ellie back to the laundry, and I would have been in trouble, no doubt. But Mary didn't. Instead she came and felt Ellie's forehead. "She certainly has a fever," she said. "We must get her out of these wet clothes. They're wringing with sweat. She needs to be tucked up in bed in a clean dry smock. We have to keep her warm, since she has a fever."

I nodded. It was a relief to have someone who knew about these things. I hardly recognized giggly plump Mary Shelton. "How do you know so much?" I asked, very impressed.

Mary shrugged. "I've helped my mother look after our tenants since I was nine years old."

Between us we took off Ellie's worn old kirtle and her dank smock and I got one of my own from the chest and put it on her. Then we tucked her up in my bed, because Mary said Ellie needed a bed with curtains around like mine, to keep her from the bad night airs.

Poor Ellie was too feverish to be quite in her right mind and she looked very worried. "I must go," she fretted. "Mrs. Fadget says I've all the stockings to wring out next—"

"Mrs. Fadget can wait," I said. Well, that isn't quite what I said, but I've made it more respectable for writing down. "You rest, Ellie. We're getting the doctor."

"What? You can't!" she said, trying to sit up. "I can't pay 'im and Mrs. Fadget—"

"It's all right," I told her, getting her to lie down again. "I'm going to fetch my Uncle Cavendish: he won't want paying."

So she sighed and rested her tangled head back down on the pillow. "Never 'ad a doctor before," she muttered. "Not even an apothecary."

But when I got up to fetch my uncle, Ellie would not let go of my hand, so Mary offered to go instead, bless her!

When she came back she had a very disapproving look on her face—rather like Mrs. Champernowne when she catches me writing my daybooke while I'm wearing my white damask. I saw why, and my heart sank a little. My Uncle Cavendish was swaying and staggering behind her. I love my uncle dearly, but he has such a weakness for the drink, and I fear it will be his undoing. Clearly, this even he had drunk far too much wine.

"Lady Graishe, my dear," he said, blinking and swaying over Ellie in my bed, "I'm shorry to shee you ill." He fumbled for her hand.

I was going to tell him it wasn't me, but then I thought he might be embarrassed by his mistake and that might distract him from his doctoring. So I kept quiet and moved behind one of the bed curtains.

He felt Ellie's forehead, his eyes slightly crossed, then her pulses, and then smelled her breath and looked down her throat. "She's got a quinsy," he said to Mary. "Quite sherious. No need to bleed, but she musht have hot drinks every hour and she musht rest and stay warm. Hic. I'll ret—ret—come back in a day or sho." And he staggered out.

Mary was still frowning. But she politely did not refer to my uncle's drunken state. "Poor Ellie," she said. "A quinsy's horrible. My sister had one last year. She said it feels like your throat is full of rusty nails." She patted Ellie's hand. "What you need is a sweet wine posset. I'll make you one."

When it was ready, Mary and I helped Ellie to sit up and sip the hot drink. There was still no sign of Lady Sarah, for which I was grateful, as I was certain she would not take kindly to Ellie's presence. I hoped we could have Ellie safely tucked up in bed and hidden by the curtains before Sarah's arrival.

When Ellie had finished her posset, she gratefully sank back down on the pillows and shut her eyes. Mary went to her bed and I climbed in next to Ellie. It was like having a bread oven in bed next to me—or a furnace even!

Lady Sarah eventually came to bed, waking me up by humming some song about "hauling 'er up-ay-oh." I was so hot then that I had to get out of bed again, so I thought I'd write all this down and cool off at the same time—maybe then I'll be able to sleep.

I woke quite late this morning. Lady Sarah was already risen and gone—off to daydream about Captain Drake, no doubt—and Mary was putting on her white samite gown to attend the Queen. It's a pity really, white looks terrible on her—it quite drains her of colour. She needs pinks and purples to look healthy.

"Grace! At last!" She smiled. "I have a drink here for Ellie—hot water, aqua vitae, honey, and citron. Give her spoonfuls one at a time, because it is hard for her to swallow. I shall be back soon."

Well, of course I was very pleased to do it, so I put on my hunting kirtle and sat spooning the hot drink into Ellie and helping her up to use the close-stool.

There was a soft knock at the door and Masou crept in, just as I was tucking Ellie up in bed again. He looked very nervous—and well he might, because no boys of any kind are supposed to come near the chambers of the Maids of Honour.

"Grace, I can't find Ellie anywhere, and I have looked in every hiding hole in the palace," he whispered. "I don't—"

I moved aside to show him Ellie, softly tucked up.

He sighed with relief. "Allah be praised, I was so full of worry for her," he said. "That hag in the laundry said she neither knew nor cared where Ellie was."

"Ellie has a bad quinsy but Mary and I are looking after her," I told him. "Don't worry, she was seen by my Uncle Cavendish last night and he says she'll be well enough if she stays warm and rests."

Masou nodded, glanced around furtively, and then headed for the door. "I must go now," he said. "Mr. Somers wants all of us who can swim to come to the watersteps and practise a new tumble for the next time the Queen goes to Tilbury by boat."

"Wait a minute, Masou." I stopped him, grabbing a piece of paper. "Will you take a note to that Fadget woman at the laundry?"

Masou bowed. "As my lady pleases."

It always embarrasses me when he does that— which is why he does it, of course. So I wrote a very haughty note to Mrs. Foul Fadget, saying I was unwell and would keep Ellie with me because I required her help, and that she would return soon enough.

Masou trotted off with it after another elaborate bow. Unfortunately, the cushion I threw at him missed and knocked a pot of face cream off Lady Sarah's table.

Mary came back then, carrying some soup from one of the nearer kitchens.

Ellie had been sleeping but she woke up as Mary entered. "Oh no!" she croaked. "Look, the sun's up! Mrs. Fadget will kill me—"

I held her shoulders. "It's all right," I assured her. "I wrote her a note and she can do without you for a bit."

"But I shouldn't ought to be in your bed!" Ellie wailed, looking frightened now. "What will Mrs. Champernowne say?"

Mary grinned cheekily. "Mrs. Champernowne has somehow got the idea that it's Lady Grace who is ill," she said. "And she won't be coming in. Now, sit up and have some soup."

So Ellie struggled up on the pillows and Mary put a napkin round her and fed her the soup. It was a special mess of chicken and dumplings, with a little egg mixed in—Mary has friends in all the kitchens. Perhaps that is why she is so plump.

When she had finished, Mary produced another bowl. "Now this here is a very nasty willow-bark tea," she said. "You have to sip it slowly and let it trickle down your throat to help with the pain. But then you can have a wet sucket to take the taste away," she added.

Suddenly Ellie was crying. "You're both so kind, I don't—"

I put my arms round her and hugged her. "Don't be silly, Ellie, you're sick," I said. "If we were in Whitehall Palace, instead of here at Greenwich with Mrs. Fadget, Mrs. Twiste would put you to bed in the laundry's back room and do just the same as us, now wouldn't she?"

Ellie nodded.

"So, if that foul Fadget woman won't treat you properly, we will," I told her. "And you shall stay right here until you are better."

Afternoon

I have slept most of today, I was so exhausted. I can't believe all that has happened since last I wrote in my daybooke! I must begin at the beginning and try and keep it all straight in my head, because if ever there was a perfect new case for Her Majesty's Lady Pursuivant, this is it!

Shortly after I'd finished my last daybooke entry, Mrs. Champernowne caught me in the corridor.

"I heard you had a quinsy, Lady Grace. I didn't expect to see you today," she said. "I must say, you don't look very ill," she observed suspiciously.

"I'm feeling a bit better," I said, trying to make my face go pale by concentrating.

"Well, in that case," Mrs. Champernowne said briskly, "I'd be grateful if you would run and find Lady Sarah for me."

So I did. Only I couldn't find Sarah anywhere.

I went all over Greenwich Palace—even in the stables and the mews—but there was no sign of her. Not in the Withdrawing Chamber, nor the Presence nor the Wardrobe nor the gardens nor the Long Gallery. No sign of Lady Sarah, and no sign of Olwen, either. Eventually, I returned to our chamber to make sure she hadn't skulked back to bed.

Mary was there, knitting a baby's biggin cap, and Ellie was asleep. But no Sarah.

Mary decided to come and help me search. As Ellie was settled, with the bed curtains closed, nobody would know she was there.

As we wandered, we tried to think where else Lady Sarah might be: hidden in an attic, high up in a tree, fallen down a ditch? It made us laugh, but none of these seemed very likely.

We were passing through a courtyard, heading for the Presence Chamber, when a pageboy came over. "Er, you're Maids of Honour, aren't you?" he asked us.

"Yes," I replied cautiously, because sometimes the pageboys try and get you to scream by showing you a spider or something. It doesn't work on me, of course. "Who are you?"

"I'm Robin, my Lady. Do you know Lady Jane Coningsby?" he asked.

"Yes, I do," I told him.

"Well, I've got a message for her from her friend," the pageboy explained.

Lady Jane has a friend? That was a wonder to me. I glanced at Mary and she looked just as surprised. "Go on then, I'll pass it on to her," I offered, keen to know from whom the message came.

"It's from Lady Sarah Bartelmy," said Robin, and he screwed up his eyes in an effort to remember it properly. "She said, 'Please tell my best friend, Lady Jane Coningsby, that I send her my love and she need not worry for me.'"

I stared at him. I'd never heard anything so unlikely in my life. "Lady Sarah said that?" I asked incredulously.

"Yes," Robin replied politely. "Down by the Thames, when the sea captain gave me her letter to deliver."

"The what?" asked Mary.

"The sea captain," Robin repeated. "I don't know his name but I know that's what he was because Lady Sarah called him Captain. He was helping Lady Sarah into his boat, and he called me over and gave me this letter from her, to deliver to Her Majesty."

Mary and I looked at each other, astounded. Lady Sarah, getting into a boat with a sea captain?

"How did you know it was Lady Sarah?" I demanded.

"Everyone knows Lady Sarah Bartelmy," Robin replied. "She's the one with the red hair and the big . . . er . . ."

I nodded hastily. "Now tell us again what happened," I ordered.

The pageboy began to look uncomfortable. "I wasn't doing anything wrong," he insisted truculently. "I'm allowed to fish off the watersteps and I—"

"Not about you, about Lady Sarah," I interrupted impatiently.

"Oh, right," Robin said, looking relieved. "Well, she was being helped into a boat by this sea captain, and he called me over to give me her letter to deliver to the Queen. And as I took the letter, Lady Sarah, she called to me, 'Please tell my best friend, Lady Jane Coningsby, that I send her my love and—'"

"'she need not worry for me,'" I finished for him.

The pageboy nodded vigorously. "Well, if you're

going to pass the message on to Lady Jane, I'd better get this delivered," he said, holding up a letter addressed to Her Majesty the Queen.

I stared at it, then looked at Mary. Her eyes were like saucers.

"Her Majesty will not see you at this hour," Mary said. "She will be dining in her Private Chambers."

Robin sighed and nodded, then went to sit down in a corner of the courtyard and wait.

Mary and I hurried off through a gateway into the next courtyard to discuss what we had discovered.

"Being helped into a boat by a sea captain!" Mary gasped. "Must be Drake—did you *see* them simpering over each other? And sending the Queen a letter . . ." She turned to me. "You know what this might mean, don't you?"

We stopped and stared at each other. I knew Mary had had the same thought as me: "Mayhap she is eloping!" I said.

Mary nodded.

I couldn't help laughing at the thought of elegant Lady Sarah as a sea captain's wife.

Mary was holding her stomach, she was laughing so much. "She'll be climbing up the mast!" she gasped. "She'll be firing a cannon!"

I laughed even harder—but then I suddenly thought of something awful, and stopped laughing. "Lord above," I said. "Think how furious the Queen will be that a Maid of Honour has eloped, to marry without Her permission. She'll send out the Gentlemen of the Guard to capture both of them. Captain Drake will be thrown in the Tower and Lady Sarah will be dragged back in disgrace!"

At that, Mary Shelton stopped laughing, too. It was always fun to watch Lady Sarah getting into trouble with the Queen for squabbling with Lady Jane, or wearing too much face paint, but neither of us wanted to see her get into *real* trouble. Not being-banished-from-Court trouble. Not even Lady Sarah I'm-so-pretty Bartelmy deserved that.

I grabbed Mary's arm. "I have to get a look at that letter!" I told her. Then I turned round and ran back to where Robin was playing knucklebones in the corner of the courtyard. Mary followed.

"Robin," I said, "if you give me that letter, I'll see that Her Majesty gets it. So you can go and get something to eat in the Great Hall rather than waiting around here."

Robin's eyes lit up at the mention of food. He pulled off his cap, bowed—quite gracefully for a nine-year-old—and then put the letter in my hand. "Thank you, my lady," he said quickly, and then sped off in the direction of the Great Hall.

I stared down at the letter, feeling a little sick, because I was now going to commit a sort of treason. After all, you're not supposed to read a message addressed to the Queen before she gets it. But I had to know what Lady Sarah said in her letter. And anyway, I reasoned, Her Majesty's clerks read most of her letters for her—she gets so many she would never have time to read them all.

"Come on!" I whispered to Mary, and hurried off towards our bedchamber, with Mary puffing along behind.

As soon as we were in our bedchamber, I blocked the door with a stool and lit one of the candles. Then I got the penknife out of my penner and heated up the blade in the candle's flame. One of the clerks showed me once how to open a letter without breaking the seal—so that you can read it and seal it up again, and no one the wiser! If this letter turned out to be boring Court business, I intended to do just that, and then take it to the Queen. Holding my breath, I put the letter on the table and used the hot knife blade to gently ease the seal off the paper. I unfolded the letter. It said:

Palace of Placentia, Greenwich
The seventh day of May, in the Year of Our Lord 1569

Your Most Gracious Majesty,
I must tell you that I am ardently in love with Captain
Drake. We are going aboard his ship, whereupon his
chaplain shall marry us and so I shall be his wife for ever.
I have taken Olwen with me.

Your humble servant,
Sarah, Lady Bartelmy

I could feel a breeze in my mouth, so I shut my jaw.

Mary, who had been squeaking about how I mustn't open the Queen's letter, peered over my shoulder and read it, too. "So! It is confirmed!" she gasped.

"What's 'appening?" asked a croaky voice from my bed. "What are you doing, Grace?"

"It seems Lady Sarah has eloped with Captain Drake," I told Ellie.

Ellie was silent for a moment. "Cor!" she said reverently.

I was thinking as hard as I possibly could, as hard as a Lady Pursuivant, trying to make sense of it all. Lady Sarah had shamelessly flirted with

59

Captain Drake, and he'd promised her presents, but was she *really* stupid enough to run away with a piratical sea captain? She would be banished from Court for a certainty, and she loves it here. Even I had to admit it was hard to believe she would act so foolishly. And yet, I had the evidence of her letter in my hand.

"What do you think the Queen will do to her?" Ellie asked ghoulishly. "Put her in the stocks? Flog her?"

"She'll be in the most terrible disgrace," said Mary seriously.

"Oh, is that all?" Ellie sounded quite disappointed.

I stood up and went over to Lady Sarah's corner of the chamber. Her jewellery casket and her ivory comb and the cochineal-pink wax she uses on her lips to make them shine were all still sitting on her dressing table. So was the smelly stuff made of crushed woodlice that she puts on her spots, and the bit of unwashed white lamb's wool she rubs her hands with to keep them soft. It just didn't make sense. "Look," I said, "she's left all her toilette behind—how will she comb her hair and cure her spots? She's even left her jewellery."

"Now that *is* odd," agreed Ellie. "I never 'eard of

anyone eloped what didn't take all the jewellery she could lay her hands on."

"I truly think she has taken leave of her senses," said Mary, shaking her head in bafflement. "What with the elopement, and that extraordinary message, sending her love to her best friend, Lady Jane! I believe she'd be more likely to send her love to that old crone Mrs. Champernowne, for the Lord's sake!"

I nodded. "You're right, Mary," I agreed. "Anyone who knows Lady Sarah would see the untruth of her message to Lady Jane." Then a thought came into my head. "But what if that was Sarah's intention?" I said slowly. "What if she was trying to alert those who know her that all is not as it seems?" I held up the letter. "Mayhap *this* is untrue, too?"

I rushed over to the window and held Sarah's letter to the Queen up to the light, to examine it more closely. Was it really Sarah's writing? "I'm not sure this is Lady Sarah's hand," I muttered as I studied the letters.

"But how can you tell?" asked Ellie, who was sitting up now, still quite flushed, but determined not to be left out even though she cannot read. "Aren't you all taught to write the same?"

"Let me see," said Mary.

I went and sat on the bed along with Mary, so that we could all see. It is true that we have all been strictly schooled in writing—and thus our letters look very alike. But Sarah's hand has one special characteristic. "Look," I said. "This letter *appears* to be from Lady Sarah, but Sarah always pens a big curly tail on her *ys*—I think she learned it deliberately, to be like the Queen."

"Oh yes," agreed Mary. "I once sat next to her when she was writing to her father complaining, as usual, that she had nothing new to wear. She took ages over her curly *ys*—I grew quite bored watching her."

I passed no comment on Mary's nosiness, as I was too excited by my discovery. "Yes: see these words, *Majesty* and *marry* and *Bartelmy*?" I said, pointing them out to Mary and Ellie. "The *ys* don't have curly tails at all. I don't think this letter *is* from Lady Sarah. I think it's a *forgery*! And that means Drake has taken Lady Sarah away against her will!"

"Cor!" breathed Ellie again.

Mary was speechless.

I paced up and down the room. "Think about it," I told them, while they both goggled at me. "Lady Sarah was flirting with Captain Drake. Maybe he misunderstood—he isn't entirely familiar with the ways of Court, after all. She won't agree to marry him, so he captures her and takes her to his ship. He's a pirate, he's used to doing dangerous things. Then, when they're well out to sea, his chaplain will marry them and the thing is done!"

Mary nodded. "It happens sometimes," she agreed. "A cousin of mine was taken by her wicked stepfather to wed his nephew. Luckily, my father, together with some other gentlemen, rode after them and saved her just in time. Once you're married, there's nothing to be done—and your husband gets all your wealth!" Mary tutted sadly, then picked up an empty wine flagon. "It's time for your next posset, Ellie," she said. "I'll be back soon." And she slipped out of the room.

How dare Captain Drake think he could abduct one of us just because he felt like it! I was so angry, it made me want to rescue Lady Sarah—even if she is the worst possible chamber-mate and does insist on using foul, smelly spot creams.

"If I tell the Queen what's happened and explain that the letter is forged, perchance the Queen will let me go and investigate and rescue Lady Sarah," I said hopefully to Ellie. "If I go down to Tilbury right away, they might not have sailed yet and I could get her back quietly."

"Don't be a Bedlamite," replied Ellie. "The Queen would never let you do that!"

"She said I was her Lady Pursuivant and I could investigate mysteries at the palace," I reminded her, feeling quite annoyed. But I knew Ellie was probably right.

Ellie shook her head, then winced. "Her Majesty might let you 'vestigate within the Verge of Court, but she'll never let you go gallivanting off down to Tilbury docks," she declared. "She'll send men, lots of them, with halberds and swords. Hey! Do you think there'll be a fight? D'you think Drake's sailors will fight them off?" Ellie started coughing again in her excitement.

"Doubtless," I agreed. It was exciting to think of the battle, but my heart was sinking like a stone as I thought of what it would mean. "But if there is any such brawl and Lady Sarah is brought back by the Queen's Gentlemen of the Guard, everyone in the Court will know of it," I pointed out to Ellie. "The gossip will be all over London in half a day, the ballad-sellers will be singing of it by dinner time! Lady Sarah's reputation will be ruined, whatever really happened—and whether she was willing *or* forced. She will have to leave Court like Katharine Broke, and her father might even disinherit her. Then she'll have to marry a barrister or somebody awful like that!"

"Well, there's nothing you can do about it," Ellie declared. "So you'll have to seal up the letter again and give it to the Queen."

I almost agreed, but then I was struck by another idea—it was the beginning of a plan, but a plan so bold that I hardly dared mention it. If I hadn't been so angry with Captain Drake I don't suppose I ever would have thought of it, but, "There *is* something I can do about it, Ellie," I said slowly, clenching my fist on the forged letter. "I can go to Tilbury *secretly*, and try to rescue Lady Sarah with no one being any the wiser. If I succeed, her reputation will not be ruined and she will not be sent from Court!"

Ellie just stared at me with her mouth open.

And I stood there, trying to look brave and determined—which I think was very noble of me considering what a nuisance Lady Sarah is!

At that moment Mary Shelton came back with the posset and I told her my intention straight away, before I had time to change my mind—because I knew I would be taking a very great risk; only my outrage at Drake's behaviour made me determined.

It took another half-hour of arguing, but in the

end neither Mary nor Ellie could think of any better way to help Sarah—unless you count sitting on our bums and wringing our hands. So we came up with a plan so that I could slip away to Tilbury: Mary would tell everyone that I had suffered a relapse, and that Lady Sarah was now ill in bed, too. She would pretend she was looking after both of us. That way, no one would come near, in case it was something infectious, and Ellie could continue to be looked after in my bed. "And I think Lady Sarah took Olwen with her. So we'd better include her, too," I added.

Mary giggled. "So now I have four patients, one visible and three invisible. Don't you think your uncle, Dr. Cavendish, will wonder . . . ?"

"My uncle won't even notice," I assured her.

Mary shook her head. "I'm not sure if you are very brave or very stupid," she said with feeling. "You don't even *like* Lady Sarah."

That is true. But I believed that Lady Sarah had already suffered the indignity of abduction, and as Lady Pursuivant I intended to do my best to see that she should not also suffer the injustice of disgrace because of it. Not even Sarah—though she is most trying—deserves that.

I made sure I had some money with me and considered taking my daybooke—only it is too precious and I would not want it to get spoiled at the docks. Tilbury is a damp and untidy place, so I resolved to leave my daybooke in my chamber but to take careful note of my adventure for writing up later.

Of course, I needed the right clothes for my mission. So I hurried down to the buttery, where Masou and the other acrobats often go after a hard practice to drink mild ale and boast.

Sure enough, Masou was there. I dragged him into an alcove and told him what had happened. His eyes nearly popped out of his head.

"Allah, forgive me!" he cried. "I saw them getting into the boat myself. It was rowed by some uglylooking ogres—and the Captain lifted my Lady Sarah and carried her on board when she didn't get in by herself. But I was busy practising a juggle and balance and I never thought anything of it, so, alas, I raised no alarm!"

"That must have been Captain Drake!" I exclaimed, then patted Masou's arm reassuringly because he looked so horrified. "Can you tell me anything else?" I asked.

"The lady was as stiff and white as paper—perhaps the Captain held her under an enchantment—" he mused.

"Masou!" I said. "This isn't the time for your romantic nonsense!"

He looked embarrassed. "I heard her asking him about Olwen and whether she was safe," he remembered.

Aha! I thought. That explains why Sarah didn't struggle or call out directly for help when Drake was putting her into the boat. He used Olwen's well-being as ransom. What a cowardly bully.

As quickly as I could I told Masou what I was going to do. "But I shall need to go in disguise—as a boy—if I am not to attract attention," I explained. "So I shall need a boy's clothes. Is there anyone's I could borrow?"

Masou thought a bit, then his eyes lit up and he nodded. "French Louis's son has a new outfit, and he is a beanplant like you. We should find his old apparel in the tiring chamber."

We crept off to where the acrobats change before a performance, a little room off the Great Hall. The clothes were old and worn and quite smelly, but I nipped into a closet, took off my kirtle and smock, and put on the shirt and hose. I came out pulling on the doublet and leather jerkin, then I put my eating knife on the belt. I thought I looked very well indeed.

But Masou sighed as he looked at me, and then he

brought out a pair of shears. I flinched and he tut-ted. "Did you ever see a boy with locks as long as yours?" he asked.

I flushed. He was right, of course, but—cut my hair? I wasn't sure if I dared. Mrs. Champernowne would have a fit if she found out—several fits!

"Come, it will grow again," Masou reassured me, and without more ado he cut it all to one short length.

I couldn't believe it was all gone—just like that! It felt very peculiar indeed, but as my mousy brown hair was hardly my crowning glory, I found I didn't mind so much. And I could always use a hairpiece to hide the damage later, I thought.

Masou then found me a blue woollen cap, helped me to put it on the right way, and showed me my reflection in the big mirror with the crack in it that the acrobats use.

I gasped. With my short hair and my flat-as-a-pancake chest (*when* will I start growing outwards as well as up?) I made a very believable boy. Not far off handsome, in fact. I did a bow—not very good.

Masou sighed. Then he took down two cloaks from a rail. "I am coming with you," he announced.

"But Mr. Somers might beat you if he finds out!" I argued. "You don't have to come."

"Of course I do," snorted Masou. "What do you know of being a boy? Nothing. And if *you* are found out, there will be a most dreadful scandal." He shook his head. "Walk over there."

I did and he sighed again. "Stride, swagger!" he instructed. "Don't smile. And stare straight at people."

I walked up and down trying to swagger. It felt very odd to have so much air around my legs, and yet cloth chafing between.

"Not bad," Masou admitted. "When you talk to anyone, remember to say 'sir' or you'll be buffeted."

I heard the clock chime one, and worried that Drake might soon have readied his ship to go to sea. "Come on, Masou," I urged, "we must hurry!"

We flitted through the back passages of Greenwich, past the bakery and the dairy and the little laundry—where Mrs. Fadget was screaming at some very tired-looking laundrywomen—and down to the kitchen steps.

Masou shouted, "Oars! Oars!"

At last a boat drew up and I looked nervously at it, waiting for the waterman to help me board.

"What are you waiting for?" Masou dug me with his elbow. "Jump in!"

Of course, boys don't get helped, so I gulped and jumped and managed to keep my balance. In fact, it was easier because I hadn't any petticoats or stays.

Masou followed me, stepping aboard lightly.

"Tilbury," I said to the man. "And as fast as you can."

"Won't make no difference," said the waterman. "Tide's still against us."

"But it's an urgent message for Captain Drake from the Queen," I told him desperately.

"You'd better help row then, lad," the waterman replied bluntly.

Masou showed me the spare pair of oars and fitted them in the little metal things on either side of the boat. He took one himself and started dipping it into the water. I tried to copy him but the oar kept popping out when I wasn't expecting it and making me fall backwards. It was very annoying and frustrating, and made the waterman laugh and shake his head.

"Clumsy, ain't you?" he remarked.

It seemed to take ages to get to Tilbury and I was puffing long before then.

"What's wrong with your mate?" grunted the waterman to Masou. "He sick, then?"

"No, he's just outgrown his strength," replied Masou with a grin. "Look what a beanpole he is."

"Humph," was all I could manage.

We rowed and rowed and at last we came to the Tilbury watersteps. They must have tidied up for the Queen for it looked messier than I remembered it, and even more muddy. I paid the waterman, and then Masou made me go behind some barrels and arrange my purse in my crotch! Under my codpiece! He said I had to or it would be stolen the first time I blinked. He turned away while I did it and I heard spattering.

"You'd best go, too," he said, gesturing.

And that was when I realized what was going to be the biggest problem of all: how on earth could I make water? It's never a problem usually: either there's a chamber pot to use or, if we are on progress or out hunting, I just find a quiet grassy spot and my farthingale hides me. But now I wore hose, and a codpiece between my legs that unlaced at the front—only that wouldn't do *me* any good!

"Um . . . Masou . . . ," I said, wondering if Lady Sarah was worth this humiliation, "um . . . how . . . ?"

"Undo all the laces except the back ones and then squat," Masou instructed. "And try and do it where nobody sees." He shook his head and tutted.

So I did just that behind a big barrel—and found it very strange and draughty.

As we hurried along the docks, Masou tried to teach me to whistle. I had never realized there were so many things you had to know to be a boy.

"And by the way," he asked, "what is your name going to be?"

Another thing I hadn't thought of. I could hardly go around calling myself Lady Grace in doublet and hose. "Um . . . Gregory? It's a bit like Grace," I suggested.

"Right, *Gregory,* please tell me you have a plan," said Masou. He was sounding a bit nervous now.

"Of course I have a plan," I blustered. "We go aboard Captain Drake's ship, find Lady Sarah, and get her off before it sails. Simple! But we don't want to meet Captain Drake, because I'm sure he'll recognize me and then who knows what he'll do?"

"If he's rogue enough to kidnap Lady Sarah," Masou pointed out, "you could end up married to the First Mate or something!"

"Well, we're not going to see him, and we're not going to get caught," I told Masou firmly, feeling a bit annoyed. Now he'd made *me* nervous too!

We passed a ship that was being built in the dry dock. It was swarming with people, full of the sounds of sawing and hammering and shouts. Then we passed the big square pond where we had raced the two model ships. The winches were still there, now being perched upon by seagulls.

We asked everybody we met which was Captain Drake's ship. One person said it was about to sail. So we rushed to the quayside where he'd pointed. The sailors were in the rigging and there were ropes everywhere, along with the sound of creaking and stamping and a song that sounded like "Oo-ay and up she rises, oo-ay and up she rises . . ."

I was in a panic to get aboard and rushed up to the pigtailed sailor standing by the gangplank. "We've got a message for Captain Drake!" I gasped, forgetting to be nervous. "Let us on the ship!"

"No," said the sailor. He gave me and Masou a knowing grin.

"Why not? We've got to talk to the Captain!" I insisted.

"Well, you won't find him on this ship," the sailor said. "This 'ere is the *Silver Arrow*—Hugh Derby, Captain. If you want Captain Drake you need to go to the *Judith* over there." He pointed at the other two-masted ship in the next quay.

Masou and I hastily stepped back from the gang-plank, as the sailors hauled up the anchor. The *Silver Arrow* started moving away from the quay. She was being pulled by ropes attached to smaller rowing boats. There were lots of shouts as one sailor removed the mooring ropes from the big tree trunks at the quayside and then leaped lightly across the gap onto the ship.

"Derby's in a hurry," commented a sailor behind us, as he watched the *Silver Arrow* move slowly out into the river. "Where's he off to? I wonder. He's too early for the ebb."

Masou and I shrugged at him, then hurried towards the *Judith*.

We found Drake's ship still moored to the quay, with sailors swarming round it. Baskets and nets full of loaves of bread were being loaded into the hold, and a boy was handing a package to the sailor guard-ing the gangplank.

"Package for Captain Drake," he said.

The sailor took it and nodded. "I'll see that 'e gets it," he replied.

The boy left and Masou swaggered up to take his place. I followed, doing my best to swagger as well. "Captain aboard?" Masou asked the sailor.

"Aye, but he's below."

Below what? I wondered, but didn't ask. I just stood there trying to look, well—boyish.

"We got a message for him," said Masou.

"I'll give it to 'im," said the sailor.

"We've been told to give it to him personally," Masou countered.

"Ah, now would you be the boys sent from the steelyard?" the sailor asked.

"Might be," said Masou, using the opening the sailor had unwittingly given him.

"In that case, you can come aboard and wait in the Great Cabin for him—but mind, no tricks now. Captain's got a short way with lads what annoy him." The sailor made a throat-slitting motion and grinned.

Masou salaamed, and I pulled at my cap as I've seen the kitchen boys do, then we made our way up the gangplank. I swaggered for all I was worth—and nearly fell off.

"Tell your mate to sober up afore he talks to the Captain!" the sailor shouted at Masou.

Masou looked at me sidelong. I could tell that he was trying not to laugh. "Less sideways, more forwards," he directed.

"This is so difficult," I complained, puffing.

"Compared with petticoats?" Masou asked. He did have a point.

We picked our way across the deck between baskets waiting to be stowed and net bags full of cannonballs and barrels. Masou told me that the Great Cabin was located in the sterncastle, at the blunt end of the ship.

I had to duck my head as I passed through a low door into the small room that was called the Great Cabin. I stared around, at the table covered with maps and papers, and the cot in one corner. A sword and a pistol in its case were hung on one wall. The others had half-finished paintings on them; they were quite clumsy, showing what appeared to be a lot of people standing on big round balls and looking out to sea. The solitary window looked out on sailors hammering on the deck. But there was no sign of Lady Sarah. And I had been so sure she would be there!

I crept into the next cabin, which had two cots in it, and the next, which had three cots and three small chests. I couldn't believe Sarah wasn't in any of them. Where had he put her?

"Any luck?" Masou whispered to me, from where he was keeping watch at the half-open door.

"No!" I whispered back.

Our hearts beating like mad, we climbed down a ladder to look in the tiny cabins below. But we didn't find her anywhere. And there was so much more ship to search than I'd expected.

Eventually, Masou shook his head. The sun was starting to go down. "Come on," he said. "She's not here—we'll have to leave."

"But we haven't even been into the front half of the ship," I pointed out. "We at least ought to look."

We crept like mice along the low space under the main deck, where the crew's bedrolls were tucked alongside the guns. A little further along we passed a little eating room for the officers, where tables hung from the ceiling. The big sullen-looking boy, who had kept the seagulls away from the feast when we visited the docks with the Queen, was listlessly scrubbing at them. Luckily, he was too busy muttering about the First Mate to notice us.

Then Masou found a ladder that went right down into the belly of the ship. Down here the darkness was full of barrels and hams hanging on beams. It looked like the dirtiest, smokiest kitchen you ever saw—and the smell was awful.

We crept past the barrels and found a fire burning in a brick grate, with a huge copper full of water above it. Benches and stools were set around it as if it were an inn. Masou poked a basket that had loaves of bread in it and I had a sniff at an open barrel where some salt beef seemed to be soaking.

"Oi! You two! What are you doing down here?" A skinny man in a dirty apron jumped down from a ladder. He had a sack over his shoulder. "Get out of it! Stealing food—I'll 'ave you!" He dropped the sack and started throwing potatoes at us, so Masou and I ran away as fast as we could. Once we had escaped, I gasped indignantly, "Stealing food! That horrible stuff? Why would anyone want to?"

Masou just shook his head and laughed.

We searched on until we reached the pointed front end of the ship, where we found a triangular room filled with folded sails, all marked with chalk symbols. I noticed a bowl on the floor—and then something moved slightly in the shadows. I peered into the darkness and saw a long, curvy shape. My heart leaped with excitement. It had to be Lady Sarah with those famous curves of hers! "She's here!" I gasped.

Shocked that she'd been tied up there in the dark,

I rushed over to release her. Masou followed, and together we pushed past the huge packages of sails to reach Lady Sarah . . .

Only it wasn't. It was just a sail, tied up so it looked like someone rather busty lying down. The movement I'd seen was a little family of cats—a mother and her kittens, nestling in the folds. The mother cat meowed at me and then gave a warning hiss.

"Ahh," I said. I couldn't help it. The kittens were adorable with their huge eyes and little paws. "It's all right, I won't harm—"

"Is she there?" Masou nudged me from behind.

"No," I said. "It's kittens. I don't know what we—"

"Shhh!" Masou whispered fiercely, staring over his shoulder.

There were voices outside the door. One of them was Captain Drake's! I dived behind the sail with the cats in it, and Masou shrank into the space behind the door.

Captain Drake's lively face appeared round the door as he peered into the dim room. "You've rousted the sails out well?" he demanded.

"Aye, Captain," said a voice behind him. "We shook 'em out and checked 'em for holes yesterday, while you were at Court."

No, you didn't, I thought, while my heart went *boom-da-da-boom*. That family of cats looks far too cosy to have been disturbed for a week. I prayed none of the cats would move and attract Captain Drake's attention. Where have you put Lady Sarah, you evil man? I thought, staring at him. She must be here somewhere.

"Very good," said Drake. And then he pulled the door shut.

As Masou and I hid there in the shadows, we heard bolts slide home on the outside of the door! We stared at each other in horror as the footsteps moved away. Then Masou began muttering to himself in his own language and pushing at the door.

I felt my way over to him, my mouth totally dry. We tried everything to slide the bolts open from the wrong side. Masou jiggled with his knife, I worked on the hinges—but to no avail.

"If only it was locked, I could pick it," Masou said, thumping his fist on the door in frustration.

"Shhh," I warned. "Don't do that, someone will hear and we'll be in terrible trouble."

"I hate it!" he panted. "I hate being locked in, I . . ." He slipped back into Arabic again.

I felt for his shoulder and patted it. "Masou," I

said, "they'll have to come and get sails sooner or later, and then they'll let us out."

"No, I have to get out now!" he insisted. He banged with his fists and shouted at the top of his voice—but he was drowned out by a sudden tramping of feet above us. A work song began: "Oo-ay and up she rises, oo-ay and up she rises . . ." The feet settled to a steady stamp and heave, and there was a creaking and clattering and a long squealing sound.

"What's that, Masou?" I caught his hands to stop them drumming. "Listen, what is it?"

He was quiet for a long time. "I think it's the capstan for the anchor," he said eventually.

"Eh?" He was talking Sailorish.

"They're pulling up the anchor," Masou clarified.

"Oh," I said. "Um . . . does that mean they're getting ready to sail?"

Masou nodded, and then he started banging again. Except nobody heard because of all the noise from the anchor.

Masou was panting heavily by now, so I took hold of his hands again and patted them. It was very frightening being locked up in the dark, and knowing that the ship was getting ready to sail soon. But trying to calm Masou helped me not to feel so frightened myself. I'd never known him be so scared before—I'd seen him juggle with fire while balancing on top of a little pole, and not so much as blink. I had been the one with my heart in my mouth then. And seeing him frightened now made me feel guilty for bringing him on such a mad escapade. We had found no trace of either Lady Sarah or Olwen anywhere.

There were thuds and bangs and shouts. The ship began to rock in a different way. There was more creaking, the sound of counting, and men shouting, "Heave!" And then two big splashes. More shouting. The ship was definitely moving—it seemed to find a new way to rock every minute.

I had thought it would be simple to rescue Lady Sarah, but now we needed rescuing ourselves! What if they didn't need sails for days and days? What if they were going to the Azores or New Spain? What if the ship got caught in a storm and sank? What if it went into battle with the Spanish? I felt horribly sick with panic, but I forced myself to keep quiet for fear of making Masou any worse.

I don't know how long I sat there in the dark, listening to the happy squeaks of the kittens with their mother, and worrying about what would happen to us. Masou calmed down a bit after a while—I could hear him breathing more steadily. The ship was rolling from side to side, which was making me feel peculiar. I tried to take my mind off it by thinking about Lady Sarah—what if Drake's regard for her had been nothing but an act and he wanted her only for her wealth? Or what if he had lost patience with her—which, heaven knows, is easy to do—and had put her in irons in the brig, with the rats? She'd be so frightened. She didn't even like *mice* and she was so silly and timid. . . .

After what felt like a very long time, there was another kind of movement—like a horse makes when it canters. It was quite soothing, really. Although I was so frightened and worried (*what* would the Queen do when I got back—*if* I got back?), the motion was comforting and I curled up on one of the sails and dozed off.

The next thing I knew there was a bright light! A loud bang! A rough man's voice calling, "Tom?" in the distance. Then the man's voice shouted, "What the—! God's teeth, what's this? What the hell are you two boys doing here?"

I was thick-headed with sleep, trying to work

out how a man with a big gold earring and a pigtail had got into the bedchamber of the Maids of
Honour. . . .

Masou scrambled to his feet, looking terrified.

The man called over his shoulder, "Mr. Price,
we'm got stowaways again, bloody little rats." Then
he turned back to Masou and me. "Come on, you!
Out of there—and you'd better not've damaged any
of they sails, you hear?"

He not only had a pigtail, he was as wide as a barrel and one of his front teeth was missing. He
grabbed hold of Masou by the arm and slung him
out into the passage, where Masou rolled neatly and
came to his feet. Then he strode towards me,
grabbed my jerkin, and did the same to me. I landed
in a heap.

"Why did you do that?" I shouted, climbing to my
feet again, outraged at his unfairness. "It's not our
fault, we got locked in!"

The man swung his arm and hit me so hard round
the head that I fell over again, my head ringing and
my ear burning. I felt too dizzy to get up for a bit.
Masou came and stood between me and the man.

"What were you doing in there at all? Looking for
vittles to steal, I'll be bound!" shouted the man.

"No, sir, we weren't," replied Masou. "We were lost."

I was very impressed at how steady his voice was.

"Call me a liar, would ye?" roared the man, and he aimed a clip round Masou's ear too—except Masou was clever enough to duck and roll so he didn't get hit.

I struggled to my knees and then decided it might be sensible to stay on the floor. "It's true," I said. "We were *lost*." But I could hardly tell him that we'd become lost while looking for the girl his Captain had kidnapped, now could I?

"A likely story!" He kicked at Masou and then at me. "Up! Get up and explain yourselves to the Mate."

At least he wasn't taking us to the Captain—yet. I rubbed the bruise on my bum where I'd landed on the floor, and my swollen ear, then scurried up the ladder after Masou.

As we got to the top, Masou muttered to me, "Shut up and let me talk. I don't want you making him so angry he throws us overboard."

"He wouldn't dare—" I began.

"Who'd know?" Masou pointed out. "You're not important now, *Gregory,* so be quiet!"

I realized with a chill that Masou was right! I was no longer Lady Grace Cavendish, with the protection of Her Majesty the Queen. I was Gregory, suspected stowaway! I could see that Masou was frightened—a different sort of frightened from when we were shut in—and it was making him fierce. I started to get frightened, too. This wasn't at all what I'd planned. We were supposed to be back at Court with Lady Sarah, safe and sound, by now!

We went up another ladder and found ourselves in the middle of the deck, next to the biggest mast. There was a strong wind blowing, and big waves, and no land anywhere around. When I looked up I could see lots of sails billowing in the wind, and ropes everywhere, all crossing each other.

The wide man who'd found us gripped us both by the shoulder and shoved us forwards, until we were standing in front of another broad man in a woollen doublet and a ruff. His hands tightened and he shoved us again so we both fell on our knees.

"Stowaways, Mr. Newman, sir," he said. "Found 'em in the sail locker."

Mr. Newman looked down at us as if we were dead rats, and sighed. "Have either of you sailed before?" he asked.

"Yes, sir," answered Masou quickly, "I have. A two-master out of Dunkirk when I was younger." I remembered Masou telling me that he'd only been six years old at the time, but I didn't think he'd want me to mention that. "I'm an acrobat now," he added. "My name is Masou—and this is my mate, Gregory."

Mr. Newman looked a bit more interested. "Acrobat, eh? Can you climb?" he asked Masou.

"Yes, and I can tumble, sir," Masou told him proudly.

"Go on then," said Mr. Newman, folding his arms.

Masou bowed, stood on tiptoe, then bounced—turned a neat somersault in the air—and came back down lightly on his feet.

"And you?" said Mr. Newman to me.

"Um, please, Mr. Newman, where's the ship going?"

He scowled. "None of your business, boy. That's up to the Captain. Now, have you sailed before?"

"Er . . . no, I haven't sailed," I said, then, as he frowned, remembered to add, "sir."

"So what can you do?" Mr. Newman enquired.

"Um, I can . . . I . . ." I thought desperately for something. "I can embroider, sir . . . I was apprenticed to the Queen's Wardrobe, but I ran away because it was boring. And . . . I . . . can paint and draw, too," I added, hoping that the patterns I'd designed for my embroideries would stand me in good stead.

"Soft as a girl, in other words," said Mr. Newman disgustedly. "You, Masou, are you afraid of heights?"

"No, sir, not at all," Masou replied.

"Good," Mr. Newman said. "The banner's snagged at the topsail yard. You and your mate go up there and free it." He pointed up and up and up the mast that was nearest the front of the ship, to where there was a sort of lump tangled in the ropes.

Masou knuckled his forehead. "Yes, sir." He went over to the rail and climbed on it.

I stared in horror at the enormous mast stretching upwards into the sky. "What if we fall?" I quavered.

"You'll die," said the man who had found us. "And that'd be an easy way out."

"You can do as you're told, boy," added Mr. Newman, "or you can go in the brig. But you get no food if you don't work. Up you go."

Well, it was long past breakfast time and I was thirsty, too, so I gulped and nodded.

Mr. Newman frowned. "I don't like your manners, Gregory," he said. "Mend 'em or you'll be in worse trouble than you can imagine."

"Y-yes, sir," I replied, and went to follow Masou.

He hadn't started climbing yet. "You go first," he whispered to me. "Then if you slip, I can catch you. Just think of it as a tree," he suggested.

"Hell's teeth!" I exclaimed nervously. I don't mind climbing trees, but this was a tree that was rocking back and forth with the waves.

"Wait for the ship to roll the other way," instructed Masou. "Now, up . . ."

I climbed, holding on as tight as I could. My knees were knocking, but at least I could hear Masou behind me. We went up and up, past the huge yellow-white sheets of the sails and about a thousand ropes. But the ladder—what was it Captain Drake had called them? Ratlines? Anyway, the rungs got narrower and narrower and then stopped under the platform, halfway up the mast, that he'd called the fighting top.

"Now what?" I wailed. "There's no more ladder!"

"See the ropes going out to the edge of the fighting top?" called Masou from below me.

I looked, and saw ratlines I hadn't noticed, stretching from the mast out to the edge of the top—

but what good were they? I'd be hanging right out over the deck, which was really far below us now. "Yes," I whispered, knowing what Masou was going to say.

He did. "We have to climb them."

"What?" I squealed, sounding almost as squeaky as Lady Sarah when she's seen a mouse. "I can't!"

"Yes, you can," Masou said firmly.

"But . . . it's too high . . . I'll be hanging by my hands. I can't, Masou!" I pleaded.

"Yes, you can!" shouted Masou fiercely. "You *can* do it, because you *have* to!"

Masou had never spoken to me like that before. Nobody had. But I still could not move.

"Allah save us," he muttered. "Grace, I cannot coax you, there's no time. You've climbed harder things; I know you can do this, but the only way for you to know it too is to try. Now *climb* the *tree*! Or else you will have to go back down and confess that you're a girl."

Suddenly I felt furious with myself. Who was acting like Lady Sarah now? Masou was right. I would *not* give up and admit to being a girl just because I was scared of climbing the ratlines.

Heart hammering, I put my hand up, gripped one rung of the rope ladder, then the other, got my toes into a narrow gap, then my other foot . . . I was leaning right out, with nothing under me for miles and miles . . . If I fell, I'd die! Toes clawing round the rung of the ladder, I reached up for the next rung, then the next. The edge of the top was the worst, I had to hold on with one hand, move the other over the edge to the new set of ratlines there, then wrap my arm around it, then reach over with the other hand . . .

Suddenly Masou was there, hauling me up onto the top by my jerkin. He must have whisked up on the other side of the mast. "Well done," he whispered in my ear. "You see? You did it!"

I lay there for a minute, gasping and shaking, and then got slowly to my feet.

Masou pointed to the next, narrower set of ratlines, which went right up to the point of the mast where the cloth was tangled in a rope.

"Oh no," I gasped, my heart thundering enough to crack my chest.

Masou grinned encouragingly at me and began to climb.

I didn't want to be left alone on the high tossing little platform. So I started following him.

He looked down at me and shook his head. "Not this one. The other side."

So I climbed down, edged over to the other set of ratlines, and started climbing again.

When I caught Masou up at the highest place on the mast, he was already struggling with the cloth bunched in the ropes. I wrapped one leg around the ratlines and tugged at the tangle. Then I stopped and looked more closely. It was pulled up too tight. I could see we'd never get it free like that. "Loosen it!" I yelled down to the deck, as loud as I could.

There was a movement down there, which I could hardly see for all the sails in the way. The ropes moved past each other a couple of times, and then I could see the bit that was caught and tease it out with my fingers.

Suddenly the banner flapped and took the wind and floated out above the ship.

Masou grinned at me. "See, my lady? You did it."

I smiled back, trying not to think about getting down. "You should call me Gregory," I reminded him.

Masou scampered back down to the fighting top like a monkey. He waited for me there as I edged my way much more carefully, trying not to look down.

When I reached him, he showed me how to slide my feet out over the edge of the fighting top, catch my toes in the rungs and then let myself down onto the main ratlines.

Then he grabbed a rope. "Now don't try to get down this way," he warned me with a mischievous gleam in his eyes. Next thing I knew, he was sliding down the rope, hand over hand, all the way down to the deck!

I climbed my way down the ratlines—but much more quickly than before, because I was so relieved to be going down, not up.

Masou flourished a bow at Mr. Newman when we landed back on the deck. I copied him.

"Hm," Mr. Newman said, looking at Masou with some respect. "You've not been a ship's boy before?"

"No, sir," Masou answered.

"You might make a very fine topman with care," Mr. Newman decided. Then he turned to me. "You, Gregory, I don't know what use you might be. Did you say you could paint?"

"Yes, sir," I lied.

"Good. Go and report to the Boatswain. In fact, both of you go," Mr. Newman ordered.

I wondered if we were going to get any dinner. My stomach was grumbling. But I didn't think it would be a good plan to ask. So I went the way he pointed and found a harassed-looking white-haired man carrying some clay pots towards the Great Cabin—the last place I wanted to go, in case the Captain saw me. I heard Masou groan behind me.

"Sir, sir, are you the Boatswain?" I asked.

"Aye. Ah yes, Mr. Newman said you claimed to be a painter and stainer," the Boatswain declared.

"Only a 'prentice, sir," I hedged quickly.

"No matter. Come this way," he said, and led us into the Great Cabin.

I followed, with my shoulders hunched. Captain Drake wasn't there, thank goodness. "Where's the Captain?" I asked.

"He's training some new gunners," the Boatswain replied. "Now then. See here, this painting needs finishing." It was the scrawl of people standing on balls looking at waves. "This is to show the Queen when she came to Tilbury."

Aha! They weren't balls, they were kirtles. I nodded and tried not to smile at how crude the picture was.

"There's the paint," said the Boatswain. "And there's the picture. Get to it." And he left us to it.

"Are you angry with me for ordering you about up there?" Masou asked me, once the Boatswain was out of earshot.

I smiled at him. "No, it helped. How did you know what to say?"

He flashed his white teeth in a grin. "It's how Mr. Somers talks to me if I think I cannot do a tumble he wants."

I looked at the paints. There were some good colours—a red and a blue and a yellow and a black and a white. I took one of the brushes—which were far too thick—and gave it to Masou, then started to improve the kirtles of the Ladies-in-Waiting. "You know, since we're stuck here," I said to him, "I think we should do more investigating. I'm determined to find some way to spoil Captain Drake's wicked plot, and if we really look, we're bound to find Lady Sarah *somewhere*."

I think Masou groaned softly but I wasn't sure. He wasn't very good at painting, so I found a bit of wood for mixing colours on, made some blue-green and set him doing the waves, which were easy.

I started to enjoy myself. It was hardly the same as embroidering a petticoat's false front, and the paints smelled terrible—I remember someone telling me once that white paint is made with mercury and sends alchemists mad—but it was interesting to try and make the scene look better. I decided I couldn't do much about the faces: they were just blobs of pink. But I was able to make the Queen's kirtle look something like it really does, and when I took a quick look about the cabin, I even found some pieces of paper left for kindling by the brazier—*and* a pen and ink on the desk.

At last I could scribble some notes on all that had happened to put in my daybooke later. I longed to write of my adventures, but of course I had not brought the daybooke with me because it is quite big and very precious and might be ruined by sea water—and what would Gregory the page want with a Maid of Honour's daybooke anyway? I would most likely have been taken for a spy—and thrown overboard or something terrible—had it been found!

Even writing a few notes took a while—and used up all the scraps of paper, which I folded and tucked in my pouch when I'd finished. Masou just shook his head at my lunacy and said nothing.

For a long time the painting and writing had kept my mind off a very serious problem, but I could not distract myself any longer. I realized I simply had to go to the jakes!

When I told Masou this he laughed and shook his head. Then he went outside to find the Boatswain. "Sir, may I show Gregory where the jakes are?" he asked.

The Boatswain, who was sitting outside like a guard, and drinking from a flask, nodded. "Mind you come back quick," he added.

Masou elbowed me. "I'll show you," he said.

We walked to the front end of the ship, where the painted beakhead jutted over the waves. Then we climbed onto it from the foredeck—which was hard, because it was going up and down quite a bit. One of the sailors was sitting there, his breeches untrussed and his bare bum over the side, as he peacefully smoked on a pipe.

I clutched Masou's hand. "Masou, there's somebody here," I gasped.

Masou squeezed my hand briefly and winked. "You can do it, Grace," he whispered, "I know you can." And then he swung himself down, unlacing as he did so, and sat next to the sailor with his bare bum hanging over the waves as well.

And I simply *had* to go. I was ready to burst. So I undid the lacing, then lowered myself down by one of the rope handles, until I was sitting on a plank with my bum bare like the other two and my shirt hanging down in front. My face was burning red, so hot I thought it would burst into flame, and even though I was so desperate, I couldn't do anything for ages. I just had to sit there with my privy parts getting colder and colder, hating Lady Sarah more and more each moment (although I knew it wasn't really her fault)!

Just as I was starting to relax, the sailor belched, farted, and sighed, banged the dottle out of his pipe into the sea, then heaved himself up and off the plank. "Best be quick, boys," he said. "No skiving on this ship, the Cap'n won't have it. He'll come down here looking for you himself, if needs must."

I could hear Masou snorting with suppressed laughter, though I don't know what he thought was so funny.

Once the sailor had gone, I concentrated hard on pretending to myself that I was just using a jakes on progress, and at last I managed to do what I had to do.

When I had got the laces done up again and heaved myself off the plank, I saw Masou waiting for me. "Never, never, never tell anyone . . . ," I whispered through gritted teeth.

"And have the Queen clap me in irons, throw me in the Tower, and then take my head off?" Masou replied, chuckling and shaking his head. "Never fear. But I wish you could see your face."

We went back to painting in the Great Cabin, with Masou still snorting with laughter every now and then. I don't know how sailors can bear it, I really don't.

A minute later the Boatswain came in and tapped me on the shoulder. "Come on," he said. "Time for vittles."

"I've got to clean the brushes first," I told him. Then I wiped them on the rag I'd been using to rub things out, and looked around for soapy water. The Boatswain pointed to another pot of bad-smelling stuff, so I dipped the brushes in that, and the paint did come off quite well. Once they were clean I left them to dry, and followed him and Masou back onto the deck.

"Well, he ain't lying about painting, at any rate," said the Boatswain to Mr. Newman. "He's done handsomely on the Captain's picture. Reckon they've both worked hard enough to get fed, now."

That was a relief. My stomach was so hollow it was making very strange *squeak-bubble* noises.

Mr. Newman nodded, so we went down steps and then more steps, down and down to the bilges where the Cook was. He was a scrawny man in a filthy shirt and jerkin and when I said "sir" to him, remembering what Masou had told me, he snorted. "You call me Cook, boy, that'll do. Squat over there to eat." He pointed to a space between two beer barrels. Then he slopped something that looked like vomit into two wooden bowls and gave them to Masou and me, along with a hunk of bread each and a big leather beaker of ale.

I drank my ale down at once, then looked at the stuff in the bowl. Masou was already hunkered down on his haunches, next to a barrel, throwing bread into his mouth. There wasn't room for us at any of the benches, and all the men were ignoring us.

"What is this?" I whispered, squatting next to him.

"Bacon and pease pottage," he whispered back. "As I am a Mussulman, I should not eat it, for the pig is unclean, but there is nothing else."

"Oh." I looked at it. I don't think I'd ever had it before. I tried a bit, and found it was very salty and strange tasting, but I was so hungry I ate half of it. Then somebody barged into me from behind and knocked me flying, so the food went on the deck.

"Watch where you're going!" I shouted, furious that my bit of bread was now on the dirty floor.

It was the sullen-looking boy again. "You watch

where you're sitting," he sneered. "You're in my way."

"No, I'm not," I defended myself. "You just did that on purpose—"

"You calling me a liar?" shouted the boy.

One of the men laughed, and tapped his neighbour. "Temper, Tom!" he called. But instead of doing something about the boy, they settled back to watch. Another man put down some pennies, and then another, and I suddenly realized they were laying bets on us.

Tom lifted up his fist and waved it under my nose. "I'm older'n you and I'm a sailor and you're not. So you do what I say."

Masou could see I was tempted to answer back and elbowed me hard. "Leave it," he whispered in my ear. "We don't want to get into a fight."

But then Tom kicked Masou's bowl over and shoved him flying into a barrel!

"What did you do that for?" I shouted at him.

"'Cause I choose," he spat. "'Cause I'm better'n you and that slave boy, and you better remember it."

I slapped him hard across the face. How *dare* he call Masou a slave?

He roared, and then hit me so hard on the side of the face, I fell to the ground. Tom had punched me! Me! A Maid of Honour to the Queen!

Masou cannoned into him, fists flying, and knocked him sideways. I stared for a second as I climbed to my feet, astonished at Masou, who was supposed to be the sensible one. Unfortunately, he isn't very big—or good at fighting—and that beefy Tom knocked him down with one of his big fists, and then kicked him.

That really made me lose my temper. Everything went all slow and cold. I'm not sure how I managed it, but I caught up some of the pottage from the floor and threw it in Tom's face, and then somehow I got my arm round his neck while he was trying to wipe it off, and started squeezing. He was terribly strong, and his arms flailed, but I just kept on squeezing while his face went red—and I hit his ear a couple of times too. . . .

Masou had climbed to his feet, with a wicked look on his face and his knife in his hand; at that, two of the men pounced on us, lifted Masou out of the way, and grabbed me by the shoulder.

"Let go," growled the one holding me. "Let go, right now."

After a moment, when the roaring in my ears had faded a bit, I did let go of Tom's neck. Tom fell to his knees, choking and gasping. Then he stood up, with a knife in his hand, too.

"Put it away, Tom," said the man behind me. "You got beat, now live with it."

Some of the other men clapped and started paying their bets. I thought we'd get some terrible punishment—but nobody said anything.

Masou picked his bread up off the floor before a hopeful rat got to it, and I did the same. Then I decided not to eat it because it had got trampled in the fight. The rat could have it, and welcome.

The three of us were ordered to clean up the mess made by the fight. I watched Tom like a hawk in case he tried to attack again, but he just scowled and did the minimum he could get away with. But I noticed that while he was cleaning, he carefully picked up all the spilled bits of bacon and put them on a bit of wood he had hidden in a corner. When he had gathered all he could find, he went to Cook and muttered something. I nearly sprained my ears trying to listen to them.

"Not again, Tom," Cook sighed.

"Captain said I could. It's for herself," Tom told him.

I was so excited I practically scrubbed a hole in the planks.

Cook shook his head and handed over a small

bowl of drinking water. "You're soft on her," he accused.

"I'm not soft!" grunted Tom, and he skulked off into the darkness.

I tried to catch Masou's eye, but he wasn't paying attention. I was desperate to talk to him. Both of them had said "her"! And this ship was full of men and boys only. Well, I was there, but nobody knew I was a girl. They must have been talking about Sarah!

I wished and wished I could follow Tom to wherever he was taking the supplies, but I couldn't. Cook was watching us. I made careful note of which direction he had gone in, and that was all I could do—which was terribly frustrating. Of course, it was awful for Sarah, being fed leftover bacon that had been on the floor, and nothing but water to drink. I could only think that Drake was sorely vexed with her—Sarah is very trying, and perhaps she had refused to give in to his wicked plans! But Masou and I weren't doing too well, either. My face was puffing up in a bruise, and Masou had a split lip.

As we finished working, Cook kept shaking his head and chuckling to himself. "Don't think any of 'em expected to see you give Tom a run for his money like that," he said to me, shaking his head. "You've got some spirit in you, lad. No wonder you've run away to sea. I done the same myself, in my time."

I saw a great opportunity: Cook would likely know everything that went on aboard the *Judith*. So I pretended to be interested in hearing how he had run away to sea—and had to listen to a very long and unlikely tale about how he'd "nearly got sunk and drownded with the King's Great Ship and then fought the French hand to hand." I made impressed noises as he told me, then, when he'd finished, I risked a question. "Do you know what the Captain's up to on this voyage, Cook?" I asked casually.

"Oh, aye, hoping for some plunder, eh?" Cook assumed. He tapped his nose. "Well, Captain did put to sea in an almighty hurry—we'd not even fully finished loading our supplies. He might've caught wind of whatever it was Captain Derby was hurrying to find. But nobody knows for sure. Captain's not said yet what we're up to."

I decided to risk another. "Um . . . have you ever known anyone . . . bring a woman to sea on the *Judith,* Cook?" I asked, busily scrubbing the pot in my hands.

Cook chuckled. "Oh, aye," he said—it seemed to be his favourite phrase. My heart leaped, thinking he was going to tell me of Lady Sarah! "There was that Sam Pike," he went on. My heart sank again. "See, he was lately wed, and desperate for to keep his wife close by him. So he smuggled her aboard dressed as a sailor and she hid in the cable tiers, and the sail locker, and even the brig. And when the Captain came round for his inspections, you never saw such a flurry, what with Sam and his mates shifting her out of the hold and into the galley one step ahead of him. I did laugh. Course, she got tired of it and fell asleep one night in Sam's bed, and the Captain found her . . . Oh, aye, he was fit to be tied, was the Captain . . . Would have flogged Sam, he said, only he was such a good topman. Mrs. Pike spent the rest of the voyage shut up in a cabin, sewing, and couldn't wait to get off the ship when we came home to Plymouth."

Cook shook his head again, grinning. "Oh, aye, the men are always trying it on, but the Captain, he just won't have it. He said, clear as clear, he said, 'I'd as soon have a raging bull on my poop deck as a woman stowed away in the cable tiers for the men to fight and grieve over.' That's what he said."

I grinned back, all the while thinking what a hypocrite Drake was—abducting Lady Sarah without a by-your-leave, and then keeping her hidden away somewhere aboard ship! I tried one last line of investigation: "Oh," I said, "it's just that I thought I saw a woman in one of the cabins, Cook. Very pretty, red hair, with a figure . . ." I made a curvy shape in the air, as I'd seen gentlemen do about Sarah when they didn't know I was watching.

Cook laughed and swatted me lightly with a ladle. "You're too young to be thinking sinful thoughts, Greg. You get your back into cleaning these here pots—that'll settle you down for the night."

Masou shook his head as we worked away at cleaning the black iron pots with sand. It was really hard work, and quite stinky, and my hands got sore from the sand. I kept thinking of Lady Sarah, in irons in the brig—which was where I thought she must be hidden since few seemed aware of her presence and she was being fed on scraps. But by the time we finished, all I could think of was how lucky she was to be sitting down and not having to work. At last Cook said we could stop.

I was exhausted. "Do you know where we are to sleep, Cook?" I asked him.

"Here, it's the last space we've got," he said, pointing at the gap between the barrels where Masou and I had eaten. "I've counted every onion and cabbage, and if there's even one missing in the morning, I'll beat you."

"But what if the rats eat them, Cook?" I asked.

"That's why you're here," he replied. "Keep 'em away, and you won't get beaten, see?" He seemed quite friendly now—he even gave us a filthy blanket to share. Then he hung a candle-lantern from a beam so we could see the rats, and left us.

I lay down awkwardly, top to tail with Masou. I'd slept on a straw pallet on the floor when on progress, but never on the *actual* floor! The planks were really hard, and I was so tired my head was spinning, plus my ear was hurting and my cheek felt like a sore pillow—and bits of me were all bruised where Tom's fists had flailed. This adventure was turning out to be a very uncomfortable one—even for a Lady Pursuivant.

Masou's lip was swollen, too, but he seemed to find something funny, chuckling away to himself.

"What?" I asked crossly.

He shook his head. "Where did Lady Grace Cavendish learn to fight like that?" he mused.

I scowled, because I was a bit embarrassed about it.

Masou reached over and patted my leg. "You make quite a boy, Gregory," he said. Then he put his head on his arm and seemed to fall asleep at once.

I kept hearing skittering in the shadows, and then a pair of small eyes shone red in the lamplight. I threw a bit of squashed bread at them.

Masou snored gently and annoyingly beside me, but I think that even if the planks had been soft as pillows, I would not have been able to sleep— because I kept thinking of Tom taking food to someone who was a "her"! Who could it be except Sarah? Cook must have been lying to me. I had to find her. And I could not leave further search a moment longer!

I considered waking Masou to let him know what I was up to, but he was in such a deep sleep, I decided against it. And anyway, it would be easier to creep around, and hide, on my own.

I got up very quietly, left my boots and socks off, and crept along to the ladder.

The hatch was down, but not bolted. I pushed it up slowly, hoisted myself out, and crept along again.

I knew, from listening to the sailors talking, that there'd be a watch kept on deck, but below decks was different. Down here, the sailors who weren't on watch were bundled up, snoring, all over the place—and every deck smelled worse than the last—of sweat mainly, but also of onions and beer and salt fish, and that thing which happens to your bowels when you eat too much pease pudding.

I went all the way aft to the stern. We hadn't been able to search the rear of the ship properly before we were shut in the sail locker. I was praying that more of the doors might be open—and some of them were—but they were storerooms with nobody in them.

There was a hatch next to the capstan and I opened it and peered in. I could see thick anchor ropes in the shadows. They smelled horrible: salty mud and rotten seaweed. "Lady Sarah?" I called softly. "Are you there?"

But there was no reply, just the creaking of the ship and the clopping of the water, and loud snoring coming from somewhere else.

Further along, I found a door with a big lock on it and guessed it was the brig, because it had a tiny hatch to pass food through. Heart thudding, I opened the hatch—and the smell from within almost knocked me down by itself! Hell's teeth! Now I hoped Lady Sarah was *not* in there! Bracing myself, I put my face to the hatch again, and called softly.

There was no answer, and I was relieved that Lady Sarah was not languishing in such a hell-hole—but where else was there to look? I wondered desperately.

Then I remembered Cook's story of Sam Pike—and how he had moved his wife around the ship, while hiding her. Captain Drake didn't have to keep Sarah in one place either, did he? I rolled my eyes. There was no help for it—I couldn't possibly go to sleep thinking about that. I would have to search everywhere afresh.

So I crept forward again, looking carefully in all the cabins, hiding in the shadows when some sailors came by.

I found myself outside the sail locker again. I opened the door and, just for a second, I thought I'd found her. There was a candle guttering on the floor and someone lying curled up there. "Lady Sarah?" I whispered cautiously.

The shape on the floor moved. By then I had realized it was too big and the wrong shape to be Lady

Sarah. It was that ugly bully, Tom. Why he was sleeping there, I didn't know, but I didn't want to get into another fight with him, so I turned to creep away.

Suddenly a hand caught my shoulder and slammed me against the wall. "What you doing here?" Tom growled.

I thought quickly, and said the first thing that came into my head: "I . . . I've come to see the kittens." Then I shut my mouth in horror. What would he think? He'd guess I was a girl now, surely!

Tom loomed over me. I couldn't see his face in the candle shadows. "If you're coming to drown them kittens—" he began.

"Of course not!" I cried, shocked at such a thought. "I just came to see them."

The big hand let go of my shoulder. "That right, then?"

"Yes. What are *you* doing here?" I demanded, remembering how Masou always fared better by standing up for himself.

Tom drew himself up straighter. "I'm guarding, that's what."

"What?" I asked, sounding very stupid.

"I'm not letting any of them sailors drown 'er kittens." He was scowling now.

"Well, of course you shouldn't," I said. "Who would want to do a thing like that?"

"Some of 'em," Tom muttered. "They reckon it's a bit of fun. But I'm not having it. And I don't *care* if they say Tom Webster's soft. Them kittens is stayin' safe until they can go to other ships. We've got plenty of rats for 'em."

I was outraged that some might see it as sport to harm the kittens. "You're *not* soft, Tom," I said, forgetting I'd fought him. "You're doing what's right."

He grunted and stood there, looking at me for a while. "You want to see 'em?"

I squatted down and peered next to the candle in its holder. There were the kittens, lying in a heap on their mother, who was purring softly.

"Don't try and stroke her, she'll scratch you," Tom warned, smiling fondly. "She's a fierce one."

I looked for a while longer. Then I had to ask him. "Tom, why did you fight me and my friend?"

Tom shrugged. "Bull's-eye Jarvis bet me a shilling I couldn't beat the two of you, so I took him on."

"But why?" I persisted. "We never did either of you any harm."

"I can't let them think I'm soft, can I?" Tom replied gruffly.

I shook my head. It all sounded daft to me: Tom didn't have to fight complete strangers to show he was tough. I thought much better of him now, though—and so would Masou. "Well, a Knight of the Queen also protects the weak, and is regarded as the bravest of the brave," I said.

"What do you know about it?" sniffed Tom.

"I was apprenticed in the Queen's Wardrobe, it's a Department of State," I told him.

"Is that why you talk funny?" Tom asked.

"Er . . . yes," I replied. "Anyway, as I was saying, a Knight of the Queen should be brave in battle against the strong to defend the weak, and gentle with the weak themselves. That's how you know he's a gentleman."

"Oh," Tom mumbled. It looked as if he needed to think hard about that one.

While he was doing so, I decided I might as well sidle away. He didn't stop me: he was too busy frowning with the effort of thinking.

I did look in a few more places, but had no luck, and by now I was feeling sadly discouraged. I was so sure Tom had been taking the bacon scraps to

Lady Sarah, but obviously they had been for the ship's cat instead—and I was no nearer to finding Sarah. My eyes felt hot and sore, and they started dropping shut by themselves. Wearily I climbed back down to the galley and lay down next to Masou under the blanket, even though I knew I would never ever get to sleep on such a hard floor, with all the smells and snores and strange sounds of the ship.

Almost instantly, it seemed, it was morning! A bell was clanging, and I felt just awful. I hurt all over. I seemed to have lumps and bumps on every bit of me, and my hands and shoulders ached.

Masou woke then—and he seemed to be in better shape. I suppose he is more used to climbing and brawling than I!

Cook came to make breakfast—which was the most horrible grey salty porridge, with more ale and bread. This time I ate the bread, which was like leather, and gave Masou my porridge. Then there was a clanging and a banging, and all the sailors rushed up the ladder.

Cook pointed at it. "All hands on deck," he said. "Captain wants to talk to the men. You want to know what we're doing—now's your chance to find out. Up you go."

Masou and I went up to the main deck and stood at the back, behind the tallest sailors we could find, in case the Captain saw me and recognized me. From here, we couldn't see Drake at all, but Masou was happy just to listen to his speech. I wanted to see Drake so I peered round the sailors and managed to get a glimpse of him.

There he was, standing on the very top, aftmost deck, his handsome face both happy and serious. He should be happy! Probably he was going to marry Lady Sarah now. I scowled at him heavily, even though he couldn't see me. How dare he do it? What an evil man—and I'd thought he was kind.

"Well, men," he said, and his Devonshire voice carried the length of the ship without his seeming to shout. "I don't doubt you're wondering why we put to sea in such an almighty hurry!"

There was a rumble of answering "Aye, sir"s.

"I'm not sure what's afoot," Captain Drake went on, "but I know that Captain Derby put to sea a day early, and I'd like to have a sniff of whatever he's after. Could be a nice fat Spanish Netherland merchant, could be sea beggars, could even be a Spanish treasure ship gone astray."

Most of the men cheered.

"So we're making the same heading as he. I know the places where he likes to cruise and if we keep a sharp lookout, we might see his prize afore he does." Drake smiled—well, he showed his teeth, really—and smacked his fist in his palm. "Then we'll snap her up!"

All the men cheered and waved their fists at that.

"I've a letter of marque from the Queen—that's Her Majesty Queen Elizabeth, her very self!" he shouted, waving a piece of paper. At the Queen's name everyone cheered again. "So we can take any ship we don't like the look of, so long as she ain't English nor Hollander nor Allemayne."

Really loud cheering.

"Now, I'm telling you what I heard," Drake added. "I heard there's a Spanish man-of-war out in the Narrow Seas, carrying the foul Duke of Alva's letter of marque, and he's been a-taking of our ships, what's more. Now we can't be having that, can we, boys?"

Roars of "No, sir, we'll have they Spaniels to our breakfast!"

"So keep a sharp lookout and be ready, and there's prize money fat and bright just waiting for the taking!" Drake finished.

Wildly enthusiastic cheering.

Masou and I looked at each other. What did Drake think he was doing, going on a privateering expedition with Lady Sarah on board? When was he going to marry her?

"What happened to that pretty Court fish you pulled out of the water the other day, Captain?" asked the Carpenter with a knowing grin, as if he'd read my mind.

Captain Drake paused and frowned. "I'll have none of the likes of you making no comments about any fair lady of Her Majesty's Court, Jim Woolley, you hear?"

"Aye, sir," said the man, sounding abashed. "Sorry, sir."

"I'll tell you the truth, men!" shouted Drake. "I'll not deny I laid suit to her for she'm the fairest I've ever seen, with all her red hair and her pretty ways. But just afore we sailed, she wrote me and told me, I'm not rich enough for her—and that's fair enough, for she's gently bred and expensive for to keep, what's more. So we're out to get rich this voyage, lads, fast as we can, and then I can go courting again with a hatful of gold!"

They all hooted and cheered at that, while Masou and I gaped at each other.

Captain Drake turned away and went to talk to Mr. Newman.

Masou and I got shouted at to go below and help Cook. While I cleared away the officers' mess, scrubbing the tables with silver sand and lye, I tried to think. It didn't make any sense. What was Drake talking about, going courting with a hatful of gold? He didn't need to if he already had Lady Sarah on board. . . .

Then Tom came and grunted at us. "Mr. Newman wants you," he said. "Best go quick."

Up on the deck, Masou and I knuckled our foreheads to Mr. Newman.

"Captain wants a sharp lookout kept," he told us. "You go up to the foremast top and stay there, until I tell you to come down or you see anything at all—a sail, a sea monster, anything."

As we went over to the rail, I turned to Masou. "I don't believe it, he—"

Somebody shoved us.

"What are you doing yapping away?" snarled the wide man who had first discovered us on the ship. "You get aloft and keep watch, and you'd better do it right."

"Aye, sir," I said, swallowing hard. I was almost

pleased we were to go up the mast again, so I could talk to Masou in peace! But Hell's teeth! Those awful ratlines again . . .

There was no help for it, so we climbed up and up and up—and I struggled up and backwards and over the side of the top again, grabbing for ropes to hold onto.

When I'd got my breath back I could see that Tom was over on the mainmast fighting top, shading his eyes to keep a lookout. We squinted into the distance, too, me facing one way, Masou the other. At last we could talk.

I spoke first. "I think that perhaps Captain Drake does not have Lady Sarah at all!" I said.

Masou looked as if he'd been thinking just the same thing. "Well, we've seen no sign of her anywhere on the ship, have we?" he muttered. "And after what Drake said in his speech . . ."

I nodded miserably. It made my stomach swoop to think we'd got ourselves trapped on a privateering ship for nothing! "So where can she be?" I asked, full of frustration.

Masou shrugged and spread his hands wide.

I took out the forged letter, which I still had in my doublet, and squinted at it. Somehow, I had read the evidence wrongly. But if Captain Drake hadn't taken Lady Sarah, who had? I sighed heavily. "I must tell Captain Drake what has been going on," I admitted. "Maybe he can take us back to Tilbury and there will be news there of Lady Sarah." I stuffed the letter away again, went to the side, and started sliding backwards over it, feeling for the ropes with my toes.

"What if he throws you in the brig?" Masou demanded anxiously.

"It can't be helped. I've still got to try," I puffed, letting myself down carefully. "You keep watch, so we don't get into more trouble."

I climbed the rest of the way, sliding a bit because I was in such a hurry. Mr. Newman was busy with a big sail at the front of the ship, so I dodged two sailors and ran to the back deck (sorry, aft), where I wasn't supposed to go at all. Facing the door of the Great Cabin, feeling sick with fright, I knocked.

"Enter," came the Captain's voice.

I opened the door and peered inside apprehensively. "Captain, sir, please may I talk with you?"

Drake was bending over charts on the table, but in fact he wasn't looking at them, he was staring at a letter. He glanced up and frowned at me.

I grabbed my hat off my head, came into the cabin, shut the door, and bowed low. "Sir, I really must talk with you," I said.

"Who are you, boy?"

He hadn't recognized me! I hesitated. Should I tell him who I really was? No, not yet. He would be surprised half to death—and he had to concentrate on what I had to say. "I'm Gregory, sir."

"Ah yes, the stowaway who's a painter," Drake remembered. "You did well on the paintings, lad. I'll have you do some more for me once we're out of dangerous waters."

"Thank you, sir." I thought fast. "But, begging your pardon, I'm really a page. Lady Sarah Bartelmy's page, sir . . ."

At the mention of Lady Sarah's name, Drake's blue eyes bored into me like needles.

"She's missing, sir," I continued. "And I thought at first that she might be on this ship, so I came to find her. . . ."

Drake frowned, and those fiery blue eyes chilled to ice. I felt terrified. Being frowned at by Drake was like being hit in the forehead.

"And then the ship set sail, and . . . um . . . here I am . . . ," I finished. "Only Lady Sarah sent this letter to the Queen, sir. . . ." I hurried forward, deciding it wouldn't hurt to be a bit courtly, as if I really were a page, and went down on one knee to give him the letter, as if he were an earl or a duke.

He snatched the letter from me in irritation, but as he read it, his ruddy face paled.

"It's a forgery, sir, I know that much," I told him. "My Lady Sarah pens her *y*s quite different."

Drake's face was a mixture of puzzlement and fury. I thought he might start shouting at me, but instead he handed me the letter he had been reading when I came in.

I read it quickly. This is what it said:

Palace of Placentia, Greenwich
The seventh day of May, in the Year of Our Lord 1569

Sir,
  My noble father hath written unto me this day that he hath found for me a husband of a like blood and land as myself. Our dalliance must be at an end for my revered parents would never countenance that I should so dispar-age myself as to wed a man of lesser breeding and wealth.
                                    Sarah, Lady Bartelmy

I squinted at the *y*s—and sure enough, they had no curly tails. "This is a forgery, too," I declared.

"But the pearl bracelet I gave her was returned with the letter," Drake said slowly. "And now she's missing, you say?"

"Yes, sir," I confirmed. "My friend Masou saw her being helped on board a boat at the Greenwich river steps."

"Where is this Masou?" Drake demanded.

"He's up the mast, keeping watch, sir," I replied. "We came on board the night before last, sir, trying to find Lady Sarah—only we got locked in the sail locker by accident, and Mr. Newman thinks we're stowaways so he sent us up the mast—"

"Stay there!" Drake commanded, already striding out of his cabin.

Just at that moment I heard a faint shout.

"Sail!" It was Masou's voice. "Sail, ho!" he shouted again.

I rushed out on deck, too.

"Where away?" shouted the Boatswain.

"That way!" came Masou's faint reply. He was much higher than the top—he was right up where we'd freed the banner, clinging like a monkey and pointing.

"Mr. Newman, make more sail!" Captain Drake bellowed.

I was puzzled—surely they didn't have time to make sails, and anyway, there were plenty in the sail locker. But then I saw that Drake meant the crew to open up more sails on the masts, to catch more wind and move the ship faster.

He jumped up to the rail and started to climb the ratlines, smoothly and surely as if he were just climbing some stairs. I scrambled up after him, after tucking both letters in my doublet.

Puffing and clawing over the side of the fighting top, I saw Drake's boots, and then felt him lift me up by my jerkin. He didn't seem to mind that I hadn't stayed where I was told. He was staring into the distance, where there were two white notches on the horizon. Masou was sliding down from his high perch, looking scared and worried.

"Tell me exactly what you saw when you watched Lady Sarah get in the boat at Greenwich," Drake ordered Masou. "Whom was she with?"

"You're Captain Drake, sir?" Masou asked, sounding very surprised.

"Aye, son, that's my name."

"Well, she was with a taller man than you, sir, with light hair," Masou told him.

I stared at Masou, incredulous. He hadn't recognized the man helping Lady Sarah into the boat as being someone other than Captain Drake? Then I realized that Masou had never seen Drake before now. It had been *I* who had told *him* that the man in the boat was Captain Drake. Because Mary and I had assumed it to be. . . .

"Straw-coloured hair? Green woollen suit?" demanded Drake, his face intent.

"Yes, sir." Masou nodded. "No chin."

"Hugh Derby," Drake concluded grimly.

Horrified, I realized what had really happened: *Derby* had abducted Lady Sarah, and had tried to make it look like Captain Drake had!

The Captain leaned casually over the edge of the platform to bellow some orders at Mr. Newman, who was staring up at us. I wasn't sure what the orders were about, because they were entirely in Sailorish—something about putting bonnets on the sails and then something about a direction. . . .

"And Mr. Newman . . . ," Drake added.

"Aye, sir?" Mr. Newman asked.

"Clear for battle stations," Drake finished coolly.

Mr. Newman's face lit up. "Aye aye, sir!"

The ship below us erupted like a stepped-on ants' nest—people were running everywhere—but it was a very organized sort of chaos. Soon more sails were unwrinkling themselves, and the yards—they're the wooden beams that support the sails—were being pulled into different positions by ropes—called lines.

The *Judith* began moving faster through the water, and changed direction towards the two distant ships that Masou had spotted.

"So Captain Derby took her," murmured Drake thoughtfully. "And tried to lay the blame on me."

Both Masou and I nodded.

Drake looked up. "I want the topsail set," he said. "We're here so we'll do it. Up you go."

My heart lurched. "I don't know what to do, sir," I told him. "I'm a page, not a sailor."

"I know that. I'll tell you what to do," Drake assured me.

He followed us up the ratlines to where the top-yard crossed the mast. Then he told us to get our toes on the toe-rope and lean over the yard and shuffle along. Masou did it first. It's a tree, I told myself; it's a tree branch and there are cherries in an awkward place. I love cherries. So I gulped again, leaned over the yard, felt for the rope, and sort of slid along on my stomach. Everything whirled for a moment.

"Don't forget to breathe, lad," I heard Drake's voice say—and it sounded as though he were sauntering in a garden. He was next to the mast, busy with ropes. "Now you'll see a reef knot in front of you. Untie it, loosen the rope, and let the sail drop."

Yes, there was a knotted rope in front of me, holding the sail tight to the yard, which was rocking wildly. It's a tree, I said to myself again, just a tree. I fumbled at the knot, picking at it one-handed, the other hand holding tight to the wooden yard. At last, after I broke a nail, it came undone.

"Come back now," said Drake.

I slid back along the yard, grabbed the ratlines, and stepped back onto them, wobbling from sheer fright. Drake caught my shoulder and held me steady until I could catch my breath and get a proper grip. Then he did more mysterious stuff with rope, shouted, and the topsail plopped out and was pulled taut from below. The ship leaned over further and picked up speed.

Drake started climbing down again. Masou and I followed, although I was still shaking.

Back on the fighting top once more, it felt almost as good as a deck.

"So you're Lady Sarah's page and you came to help her, though you know nothing of the sea?" Drake asked, staring at me shrewdly. I nodded.

Masou was listening to this with fascination.

Drake turned to him next. "And you came to help your friend here?" he asked. Masou nodded, too.

Then Drake held out his hand for us to shake, so we did, fumbling with surprise. "I like courage and enterprise in any man, and faithfulness in any friend," he said soberly. I felt my heart swell with pride. "Can either of you use weapons?" he then asked.

"I can shoot with a bow, sir," I said, which is true, since I've been taught archery to go hunting with the Queen—except I've never had the heart to shoot anything alive. But I'm quite good at targets.

"A knife," said Masou, eyes narrowing. "I can throw a knife."

"Hm," said Drake with a smile, "so can I. We'll have a contest one day." He shaded his eyes and peered out over the water. Suddenly he grinned most ferociously. "Unless I've gone blind, I'd say that smaller ship is Captain Derby's *Silver Arrow*," he observed. "And he's in trouble by the looks of it, for that larger one is the Spaniard that's been taking of our ships."

"But aren't they both flying the English flag?" I asked, squinting in the same direction.

"Aye, well, just a little entertainment for us,"

Drake said. "Me, I'd say that bigger ship's rigging is from Vigo—Spain."

He leaned over and shouted to Mr. Newman again. A flag travelled up the mainmast and flapped in the wind—I recognized the double eagle of the Habsburgs of Spain.

"Something to entertain them, too," said Drake with a laugh. "Now, boys, my thinking is that they Spaniels are shaping to take Captain Derby's ship, which would be a pity seeing it's his only livelihood."

"And what about Lady Sarah?" I asked anxiously.

"Derby was smitten with her, I know that, for he nearly challenged me to a duel for sending her that bracelet," Drake explained. "And so I think he did, in sooth, take her by force." His eyes then turned all soft. "I hope such a delicate lady stays out of harm's way in the next hour," he added.

He wasn't looking at me, thank goodness, he was staring into space, mooning about Sarah Copperlocks Bartelmy again. Hell's teeth! Even as his ship was preparing to go into battle! What *is* it men see in her?

I was more worried about being caught up in a battle—for myself *and* Lady Sarah! I could see the two ships in the distance drawing steadily closer. A mixture of fear and excitement made my stomach feel like a posset-cup. My mouth was all dry, too. Was there really going to be a sea battle? I couldn't believe it. How had it happened?

"Now," said Captain Drake, holding onto a line. "Two likely boys like you, I expect you'll want to be right in the thick of the fighting. Alas, I must disappoint you, and there'll be no gainsaying me. I can't have you down on the deck, for you might get in the way of us boarding. But you can fight from up here, understand?"

Masou and I both nodded—me because my mouth was so dry, my lips were stuck together. Want to be in the thick of the fight? In on a battle? Me? What if I got hurt or killed? (I thought killed might be better—much less embarrassing.)

"Masou, you run down and fetch a bow and quivers for your mate, and some fire pots and slow match for yourself, then come straight back up again," Drake ordered.

"Aye, sir," croaked Masou, then he swung himself over the side to go down.

"You, lad," said Drake, staring at me very hard. "What's your name?"

"Gra—Gregory," I stammered. I'd nearly told him my name was Grace!

"Hm. Well, Gregory, there's more to you than meets the eye, something not quite right. I know I've seen you before, but I cannot place you."

"Maybe you saw me attending my Lady Sarah," I said, trying not to squeak with nerves.

"Perhaps," the Captain acknowledged. "At any rate, I can't put my finger on it. Are you dealing straight with me, lad?"

"I came to find Lady Sarah," I said. "I never meant to stow—"

"No, I believe you on that matter," Drake cut in. "It's something else."

I felt as if his eyes were drilling holes in me.

He stared for a little longer and then seemed to come to a decision. "Aye, well, I've not leisure for it now, but you'll tell me after, if you're spared." He wasn't asking a question, he was stating a fact.

I swallowed hard.

There was a sound of climbing, and Masou reappeared, with bags and a bow slung over his back, and some slow match wrapped around his wrist.

"Ah, Masou, well done. Listen to what I want you to do." The Captain had his tinder box out of his belt pouch and was lighting a candle, and then, carefully, the slow match. "Here's your slow match—keep it away from the fire pots. Light the fuses one at a time, then throw the fire pot nice and easy into the rigging of the Spaniel ship, understand?"

"Aye, sir," Masou said.

The Captain then turned to me. "Now, Gregory, these are fire arrows. Light them from Masou's slow match and aim 'em for the sails, understand? When we're grappled for boarding, shoot the ordinary arrows at the Spaniels, but once I lead the men across the boarding plank, stop shooting, for you might shoot me!"

"Aye, sir," I said.

Drake smiled, his eyes serious and yet somehow also full of excitement. He seemed to be looking forward to the fight.

He clapped both of us on the back, then swung himself over the edge of the top and slid, hand over hand, down a rope.

Masou and I stared at each other, and then Masou crowed with laughter and punched the air with his fist. "I always wanted to be in a battle!" he shouted. "I am a warrior—and the finest acrobat in Mr. Somers's troop. *Allah akhbar!*"

I think boys—men—are all complete Bedlamites. They're all mad. Adventures are one thing, but a battle! My heart was thudding away, my palms all sweaty. I needed to make water, but I couldn't on the draughty top.

To have something to do, I got the bow Masou had brought up to me and strung it. It was quite small and not too stiff—I had bent stronger bows before. But I was scared of shooting a fire arrow. There were twelve of them, with pitch-soaked wadding wrapped round the head and a lump of clay behind the fletching to balance them. There were twenty-four of the ordinary arrows, too—along with a bracer and gloves, which I put on.

Then I noticed her, the mother cat, climbing determinedly up the rigging towards me, with a kitten in her mouth. I stared disbelievingly. What was she doing?

I realized she must have been ousted from her nice warm nest in the sail locker, and now she was looking for a safe place. I heard a squeak nearby and looked round—there were three little furry, big-eyed faces peering over the side of a coil of rope just next to the mast. I stared at the mother as she climbed higher and higher, clinging with her claws. As if I didn't have enough to worry about already! Once she almost slipped, but a sailor who was lacing another bit to the bottom of a sail to make it bigger just caught her in his hand and placed her higher up. And on she climbed with her kitten.

A drum started beating down on the deck. *Boom-boom-boom, boom-da-da boom-da-da boom!* There was something wild and dangerous and threatening about the beat—it made my heart beat along with it. The sailors were singing something, growling deep and loud. It sounded very fierce.

The two other ships were quite close now, and they were joined together by a plank and grappling hooks. You could easily see that one of the ships was much bigger—it was flying a Habsburg double eagle now and it had three masts. The smaller ship only had two masts—and a big pile of wreckage lay on the deck where half of one had fallen down. There were white splintery scrapes where cannon-balls had hit, and what looked like bloodstains on the deck. Some kind of swirling battle was raging on the smaller ship, the *Silver Arrow,* but a few of the fighters were scrambling back across ropes to the Spanish ship.

I looked up at the *Judith*'s mainmast. The Habsburg double eagle was coming down and the red-on-white Cross of St. George was just flying free.

The mother cat appeared over the edge of the fighting top and leaped into the coil of rope, where she settled down. All the kittens started feeding and kneading her with their paws.

BOOM!

It was the loudest noise I'd ever heard, and I nearly fell off the fighting top with fright. One of the guns on the deck had fired. Drake was on the poop deck, bellowing more Sailorish orders. The yards moved, and sent our ship leaning in towards the other two. Another gun fired. The *Judith* sailed past the grappled ships, on the other side of the Spaniard. Oh, good, I thought, maybe no battle. But then the guns poking out of the side of the *Judith* started firing.

BOOM! BOOM! BOOM! BOOM! BOOM!

The whole ship quivered. Clouds of smoke made it look as if we were sitting on a little island above the clouds. There was screaming from the Spanish ship. One of its cannons fired back, and splinters showered from the place where the cannonball had struck the *Judith*.

Drake yelled up to us. Masou licked his lips, lit a fire pot from the slow match, and lobbed it carefully into the Spanish ship's fighting top. Flames rose up, followed by hissing as someone doused it with water. I nocked an arrow and Masou blew on the glowing slow match and lit the pitch-soaked wadding. It felt very hot, even through the leather glove. I felt the heat on my face, and fired without really aiming, high in an arch, just to get rid of it. I don't think I hit anything.

Masou was already throwing again. I glimpsed Tom firing arrows, too, so I lit another one of mine, aimed for a sail as a target—and hit it. I watched the fire catch and spread.

Every so often, Tom would stare wildly in our direction. I wondered why, until suddenly I smelled burning close by. I stared wildly around. The cat was cowering deep in the coil of rope, with her kittens beneath her—too late she must have realized what an unwise place she had chosen. When one kitten tried to struggle out to look, she whacked it with a paw and pushed it back. Her fur was all on end and she was hissing. She was so small and so brave, it made me feel better at once.

I smelled a horrible stink. Some of the tarry ropes in our rigging were burning—there was a fire arrow stuck there from the boys in the Spanish ship's top. They jeered in Spanish—they hadn't noticed that their own sail was burning.

"Masou!" I gasped, pointing at the flames in the rigging.

"Later," said Masou, narrowing his eyes and lobbing another fire pot into the crow's nest of the other ship.

I couldn't believe he was ignoring the fact that we might get burned to death! But I lit another fire arrow, too—fired, and fired again, always aiming away from the people. I just didn't want to kill anyone, not even a Spaniard. They hadn't done me any harm, even if they were trying to now!

Masou had thrown all the fire pots and had started several fires in the Spanish ship's rigging. Now he took one of the bags of sand hanging above the fighting top platform, and climbed out along the ropes to get at the fire in our own rigging, which was now spreading.

I watched in horror as he hung by his knees, slit the sandbag, and poured sand into the place where the flames were leaping, then banged the place with the empty bag, until the flames were all gone and only smoke was left. Arrows fired by the Spanish whizzed past him, and something banged and cracked splinters off the wood right next to me. It was a musket ball. Suddenly I realized properly that the Spaniards really were trying to kill us!

I grabbed my bow and fired back at them, so they had to stop shooting and duck down. I was furious. How dare they try to shoot Masou like that! As soon as I paused, more Spanish arrows came flying over, and I had to duck myself. Fortunately, the Spanish didn't aim very well, and several of their arrows stuck in the wood—which was good, because I could pull them out and shoot them back.

Next there was a dreadful grinding crash, and the whole ship shook like a leaf. Masou cried out. I peered over again. The rope he'd been hanging from had suddenly given way—he'd caught another one and was hanging by his hands, dangling over the deck, fifty feet below!

I heard a slam—they'd dropped the boarding plank onto the Spaniard's rail.

"Follow me!" roared Drake, and he ran across the plank with his sword in his right hand and his pistol in his left, followed by his drummer hammering the drum, and a horde of sailors, all waving short swords and axes. Some of them were swinging across from the rigging onto the boarding nets, and climbing up— while the Spanish sailors tried to stab them with spears. The two ships rocked and jolted and there was the most terrible clanging and screaming.

Nobody was going to help Masou except me. So I squinted at the rope he was dangling from, trying to work out which one it was, out of all the many ropes criss-crossing the sails. Masou wasn't far from the top of the big sail below us. At last I identified it— and luckily, the other end was attached to the fighting top. I unwound it part way, passed it round the mast, and then, holding my breath, unwound the rest of it and let it out a little at a time. Masou was very heavy, despite being small. I couldn't possibly pull him up, so I eased him down bit by bit, while trying to keep away from the flying arrows. "I'm letting you down to the yard!" I shouted.

Masou was staying absolutely still to make it easier for me, reaching with his toes for the yard. Once he touched it, I felt the weight lighten. I lowered him a little more, and then—I couldn't believe my eyes!—he just let go of the rope he'd been clinging to, and ran along the yard to the ratlines! He ran. Along a pole fifty feet up! And then, when he got to the ratlines, he reached out and swung onto them, then climbed up them to the fighting top. "Phew!" he said, and mopped his brow theatrically.

That was when I burst into tears, because I'd been so scared for him. He gave me a hug.

When I'd recovered, we peered over the top again—I'd run out of arrows by then. I saw Tom staring anxiously over again, so I waved and shouted, "The cat's all right! She's here!" I pointed to where the mother cat was still protecting her kittens in her coil of rope—thank goodness no arrows or fire pots had fallen there. After a moment, Tom smiled.

"What was that about?" asked Masou, frowning in puzzlement. "Why are you waving at that fat pig?"

"Oh, he's not so bad," I said. "Somebody put him up to bullying us. He's been looking after the kittens."

Masou blinked and then shook his head, looking bewildered.

When we looked over at the battle again, the huge swirling mass of fighting men had changed. It had now split into three groups, because the men on the *Silver Arrow* were helping Drake's men, and the Spanish were getting pushed back to the front part of their own ship. I saw something white flapping on the Spanish ship, and pointed it out to Masou.

The next moment, all the clanging and fighting and noise began to fade, then stopped. All I could hear was a lot of men panting and gasping for breath, and someone moaning in pain.

"Come on!" said Masou. "The Spanish have surrendered."

We climbed down in a hurry, and found that the men on the *Arrow* were cutting the Spaniard grappling ropes and trying to heave up the spiked boarding plank. I could see a tall man on the poop deck, shouting orders as Drake did, though he was too far away for me to be sure it was Derby.

Suddenly Drake was shouting orders, too. He stood on the rail of the highest deck on the Spaniard ship and jumped straight across onto the *Arrow*. Some of his men followed him. Meanwhile, Mr. Newman was aiming a pistol at the Spanish Captain, who was laying down his weapons.

Desperate to know what was happening, Masou and I picked our way across the deck, passing a man lying dead, an axe in his head. It made me want to be sick, so I tried not to look.

Masou jumped onto the boarding plank. "Come on, Gregory!" he shouted at me, then he ran along it, just as Drake had.

I ran after him, telling myself it was just like the top of the Orchard wall at Whitehall—which is easy

to walk along. The next thing I knew, we were cross-
ing the Spanish deck and then climbing onto the
Spaniard's boarding plank, to cross over to the
Arrow.

And then, at last, we were scrambling onto the
Arrow's aft-deck. We pushed to the front of the
crowd of sweaty sailors, and there was Captain
Drake, pointing his pistol at Derby. There was blood
on Drake's doublet, and his knuckles were grazed.

"All I want is a look in your Great Cabin, Derby,"
Drake was saying softly. "No more. We are old
friends, and besides, you owe me that for taking the
Spaniel for you."

Derby scowled. "What are you looking for?" he
demanded. "There's no treasure in there. The
booty's in the Spanish ship—bolts and bolts of silk
that he must have had off a merchant."

"Ah, but I think there *is* a treasure in that cabin,"
said Drake. "Will I have to kill you to find it then,
Derby? And you know I will, for all that we were
friends once."

Derby scowled and then shrugged. "Good luck to
you," he muttered. "She locked herself in last night,
while we were busy trying to outsail the Spaniard,
and she won't open up."

I nearly cheered.

"*She*, eh?" said Drake quietly.

"And her bloody tiring woman, too. I have had enough of the pair of them," Derby declared. He stepped up to the door of his cabin and banged on it. "Open up, you foolish woman, it's over!"

"No!" shrieked Lady Sarah's voice. "Take me back to the Queen—at once!" Only she said a lot more about Derby and his parents, which I am leaving out to save her reputation.

Drake smiled coldly. "So it's true, then. I counted you a friend, Hugh, for all we're so different. And you betrayed me! You stole a woman from the Queen's Court and had not the stomach to admit it, so you tried to lay the blame on me. I could have gone to the Tower and not even known why, thanks to you, *friend*."

Derby stared at the deck.

Drake moved close to the cabin door, keeping Derby covered with his pistol. "Lady Sarah," he called, "it is Captain Francis Drake here, ma'am. Will you open to me? I've come for to take you back to Court."

There was silence. Then the door was unlatched and unbolted, and Lady Sarah peered out, with

Olwen beside her. They both looked very tired and dishevelled, and Lady Sarah's bright hair was tumbling down her back.

"I'll never marry you!" she screamed at Captain Derby. "How dare you abduct me and disparage me like this? I hope the Queen puts you in the Tower and hangs and draws and quarters you, you—"

Captain Drake stopped her furious tirade by raising his free hand. "My lady . . . ma'am," he said, "have you taken any hurt or . . . injury?"

"That man would have made me marry him last night," shouted Lady Sarah, "if Olwen and I had not knocked out his guard and barred the door when he went out on deck! And who knows what would have happened, if you had not come to rescue me, Captain Drake!"

Drake bowed, then looked around for me and Masou. "Indeed, you owe your thanks to your faithful friends, my lady: your page, Gregory, and his friend, Masou."

The Captain gestured for us to step forward.

I scowled at Lady Sarah, hoping and praying she wouldn't be too bone-headed and give away my true identity. "But that's not a pageboy!" she gasped. "That's—"

There was a sudden flurry. Captain Derby had

thrown himself at Sarah. Drake's gun fired, but Derby had moved too fast. Everyone froze again. Derby was backing away from Drake towards the rail. He had his fist tangled in Sarah's hair and his knife at her throat. She sobbed in fear.

"You'll lay down that pistol and get your men off my ship," he said to Drake, breathing fast. "And I'll be on my way with my Sarah, or no one shall marry her, ever."

Drake dropped his pistol to the deck, lifted his hands away from his sword belt, and stood quietly watching, his face focused and intent.

I could not bear the silence—I had to say something. "If you truly loved her, Captain Derby, you would let her go!" I burst out.

Derby blinked, and then stared at me. "What?"

"That is what true love is," I told him, and I knew it was true for my mother had taught me. "Not capturing her and threatening her and trying to marry her against her will. Let her go."

Derby looked confused for a second. Then he took his knife from Sarah's throat to point it at me. "One more word from you—"

There was a smooth movement from Drake—a bright flash through the air—and a horrible gristly thud! A knife was pinning Derby's right hand to the block next to his head. His own blade clattered to the floor. He stared disbelievingly at his wounded hand, then cried out with pain and shock.

Moments later, Sarah had stamped on his foot, wrenched his hand out of her hair, and taken refuge behind Drake.

Masou whistled and applauded.

"Now," said Drake, scooping his pistol off the deck again, "where's the First Mate of this ship?"

A stout man, who had been watching all the drama with interest, stepped forward. "Mr. Ketcham, sir," he said.

"Well, Mr. Ketcham, see the *Arrow* back to Tilbury—I'll not take her as a prize—we can talk about salvage later. I'll have your Captain and the Lady Sarah to my ship."

"Aye, sir."

There were wounded men to look after, and Derby's hand was freed from the block and roughly bandaged. He seemed to have lost all his energy and just stared at the deck listlessly. The Spaniards had already been rounded up and locked in their own hold by Mr. Newman and the boarding party, who were putting out the fires and setting the sails.

At last we all went back across the boarding

planks, with Lady Sarah holding onto Drake's arm and trembling. I ran across—because it is really much less frightening that way—and waited at the other end to help her down. As I did so, I whispered at her fiercely, "I'm Gregory, your pageboy! Until I say."

Sarah blinked at me, catching on slowly; at last she nodded. "Thank you, Gregory," she said, and smiled.

It was afternoon before everything was organized and the *Judith* was sailing back to the Thames mouth. At least a strong easterly wind had sprung up, which filled all the sails and made the ship lean over and plough through the water very fast. Lady Sarah and Olwen were nicely ensconced in Drake's Great Cabin, while Derby was in the brig.

At supper time Drake sent for me to attend on my lady, which I did, just as if I were serving the Queen. Lady Sarah sat at table with Drake, her hair still tumbling extravagantly down her back, and he blinked at her as if he found her too bright to look at.

"Will you tell me what happened to you, Lady

Sarah?" he asked at last, as I brought some boxes of sweetmeats for them to finish the meal.

"Oh, it was terrible!" Sarah began. "I knew Captain Derby was mooning after me a bit, but a lot of men do, you know. I didn't think anything much about it. And he never sent me a bracelet as you did, or wrote me a poem or anything. He just stood and stared. And then he sent me a message saying Olwen had met with an accident—"

"I hadn't, look you," interrupted Olwen. "And I got a message, supposedly from Lady Sarah, which asked me to collect a bag of pearls from a sea captain who had got some—"

"Which I never sent," put in Sarah. "Captain Derby forged my handwriting—"

"Well, I didn't think anything of it, and why would I?" continued Olwen's singsong voice. "So I went down to the watersteps, and the next thing I knew, two sailors had put a bag over my head, and no matter what I did, they trussed me up like a pig going to market. Well, I was in a terrible state, all the way down the river, and lying in the bottom of the boat, getting wet and—"

"They did it to use her as a hostage against me—" said Lady Sarah, drinking some more wine.

"And then they carried me onto a ship—and when

they took the bag off, there I was, trussed up in Captain Derby's Great Cabin, with an evil-looking ruffian holding a knife to my neck. I was terrified." Olwen ate two more marmelada sweetmeats and shook her head. "Quite terrified."

"I was already looking for Olwen to help me with my bodice when I got the message that she had had an accident," Lady Sarah continued. "I hurried to the stables, and when I arrived"—she popped a marmelada square in her mouth, too, and I sighed, because I love them and it looked as if she and Olwen between them were going to finish them all up—"there was Captain Derby, with some of his sailors. He told me he had Olwen on his ship and would do . . . awful things to her if I didn't come quietly with him. And his sailors would knife me if I screamed. So obviously, I fainted."

Obviously, I thought.

"When I came to again, Captain Derby was very impatient and not at all nice to me. He said I must come with him to the watersteps, or Olwen would die. But first I had to write a note to the Queen and another one to Captain Drake. I said I could not for I had sprained my right wrist when I fainted, and I cried about it (though it was not true)—so he had one of his men bandage my wrist, and hastily wrote the letters himself. Then he made me walk arm in arm with him down to the watersteps—and nobody noticed my plight at all—not young Robin, nor any of the tumblers." She pouted accusingly at Masou. "And I was in a terrible state, because he told me he was going to marry me, and I wouldn't dream of marrying a sea captain—even if my parents gave their consent, which they certainly would not. So all I could think of to do was give Robin a message that would not alert my captor, but which would alert those who know me. Everyone at Court knows that Lady Jane is no friend of mine!" Lady Sarah paused to draw breath, then she carried on. "We were rowed down the river to Captain Derby's ship. Once we were aboard, his crew made ready to weigh anchor, and Captain Derby sent a boy to take the other letter to Captain Drake, together with my pearl bracelet—which really seemed a most unnecessary gesture. And about an hour later we sailed from Tilbury."

"Aye," said Drake, "I was wondering why he was in such a hurry to leave—I thought he had heard word of a fine fat prize to take in the Narrow Seas, though I wasn't ready for sea myself."

"Masou and I saw the boy deliver the package to Captain Drake's ship, my lady," I put in. "If we had but known what was inside, we would have guessed your whereabouts all the sooner."

Lady Sarah nodded. "Captain Derby kept me and Olwen locked in the Great Cabin—which was very bad for Olwen, who got seasick. And that really was not too pleasant for me, either! He said his chaplain would marry us as soon as it was evening, and if I didn't say 'I do' he'd have me gagged, and the chaplain would hear whatever Derby told him to hear and then he'd cut off . . . he'd cut off Olwen's hands. . . ." Lady Sarah's voice trembled and two big glistening tears trickled down her face.

What a terrible thing to do to anybody, I thought. I tried to imagine what I'd do if somebody threatened to cut Ellie's hands off if I didn't marry him, and I thought I'd probably marry him, no matter how horrible he was. So all the nasty food, and fighting Tom—and even the sea battle—had really been in a good cause: to stop Derby's greedy selfish plans. I felt quite proud of Masou and myself.

Olwen put her arm around Lady Sarah and clucked over her. "Ah, now then, my lady, he didn't do it, so now."

Lady Sarah took a deep breath and shook her head. "And then there was a shout that they'd seen the Spanish ship sent out by the Duke of Alva—who is apparently a terrible pirate, and attacks any English and Dutch ships he can find. And then the Spanish ship started chasing us, which was even more frightening, so Captain Derby went out on deck. And while he was gone, I noticed that our guard had had quite a lot to drink, so I played cards with him and got him more drunk, and then Olwen crept up behind him and hit him on the head with a tray. Then we locked the door and barred the windows, so when Captain Derby came back with his chaplain, ready to marry me, he couldn't get in." Lady Sarah shook her head. "He was furious—and he called me so many evil names, I was quite sure I didn't want to marry such a raving bully.

"Olwen and I stayed up all night, to make sure he didn't break in—when he wasn't busy trying to sail away from the Spaniard, that is. And in the morning, there was cannon fire—which was terribly frightening—so we hid under the table. There was such a creaking and banging, and then a big roaring, clattering fight that went on and on! And finally, I heard *your* voice, Captain Drake!" she finished, fluttering her eyelashes at him. "I am *so* grateful to you!"

I had to choke back a laugh at that—typical Lady Sarah, I thought. There she was, just rescued from a fate worse than death—and still, she couldn't help flirting!

"I'll not take all the credit, my lady," said Drake with a tilt of his head. "Hugh Derby was one of my best friends. I would have trusted him with my life—my ship, even. The first I knew of what had happened to you was when your pageboy showed me the letter that was supposed to have come from you to the Queen, saying you were eloping with me. He's a good lad, my lady—I'd keep him by you if I was you. He slipped away from Court and crept onto the *Judith* because he thought I had you locked up here somewhere. And then, when he found out the truth, he came to me with the letter and told all he knew."

"But *you* did all the fighting to save me, didn't you, Captain?" Sarah gave Drake a dazzling smile. She didn't look grateful for all *my* hard work at all. And there was only one more marmelada sweetmeat left in the box, which I just knew she was going to take. And there it went. Typical!

"I'm always happy to fight—me and my crew with me." Drake grinned that ferocious piratical grin of his, and laughed. "It's a good Sunday's sport for us. And your young Gregory, and Masou, they fought from the top, shooting arrows and throwing fire pots. They'll be fine men one day. If you have thanks to give for your rescue, you should reward them, too."

I felt myself blushing because I was so pleased to have Drake's respect. He is one of those people who makes you feel like a king—or a queen—if he praises you. I would far rather have his respect than any amount of cooing from Lady Sarah.

Sarah nodded to Masou and me—but then she looked down and sighed. "Though all is lost, anyway—for my reputation is now ruined," she said quietly. "I will have to marry a merchant—or even a lawyer."

I had to say something, so I bent on one knee, as a pageboy should, and said, "No, you won't, my lady. For nobody knows you've been gone."

Sarah blinked at me dimly. "Why not?" she asked.

"Because I've had Mary Shelton give out that you and—you have a quinsy and have been in bed," I explained.

"You have? Really?" Sarah said incredulously, her face brightening.

"Yes, my lady. All we have to do is smuggle you back into the palace without anyone noticing, and then to our—your chamber, and nobody will ever know what happened."

Lady Sarah clapped her hands and laughed in delight. "Are you sure?"

"So long as you and Olwen don't tell anybody," I added, knowing Lady Sarah.

"Why, that's a wonderful idea." Then her face fell. "Except it means that Derby won't go to the Tower for abducting me."

Drake poured Lady Sarah some more wine. "I'll free him when we get to Tilbury," he told her. "It's not justice, right enough, but I doubt he'll set sail in his own ship again, for he was in debt to fit out the *Arrow,* and she'll need a new mast and yards as well. He'll have to sell her, and then the only way he can set to sea is sailing as someone else's mate or purser."

"You sound sorry for him, Captain Drake," said Lady Sarah, a little petulantly.

"I *am* sorry for him, even though he betrayed our friendship and tried to have me blamed for his crime," Drake replied. "By his own fault and sinfulness he has lost the finest thing a man can have."

"A wife," said Olwen knowingly to Lady Sarah.

Drake looked puzzled. "No, a ship," he corrected.

Lady Sarah and Olwen both looked a little put out at that. They were used to courtly gentlemen, after all.

Drake waved a hand, completely unaware of this. "When you're master of your own ship, you're as free as the wind. You can set sail upon a day, and go all round the world, visiting strange and wonderful lands—and all the time you are in your own house, with your household around you."

"Will you ever marry, Captain Drake?" Lady Sarah asked, a little flirtatiously.

"Aye." He smiled at her. "I'm minded to ask Mr. Newman for his daughter's hand, for she's a pretty little thing, and used to sailors—and I've the money to keep a wife like her, now."

Sarah now looked *very* put out. "Oh," she said pointedly. "You are not ambitious in your choice of wife, then?"

I saw Drake's blue eyes turn sharp, and thought, You have lost him now, Lady Sarah—if ever you truly had him.

Drake laughed. "Ambitious? Not for a wife wealthier and of higher blood than me, no. But ambitious to sail about the world and take satisfaction in blood from the treacherous Spaniards? Yes. That I am." He put his silver goblet down with a sharp tap and stood up. "Now, ladies, I know you must be weary from watching all night, and in need of rest. I'll bunk down in the Mate's cabin, and I desire you to make yourself free with anything you need in here."

Sarah nodded her thanks. "Oh, and Captain," she trilled, "may we have Masou and Gr—egory, to guard us in the night?"

Drake frowned. "You are in no danger on this ship, my lady," he said.

Sarah's eyes opened wide. "From the mice, Captain. There were dreadfully big ones on Derby's ship, you know."

Drake shook his head and chuckled. "Of course," he said. "Gregory and Masou, you stay here—and behave yourselves, or I'll give you what for in the morning."

"Aye, Captain," said Masou and I together, nearly dying of trying not to laugh.

"Goodnight, ladies," said Drake as he went to the door. "By the early hours of the morning, with this wind and God willing, we'll be in Tilbury." And he bowed courteously.

Lady Sarah and Olwen curtsied back. I caught myself just in time, and bowed like Masou.

As soon as the Captain had shut the door behind

him, Masou and I fell on the remains of the dinner. I don't think I'd like to be a pageboy. It's agony watching people gobble up all the sweetmeats when you're really hungry for one.

"Grace?" asked Lady Sarah, not sounding quite sure. "Is it really Grace?"

"Mmph," I said, nodding. My mouth was full of game pie.

Olwen stared at me, gave a little shriek, and sat down suddenly. "What . . . ?" she gasped. "What have you done with your hair?"

Honestly! What a daft question. "I cut it off, of course," I said impatiently.

"Is it true, what Captain Drake said you did, Grace?" Lady Sarah asked incredulously. "You came to find me, and you were in the battle?"

I nodded. "Well, high up above it," I dismissed, not wanting Lady Sarah to make her usual fuss. "And Masou was there, too, of course."

"Oh," said Lady Sarah, shaking her head. "How extraordinary. . . . Was it very hard work?"

I thought about this. "Yes," I said, "it was. So—are there any more marmelada sweetmeats?"

As we were arranging the little cabin for the night, there came a knock on the door. The Boatswain entered, carrying a basket. He was smiling fondly.

"Now then, m'dears, these here ladies'll take care of you . . . ," he said—which puzzled me until I realized he was talking to something in the basket.

He put it on the table and Sarah and Olwen peered in, then started to coo and exclaim. I peeked, too, and saw the mother cat and her kittens, now looking much happier. The kittens were asleep, with their paws curled on their fat little tummies, and the mother cat was purring.

"She'm the maddest cat I ever saw! Fancy her taking her kittens all the way up the mast! Tom fetched her down," said the Boatswain, who now didn't seem nearly so fierce. "Can you take care of her, ladies?" he asked. "She's a fine ratter, and her kittens are shaping well, what's more."

It was a silly question, really. Nobody could resist them, and soon they were in the warmest, safest corner, with Olwen feeding the mother scraps of meat-pie filling and Sarah dangling a bit of thread to see if the kittens would play.

We did sleep a little, me and Sarah sharing the little cot, and Olwen on a pallet, with poor Masou by the door. But we had to wake up again at about two in the morning because we were nearly there.

As we sailed back into Tilbury, Drake had his gig ready to go up the Thames, and we came to

Greenwich watersteps before it was light. Obviously, the great watergate was closed and locked, but there was a boat unloading loaves of bread by the kitchen steps already.

Lady Sarah and Olwen were muffled up in cloaks, and I led them in—still disguised as a page—telling the Yeoman that they were friends visiting Lady Sarah. I could tell he didn't believe me, though. He probably thought there was something scandalous going on with the courtiers.

We went through some of the rarely used back passages that Masou knew of, and slipped into our own bedchamber, while Masou kept watch. Then he went off to his own sleeping place to rest.

"I am utterly exhausted," Sarah said loudly, as Olwen helped her off with her stays. "I am sure it will take me several days to recover from such a terrible ordeal."

Mary Shelton woke up, and sighed in relief when she saw that we had all returned safely. She was looking quite ill herself, with red eyes and bags under them as well.

Ellie awoke, too, and sat up looking ever so much better—no fever, rosy cheeks. I'd say she was even a little less thin.

Mary climbed out of bed. "What happened to you, Grace?" she demanded, clasping her hands. "Where have you been? I was so desperately *worried*! I've been praying and praying for your safe return. I nearly went and told the Queen when you weren't back by last night!"

"Good thing I had the sense to stop you, eh?" said Ellie. "I know Grace." She gave me a big hug, and squawked with laughter at how I looked with my hair short, and in boys' clothes. I took them off and bundled them up for her to take back to the tumblers' tiring room. Then I changed my shift and got into bed, with every bone in my body aching with relief and tiredness.

Mary Shelton was so kind, she even said she'd wait to hear the whole story until I had slept. And then my eyes closed by themselves, as Lady Sarah got on with telling of her adventures.

⸺

Before I knew it, it was midday and Mary Shelton was shaking me awake for dinner. She had brought a tray of food, which we demolished. I was absolutely starving, and even Ellie was impressed at how much I ate.

I have spent the afternoon writing everything I

could remember of my adventures in my daybooke. After all, I was ill with a quinsy, wasn't I? And so was Lady Sarah. It was essential that nobody find out where Sarah had really been, for even though she was kidnapped and taken against her will, her reputation would still be ruined if the truth came out. So we stayed in our chamber and let it be known that we couldn't possibly attend the Queen when we were both still so ill.

When I'd written down my adventures (thank goodness I'd been able to make some notes or I'd never have remembered everything), I read selected bits out to Mary and Ellie, and Sarah and Olwen, and they laughed and gasped and oohed, just as if I were a proper storyteller.

By then, Ellie was so much better that, when the coast was clear, she crept out of the bedchamber and went back to the laundry.

Mary Shelton went to fetch my Uncle Cavendish this evening, so that he could examine Sarah and me, and pronounce us recovered from the quinsy. He came and looked at our throats, felt our pulses and foreheads—then solemnly pronounced our quinsies quite abated, thanks to his care.

Masou came creeping in to see us, too, and I had to read my account to them all again, with Masou adding comments when he thought I had forgotten something important. Mary, Sarah, and Olwen all listened and gasped in disbelief and clapped. I've even started to wonder myself if I really did all that— did I really climb a mast, fight in a battle?

I think Her Majesty is wonderful, the way she understands.

This morning Mrs. Champernowne came bustling in: Sarah and I were to attend the Queen in the Presence Chamber, now we had been pronounced well again.

Lady Sarah helped me to pin up my short hair with a hairpiece, to make it look as if I still had it long, and then, damasked and pearled, off we all went to the Presence.

Lady Jane gasped when she saw Lady Sarah, who ignored her with great aplomb as she sailed past. "Are you recovered of your illness now, dear Lady Sarah?" she asked.

"Yes, thank you," said Sarah. "My quinsy is quite gone."

"It has been very quiet without you." Lady Jane's arched eyebrows went up a bit when she said this.

"How kind of you to say so . . ." Sarah was positively simpering.

The trumpets blared and we all rose to curtsy and dispose ourselves neatly. Her Majesty was staring hard at me—which worried me a little—but then she smiled, and I thought she probably wasn't angry.

And then in came Captain Drake himself, followed by Mr. Newman, who was carrying a bolt of beautiful samite silk, which he placed in front of the Queen on the dais.

"Your Majesty," said the Captain with a bow. "With your permission, I would like to present this bolt of silk to my Lady Sarah Bartelmy, as a compensation for the gown that was ruined when she fell—" He'd turned to smile at Lady Sarah, and seen me sitting demurely with my needlework. "That was . . . er . . . ruined by sea water . . ." He trailed off, still staring at me.

"Ah yes, Captain," the Queen replied smoothly, "perhaps you remember my Lady Grace Cavendish, our youngest Maid of Honour. She turned the winch for the most notable contest between the Spanish galleon and the purposed English race-built ship." And she gestured for me to come forward.

I stood up and went to Her Majesty.

Drake looked from me to the Queen and his

mouth was opening and shutting like a codfish. "She . . . ah . . . Do you have a brother, my lady?" he asked.

I curtsied to him and looked demurely at the floor. "No, sir, I am an only child."

"Perhaps a cousin named Gregory?" he pressed.

"No, sir." I stared straight up at those vivid blue eyes and I couldn't resist it. I winked. Then I looked at the Queen, who had a very peculiar expression on her face—half disapproval, half amusement. She knows! I thought at once.

I'd wager all London to a turnip that, last eventide, Captain Drake had told Her Majesty the tale of what happened, as a wild romantical sea captain's tall tale. The Queen will have formed her own conclusions about that enterprising pageboy, Gregory. And she dearly loves to tease a handsome man.

"Ah . . . And what have you been doing these last few days, my lady?" Captain Drake asked me, recovering swiftly.

"Oh, sir, I have been in bed with a terrible quinsy," I replied, and then felt reckless: "Why, I had such a fever I dreamed I was in a sea battle and that a cat brought her kittens up to the fighting top while the cannons were firing!" Just for a second I caught the Queen's eye and nearly ruined all by laughing—for I could see that she was near to bursting, too.

The Queen can be most subtle and tactful when she wants. She would have stopped me going if she had known in advance, just as Ellie said, and I would have been in terrible trouble if I had been caught. But to bring off such a venture with no mishap, and save Lady Sarah from disgrace as well—that pleased her. If ever she should ask me whether I was Gregory, I will tell her the truth, of course. But I'll wager she never will—and will be most careful not to find out about it, either . . . *officially*.

Drake was staring at me, blue eyes boring into mine—but I didn't mind a bit, and just stared him right back. I'm a Maid of Honour. Only a madman would accuse a Maid of Honour of being in a sea battle.

Suddenly Drake shouted with laughter and bowed to me and the Queen together. "By God, Your Majesty," he said. "By God, when we have Maids of Honour such as these in England, no wonder all the world is in awe of us!"

And for the rest of the audience, while the Queen thanked him for his gift of treasure and a prize ship for the rebuilding of the Navy, he would look at me every so often, and grin suddenly, like a boy.

Meanwhile, Lady Sarah sat with a satisfied little smile on her face like a cat at a cream bowl, while Lady Jane scowled down at her blackwork with a face of thunder.

And I smiled secretly to myself, for here was another mystery successfully unravelled by Her Majesty's own Lady Pursuivant—with not a little help from Masou—and Gregory the page, of course. . . .

alchemist—a name given to a kind of chemist who sought to turn ordinary metals into gold. Some alchemists also sought the key to eternal life and a universal cure for disease.

Allah akhbar—an Islamic war cry. It means "God is great."

Allemayne—Germany

aqua vitae—brandy

banshee—a spirit in Irish folklore well known for wailing loudly

Bedlam—the major asylum for the insane in London during Elizabethan times—the name came from the Hospital of St. Mary of Bethlehem

biggin cap—a child's hat

blackwork—black embroidery on white linen

bracer—an arm or wrist protector used by an archer

brig—a small ship with two square-rigged sails, often used for piracy *brocade*—a rich, gold-embroidered fabric

bumroll—a sausage-shaped piece of padding worn round the hips to make them look bigger

buttery—confusingly, this was where barrels of beer, wine, and brandy were kept for people to fetch drinks from

cable tiers—the area on a ship where the anchor chain (or cable) was stored

capstan—a large winch, often used for hauling up the anchor or anything else that was particularly heavy

Chamberer—a servant of the Queen who cleaned her chamber for her, which the Maids of Honour and Ladies-in-Waiting, of course, could not be expected to do

citron—a citrus fruit similar to a lemon but with a very thick rind

close-stool—a portable toilet comprising a seat with a hole in it on top of a box with a chamber pot inside

Cloth of Estate—a kind of awning that went over the Queen's chair to indicate that she was the Queen

Clown's All-Heal—a plant, also known as St. John's wort

codpiece—a flap or bag that concealed the opening in the front of a man's breeches *copper*—usually a copper saucepan or cauldron used for cooking

damask—a beautiful, self-patterned silk cloth woven in Flanders. It originally came from Damascus— hence the name.

daybooke—a book in which you would record your sins each day so that you could pray about them. The idea of keeping a diary or journal grew out of this. Grace uses her daybooke as a journal.

dottle—partly burned tobacco in the bowl of a pipe

doublet—a close-fitting padded jacket worn by men

Duke of Alva—the Spanish ruler in the Netherlands during Elizabethan times

false front—a pretty piece of material sewn to the front of a plain petticoat so that it would show under the kirtle

farthingale—a bell- or barrel-shaped petticoat held out with hoops of whalebone

fighting top—a platform halfway up a ship's mast where a Navy man could stand and shoot

fire pot—a clay pot, filled with material that would easily catch fire, used as a missile in battle and to carry hot coals

fletching—the feathers on an arrow

forecastle—the foremost part of the upper deck of a ship

French cut—fashionably tight and curvy

galleon—a heavy square-rigged sailing ship used for war or trade, especially by the Spanish

galley—the area of a ship where the crew's meals were cooked. In Elizabethan times the galley was deep down in the ship's bilges, where there was maximum stability and where the cooking fire could be put out easily if necessary.

gig—a long, narrow rowing boat

grappling irons—large hooks on ropes. These were thrown from one ship onto another to pull it closer so that it could be boarded and captured.

Hubsburg—the family name of Philip II and one of the great ruling dynasties of Europe

halberd—a weapon consisting of a battle-axe and pike mounted on a long handle

harbinger—a courtier who went ahead to announce the monarch

henbane of Peru—also known as tobacco. In Elizabethan times it was regarded as a great cure for phlegm.

Henchman—a young serving man, often related to the person he was serving. His work might well involve acting as a bodyguard.

hose—tight-fitting cloth trousers worn by men

jakes—an Elizabethan term for an outside toilet

jerkin—a close-fitting, hip-length, usually sleeveless jacket

kirtle—the skirt section of an Elizabethan dress

Lady-in-Waiting—one of the ladies who helped look after the Queen and who kept her company

lateen—a narrow, triangular sail on a very long yard set at an angle to the mast

lye—a strongly alkaline ingredient in soap

Maid of Honour—a younger girl who helped to look after the Queen like a Lady-in-Waiting

man-of-war—a warship

marmelada—a very thick jammy sweet often made from quinces

Mary Shelton—one of Queen Elizabeth's Maids of Honor (a Maid of Honor of this name really did exist; see below). Most Maids of Honor were not officially "Ladies" (like Lady Grace), but they had to be born of gentry.

merchant venturer—a person who invested in overseas trade

merchanter or *merchantman*—a trading ship

Muscovy—the kingdom of Moscow; Old Russia

Mussulman—an old name for a Muslim

Narrow Seas—the English Channel

New Spain—South America

New World—South and North America together

on progress—a term used when the Queen was touring parts of her realm. Such travel was a kind of summer holiday for her.

Parlour—a room off the Hall that was just beginning to be used for eating, among other things

penner—a small leather case that would attach to a belt. It was used for holding quills, ink, knife, and any other equipment needed for writing.

pitch—a black substance similar to tar

poop deck—a deck right at the stern of a ship

popinjay—a parrot

posset—a hot drink made from sweetened and spiced milk curdled with ale or wine

potherbs—vegetables

pottage—a thick soup

Presence Chamber—the room where Queen Elizabeth would receive people

Privy Garden—Queen Elizabeth's private garden

pursuivant—one who pursues someone else

Queen's Guard—these were more commonly known as the Gentlemen Pensioners, young noblemen who guarded the Queen from physical attacks

quinsy—very bad tonsillitis

raiment—clothing

Royal Standard—Queen Elizabeth's flag (*not* the Union Jack)

samite—a heavy satin fabric

sea beggars—a derogatory term for the Dutch rebels who fought the Spanish at sea

Secretary to the Admiralty—the man in charge of the Navy (as it existed then)

shipworm—teredo worm; a wood-boring beetle that rendered most ships unusable after twenty years, until copper-bottoming came in during the eighteenth century

shipwright—a carpenter expert in shipbuilding and repair

slow match—rope soaked in saltpeter to make it burn slowly and steadily

snips—an early form of scissors without the pivot—a little like small sheep shears

Spaniels—a mispronunciation of *Espagnols* (*Spanish*) by the English

statute cap—a blue woollen cap worn by all apprentices to support the woollen industry

stays—the boned, laced bodice worn around the body under the clothes. Victorians called the stays a corset.

sterncastle—the back of a warship, built up to allow the crew to board other ships

stomacher—a heavily embroidered or jeweled piece for the center front of a bodice

tinder box—small box containing some quick-burning tinder, a piece of flint, a piece of steel, and a candle for making fire and thus light

tiring room—a room for dressing or changing clothes in

tiring woman—a woman who helped a lady to dress

topman—the aristocrats of the lower deck, these were the sailors who worked high up on the mast and in the yards

tumbler—an acrobat

vein or *open a vein*—a cut made in a vein to let out "bad" blood. This was used as a cure for almost anything!

Verge of the Court—anywhere within a mile of the Queen's person

vittles—food

waterman—a man who rowed a ferry boat on the Thames; he was a kind of Elizabethan cabdriver

watersteps—steps leading down to the river

wherry—a Thames boat

willow-bark tincture—a solution made from willow bark, which was good for pain relief but very bad for the stomach. It was later developed into aspirin.

Withdrawing Chamber—the Queen's private rooms

yard—a long pole on which a sail hangs

Forget everything you thought you knew about sea battles and pirates, because in Elizabethan times, war at sea wasn't as clear-cut as you might imagine!

In the sixteenth century there were no naval uniforms, no press gangs (men who later forced civilians into joining the army and navy), and only a few purpose-built warships, which often doubled as privateer vessels. A privateer was a pirate who preyed upon the ships of one or two countries, as allowed by his sovereign in a letter of marque.

At this time, the Royal Navy was basically a random collection of privateers and armed merchants who volunteered to serve the Queen whenever it was necessary. Very often they weren't paid unless they captured another ship, and then they received prize money for it.

Later in Elizabeth's reign, Sir Francis Drake was one of the most successful of these pirates—with investments from the Queen as well as many of her courtiers. The early Elizabethan ships were quite primitive, but the technology was evolving at a tremendous rate. And when the Armada came in 1588, it was thanks to the race-built galleons—designed by John Hawkins—that the English ships were able to outsail and outgun the Spanish.

In 1485, Queen Elizabeth I's grandfather, Henry Tudor, won the battle of Bosworth Field against Richard III and took the throne of England. He was known as Henry VII. He had two sons, Arthur and Henry. Arthur died while still a boy, so when Henry VII died in 1509, Elizabeth's father came to the throne and England got an eighth king called Henry—the notorious one who had six wives.

Wife number one—Catherine of Aragon—gave Henry one daughter called Mary (who was brought up as a Catholic) but no living sons. To Henry VIII this was a disaster, because nobody believed a queen could ever govern England. He needed a male heir.

Henry wanted to divorce Catherine so he could marry his pregnant mistress, Anne Boleyn. The Pope, the head of the Catholic Church, wouldn't allow him to annul his marriage, so Henry broke with the Catholic Church and set up the Protestant

Church of England—or the Episcopal Church, as it's known in the United States.

Wife number two—Anne Boleyn—gave Henry another daughter, Elizabeth (who was brought up as a Protestant). When Anne then miscarried a baby boy, Henry decided he'd better get somebody new, so he accused Anne of infidelity and had her executed.

Wife number three—Jane Seymour—gave Henry a son called Edward and died of childbed fever a couple of weeks later.

Wife number four—Anne of Cleves—had no children. It was a diplomatic marriage and Henry didn't fancy her, so she agreed to a divorce (wouldn't you?).

Wife number five—Catherine Howard—had no children, either. Like Anne Boleyn, she was accused of infidelity and executed.

Wife number six—Catherine Parr—also had no children. She did manage to outlive Henry, though, but only by the skin of her teeth. Nice guy, eh?

Henry VIII died in 1547, and in accordance with the rules of primogeniture (whereby the firstborn son inherits from his father), the person who succeeded him was the boy Edward. He became Edward VI. He was strongly Protestant but died young, in 1553.

Next came Catherine of Aragon's daughter, Mary, who became Mary I, known as Bloody Mary. She was strongly Catholic, married Philip II of Spain in a diplomatic match, but died childless five years later. She also burned a lot of Protestants for the good of their souls.

Finally, in 1558, Elizabeth came to the throne. She reigned until her death in 1603. She played the marriage game—that is, she kept a lot of important and influential men hanging on in hopes of marrying her—for a long time. At one time it looked as if she would marry her favorite, Robert Dudley, Earl of Leicester. She didn't, though, and I think she probably never intended to get married—would you, if you'd had a dad like hers? So she never had any children.

She was an extraordinary and brilliant woman, and during her reign, England first started to become important as a world power. Sir Francis Drake sailed round the world—raiding the Spanish colonies of South America for loot as he went. And one of Elizabeth's favorite courtiers, Sir Walter Raleigh, tried to plant the first English colony in North America—at the site of Roanoke in 1585. It failed, but the idea stuck.

The Spanish King Philip II tried to conquer

England in 1588. He sent a huge fleet of 150 ships, known as the Invincible Armada, to do it. It failed miserably—defeated by Drake at the head of the English fleet—and most of the ships were wrecked trying to sail home. There were many other great Elizabethans, too—including William Shakespeare and Christopher Marlowe.

After her death, Elizabeth was succeeded by James VI of Scotland, who became James I of England and Scotland. He was almost the last eligible person available! He was the son of Mary, Queen of Scots, who was Elizabeth's cousin, via Henry VIII's sister.

James's son was Charles I—the king who was beheaded after losing the English Civil War.

❧

The stories about Lady Grace Cavendish are set in the year 1569, when Elizabeth was thirty-six and still playing the marriage game for all she was worth. The Ladies-in-Waiting and Maids of Honor at her Court weren't servants—they were companions and friends, supplied from upper-class families. Not all of them were officially "Ladies"—only those with titled husbands or fathers; in fact, many of them were unmar-

ried younger daughters sent to Court to find themselves a nice rich lord to marry.

All the Lady Grace Mysteries are invented, but some of the characters in the stories are real people—Queen Elizabeth herself, of course, and Mrs. Champernowne and Mary Shelton as well. There never was a Lady Grace Cavendish (as far as we know!)—but there were plenty of girls like her at Elizabeth's Court. The real Mary Shelton foolishly made fun of the Queen herself on one occasion—and got slapped in the face by Elizabeth for her trouble! But most of the time, the Queen seems to have been protective of and kind to her Maids of Honor. She was very strict about boyfriends, though. There was one simple rule for boyfriends in those days: you couldn't have one. No boyfriends at all. You would get married to a person your parents chose for you and that was that. Of course, the girls often had other ideas!

Later on in her reign, the Queen had a full-scale secret service run by her great spymaster, Sir Francis Walsingham. His men, who hunted down priests and assassins, were called Pursuivants. There are also tantalizing hints that Elizabeth may have had her own personal sources of information—she

certainly was very well informed, even when her counselors tried to keep her in the dark. And who knows whom she might have recruited to find things out for her? There may even have been a Lady Grace Cavendish, after all!